USA TODAY Bestselling Author

JANICE KAY JOHNSON

In Hope's Shadow

ISBN-13: 978-0-373-60928-4

In Hope's Shadow

Copyright © 2015 by Janice Kay Johnson

Printed in U.S.A.

An author of more than eighty books for children and adults, *USA TODAY* bestselling author **Janice Kay Johnson** is especially well-known for her Harlequin Superromance novels about love and family—about the way generations connect and the power our earliest experiences have on us throughout life. Her 2007 novel *Snowbound* won a RITA® Award from Romance Writers of America for Best Contemporary Series Romance. A former librarian, Janice raised two daughters in a small rural town north of Seattle, Washington. She loves to read and is an active volunteer and board member for Purrfect Pals, a no-kill cat shelter. Visit her online at janicekayjohnson.com.

Books by Janice Kay Johnson

Visit the Author Profile page
at Harlequin.com for more titles.

Other titles by this author available in ebook format.

CHAPTER ONE

Eve Lawson wondered whether her fellow social service caseworkers ever met with one of their kids on the sidewalk outside a foster home. Especially on a bitterly cold February day.

They'd probably all agree with her that you did whatever was necessary. And the truth was, Joel had looked relieved when she asked him to walk her out to her car.

Hoping her shivers weren't obvious, Eve wrapped her fleece scarf more snugly around her neck and leaned against the fender of her car, feeling the chill of the metal penetrating even through her wool peacoat.

However alone they were out here, she was unsettlingly aware that they were being watched.

"So what's going on, Joel?" she asked.

She had been Joel Kekoa's caseworker for the past three years. He'd been fourteen years old when they'd first met, sullen, hulking and clumsy. The first thing she'd had to do was move him to a new foster home at the request of the previous foster parents, which left him feeling rejected again. Something she understood too well. The one bright spot she'd been able to see then had been his performance in school.

The move had been positive, though. He and the new foster father, Rod Carter, had bonded right away. Joel had seemingly grown into his extra-large body not long after, starring as an offensive guard on the football team these past two years. Eve had gone to a few games to cheer him on. Several major colleges had recruited him, and on signing day he'd committed to the University of Oregon because of their nationally ranked football program. Seventeen now, he was a senior in high school with a solid GPA. In fact, until this morning's call, she'd felt good enough about Joel to let him slip to the bottom of her list of priorities, which meant she'd done little but check in with him by phone occasionally.

The dynamics in the home had recently changed when Carter married a woman who also had a teenage son. Eve had just met mother and son for the first time, and her antennae were quivering.

Honestly, seeing the boy, Gavin Shaffer, watching them now from the picture window in the living room gave her the creeps. He wasn't making any effort to be surreptitious, just stood there looking relaxed, faintly amused, possibly smug. Eve had disliked him on sight, rare for a woman who worked with many troubled children and believed they could overcome the odds.

When she first arrived, she had also seen the drapes twitch in the window of the house next door and was uneasily aware that a couple-inch gap had opened when she and Joel walked to the car. The apparently curmudgeonly next-door neighbor, Clement Rowe, was also keeping his eye on them.

Her inner child wanted to stick out her tongue at them both.

Head hanging, Joel shifted from foot to foot at her question. Having not grabbed a coat on his way out the door, he had to be even more miserable than she was, but he didn't show it. His one concession to a temperature in the thirties was to shove his hands in his jeans pockets.

"Things are kinda tense right now," he said finally. "I guess you could tell that, huh?"

"I'm disconcerted that Rod couldn't be here," she said, sliding away from directly answering.

Joel scowled. "He says I have to listen to Lynne 'cause she's my foster mom now."

"How does she feel about that?"

"She doesn't like me." The sullenness Eve remembered from years past imbued his voice. "She's mostly nice in front of Rod. You know. She's got this supersweet smile while she gets a dig in."

Having just seen the woman in action, Eve couldn't help thinking he'd nailed the description. Eve hadn't liked Lynne Carter nee Shaffer *or* her son.

"What about Gavin?" she asked, almost reluctantly.

"I don't know." Head down, he toed a crack in the sidewalk. "We're not, like, friends, but he's been okay."

"Is he a good student?"

"Yeah, better than me. I can tell he thinks he's smarter."

Eve fixed the boy in front of her with a stern look. "I really doubt if he is. You've had to overcome some obstacles."

He shrugged, maybe in acknowledgment, maybe just because he didn't want to argue. Joel's biological father hadn't been abusive so much as neglectful. He had been known to leave his young son alone for days at a time, moved them frequently and not always bothered enrolling him in school. When he was arrested for armed robbery and sentenced to ten years in the Monroe Correctional Institute, Joel had been placed in foster care and enrolled in the Stimson School District. Then twelve, he had tested years behind his age group. The gains he'd made since were extraordinary.

But she let it go right now. "Does he do sports?"

"He's on the wrestling team," Joel mumbled. "Plus, I guess he's into drama. *She* says he always gets the leading roles."

Gavin had had to transfer from Cascade High

School in Everett to Stimson when his mother remarried. To be fair, Eve reflected, it had to have been tough to have to move to a new district in his junior year.

All she could think to say was, "I see." *Ugh*. Truthfully, she didn't see much of anything yet. She suspected Lynne did not want to parent this hulking young man who didn't look anything like her own, gilded boy. As sweetly as she'd tried to speak, there'd been an edge in her voice when she was addressing Joel. Eve hadn't liked hearing it. She also didn't like seeing that Joel had regressed some. He seemed to be avoiding meeting her eyes. His sulkiness told her he no longer felt secure, which was dangerous in a boy who'd known so little real security.

But none of this had anything to do with the phone call that had brought her out here this morning.

"Okay," she said on a sigh. "Tell me about Mr. Rowe."

"He hates kids." Joel grimaced. "Actually, I think he hates everyone. But he doesn't have anything to do with most grown-ups. Some of the kids who live on the block have accidently kicked balls into his yard, stuff like that. He comes out screaming if you set one *foot* onto his property." He sneered. "Like the sole of my shoe is going to poison his grass."

Clement Rowe's lawn was undeniably superior

to his neighbors'. It bore more than a passing resemblance to a putting green at an upscale golf course. Along with kids, Mr. Rowe must particularly hate the neighbor a couple of houses down whose winter-brown lawn was tufted with dandelions.

"Tuesday I was walking with some other guys," Joel continued. "We were kind of pushing each other, you know, just having fun, and I stumbled into old man Rowe's flower bed. He roared out, so I stared him in the eye and cut right across his yard to get to my front door. It was like, in your face."

Eve suspected she might have done the same at his age. She nodded.

"So, he comes over last night, really mad. Somebody had smashed some of his rosebushes."

Her gaze strayed to the torn, stunted canes of hybrid tea roses. All were evenly spaced in a row and appeared to have been recently pruned, which seemed a little early. February was the month to do it in the Northwest, sure, but this was only the twelfth, and the weather had been bitterly cold until a couple of days ago. Well, the pruning job wasn't the point, not now. Eve had no idea whether these roses could be salvaged.

"He said it had to be me. And Lynne, she just started telling him she was so sorry and that there'd be consequences for me without even *asking* me whether I had anything to do with it!" His voice had risen in outrage. "And I didn't! I swear,

Ms. Lawson. He's a jerk, but it's like, why would I care that much?"

Eve searched his angry dark eyes and thought she saw sincerity. She could also see that he was braced in anticipation of her disbelief.

Would he have lashed out at the mean old man who regularly yelled at him? Eve didn't want to think so; she'd have sworn Joel was more mature than that. But she also knew that maturity had been erected on a newly poured foundation that could have been damaged by the recent, drastic changes in his home life.

Still, she nodded. "Okay, Joel. Just stay away from Mr. Rowe's property. Cross the street if you need to go by."

His shoulders relaxed. "You believe me?"

Throw the dice. Somebody had to believe in him. "I do. You're a good kid." She smiled crookedly. "That's why I neglect you."

His broad face lit with a grin. "You mean, if I screw up you'd come see me more often?"

"Yes, but please don't. I'm running from morning to night already."

"Yeah, well, it wasn't me who called you." All too quickly, he was back to smoldering.

"It's okay. I've been intending to drop by to meet Rod's new wife and her son anyway." She hesitated. "I'm a lot more concerned about your relationship with them than I am with Mr. Rowe's grumblings."

He shrugged. She glanced toward Clement Rowe's house and this time saw fingers pulling the drapes back and a shadow in the opening.

Shivering again, Eve told herself she just didn't like winter. No ghost had brushed by; she hadn't just spoken what sounded way too much like famous last words.

BEN KEMPER SIGHED and leaned back, causing his chair to squeak. "Thank you, I don't mind waiting on hold."

Actually, he did, but he'd become resigned. Nobody had told him before his promotion to detective that he would spend more time poring over his computer or on hold—and often both at the same time—than he would out in the field. The chills and thrills of police work were few and far between these days.

The hours, though, those still sucked. The lengthy and erratic hours he worked explained why he was now a divorced man who counted his blessings when he was permitted to have his six-year-old daughter two days out of every fourteen.

Not a minute later, the cell phone lying on his desk rang. The name appearing on the screen was his ex-wife's. As always, he couldn't help feeling a spurt of hope. He missed Nicole every day.

Juggling phones, he answered. "Nic."

"You got a sec?" Nicole asked.

"I'm on hold. I'll have to call you back if some-one comes on."

"You can't hang up on whoever it is and call back?"

"It's important, and I've already been waiting for a while."

"What, I'm not entitled to two minutes of your concentration?" she snapped.

Irritation rose to poison the hope. "I am at work," he pointed out.

"Like you aren't always."

He closed his eyes. "Can we not do this?"

Silence. Finally, "I know you're supposed to have Rachel tomorrow, but something has come up and we need to change weekends."

Of course it had. He'd decided last time that he wasn't taking this shit anymore.

"I've already made plans," he said with a sem-blance of calm. "This is my weekend, Nicole. You have her the majority of the time. You need to schedule anything that includes Rachel on your days."

"We agreed we'd be flexible—"

"You've abused my willingness too many times. Please have Rachel ready when I pick her up at five tomorrow." He stabbed his phone to end the call, anger burning beneath his breastbone.

His phone immediately buzzed. Nicole. This time, Ben muted it.

The detective who sat directly in front of him

in the bull pen swiveled his chair to look at Ben. Seth Chandler was near Ben's age of thirty-three. Both worked cases individually, but often partnered. Even when they weren't conducting an investigation together, they bounced ideas off each other. In the past year, they'd moved toward real friendship. In fact, Seth had invited Ben to bring his daughter to dinner tomorrow night. Seth's fiancée, Bailey, was arriving for a long weekend. Seth was champing at the bit for her to get her degree in May and move up here from Southern California. They were hanging in there with a long-distance relationship, but Ben imagined it was tough.

Had to beat having no relationship, though, he thought grumpily.

A woman's voice in his ear pulled his attention back to the moment.

"Uh-huh," he said, writing fast. He recited back the address and two phone numbers she had just given him as well as a string of dates for insurance claims, then thanked her and hung up. Seth had wandered away to refill his coffee cup, but returned just then.

"That your ex who called?" he asked.

"Unfortunately," Ben growled.

"Wanted to change your weekend again?"

"That was the idea. Funny how 'change' always ends up with me losing a weekend with Rachel."

"It sounded like she backed down this time."

"I didn't give her a chance to do anything else. It's a great weekend for me to have Rachel. I'm not tied up with anything big, so I can concentrate on her. I'm taking her sledding on Saturday. Nic hates to get cold, so she never does anything like that with Rachel." He hesitated. "You sure you don't mind me bringing her tomorrow night? If she'll be the only kid…" As far as he knew, the only other guests were Bailey's parents.

Seth smiled. "Hey, she'll get all the attention." His phone rang and he started to turn around, but then looked over his shoulder. "Forgot to tell you Eve will be there, too. You know, Bailey's sister."

Adoptive sister. Without knowing Bailey well and having never met Eve, Ben had heard enough from Seth to know how complicated a relationship the two women had. Bailey—whose birth name was Hope Lawson—had been abducted as a little girl, sexually molested and eventually abandoned by the man who'd taken her. By then she'd forgotten her name and where she came from and went into foster care in California. Seth liked to take up a cold case now and then, and had pursued finding pretty, blonde Hope Lawson, expecting improved DNA technology and databases that allowed law enforcement agencies to communicate better might help him bring the little girl's body home for her parents to bury. Instead, Hope had walked into the sheriff's department one day, stunning Seth, her grieving parents—

and the woman her parents had adopted several years after her disappearance.

Seth had once told Ben privately that the first words out of Eve's mouth had been, "The *real* daughter returns." Probably said sardonically. And who could blame her for feeling that way? However much the Lawsons loved the girl they adopted, she had to have grown up conscious of the shadow cast by their beloved missing daughter.

Now, staring at the other man's back, Ben wondered if this was intended to be just a family gathering that happened to include him and Rachel, or whether Seth was trying subtly to hook him up with Eve. Ben remembered, after seeing a press conference on TV about Hope's miraculous return, telling Seth that he thought Eve was the beauty of the two "sisters." Had that given Seth the idea?

But he shook his head. No, of course not; if Seth had anything like that in mind, he'd have done it a long time ago. That press conference had taken place last August, six months ago.

Yeah, but the Lawsons had invited Ben to have Thanksgiving with them. He'd declined because Nicole had asked him to join her and their daughter. There'd been a party at Christmas, too, which Ben had gone to but Eve had missed. Supposedly she'd been sick. Ben had wondered idly if she really did feel crappy or was dodging seeing Seth. The two of them had gone out some before Bai-

ley's reappearance. Eve might still find it tough
seeing him crazy in love with another woman.

So…maybe this dinner party *was* a setup.
Maybe Seth was desperate to find her a boyfriend
and get her off his conscience.

Ben grunted at that thought, remembering
the petite woman he'd seen on television. Heart-
shaped face, big, melting dark eyes, masses
of dark, curly hair, slender body. Yeah, safe to
say Eve Lawson could find her own dates and
wouldn't appreciate any help from a guy she
once had a thing with. And what would make
Seth think she'd look twice at Ben? Women probably had a type, just like men did, and Ben and
Seth were…well, not quite opposites, but certainly
didn't look much alike.

Anyway, if he had a type, it was china-doll-
beautiful, blue-eyed blondes.

Uh-huh. If that was true, why had Eve caught
his eye instead of Bailey, with her spectacular
cheekbones, blue eyes and ash-blond hair?

He didn't know. Maybe he'd needed an anti-
Nicole to spark his interest. He'd definitely reacted
to Eve's appearance back then, and, damn, it was
past time he started something that included regular sex. Long-term, though, that he couldn't see.
His commitment to his daughter and, yeah, even
Nicole, didn't leave much leftover.

Might be interesting actually meeting Eve,
though, he decided, then had no trouble putting

her out of his mind as he studied the notes he'd made a minute before and reached for the phone to dial the first of the two numbers.

EVE STILL FELT a tiny bit of sting every time she saw Seth and Bailey together, but she knew that had more to do with Bailey aka Hope than it did Seth. It did figure the long-missing Hope had not only returned triumphantly to the joy of her—and Eve's—parents, but had also snagged the guy Eve had been seeing.

Get over it, she'd told herself a few dozen times, and really she had. Mostly.

As far as she knew, her parents were the only other guests tonight, so she was surprised when the big, dark SUV she'd been following for the last couple blocks parked at the curb in front of Seth's rambler. Hmm. The silver sedan in the driveway beside her parents' car was probably a rental Bailey had picked up at the airport. No reason Eve couldn't block it in. She and Seth probably wouldn't leave the house all weekend.

Yep, minor sting.

After parking in the driveway and getting out, Eve glanced back to see a man lifting a girl from the backseat of the SUV, laughing up at her as he swung her high before setting her carefully on her feet on the sidewalk.

Her own feet declined to move. So, okay, it was dark, but the streetlight was only half a block away, and unless her eyes were failing her, this guy was absolutely gorgeous. Long, lean and movie-star handsome.

He took the girl's hand and they started up the driveway to where Eve was planted in their way.

His eyebrows rose as he took her in and drew the girl—had to be his daughter—to a stop. "You must be Eve," he said, in a voice just gritty enough to be sexy aside from his looks.

"I— Yes. Are you, um, a friend of Seth's?"

Or, horrors, a relative of the Lawsons she somehow had never met? Because, oh, God, he could have been Bailey's brother. Blond and beautiful. As was the girl, whose pale blond hair was French-braided and whose face was delicately pretty.

"He didn't tell you I'd be here? I'm Seth's partner. A detective with the sheriff's department," he added. "Ben Kemper. This is my daughter, Rachel. Rachel, meet Eve Lawson."

"Hi," the little girl whispered shyly.

Eve's smile came easily. "Nice to meet you. And your dad. What say we go in before we all freeze? Looks like my parents are already here." No way could she ask where Rachel's mommy was.

"I hear Bailey's a good cook," he said behind her, as she started for the porch.

"She is. Lucky for Seth."

He chuckled. "Yes, it is. If he's like me, when

he's on his own most of his meals come out of the freezer case at the grocery store."

"Tut-tut. Haven't you ever wanted to defy the sexual stereotype?" She smiled again at his daughter, softening her voice. "Would you like to ring the doorbell?"

Rachel would. She lifted a pink gloved hand and pushed the button, then jumped at the sound of a ding-dong within. A moment later Bailey let them all in.

"Eve!" Her pleasure appeared genuine.

Eve leaned in to hug her despite the touch-me-not air that usually only Seth violated. Eve had noticed that even their parents hesitated before embracing their daughter. Bailey had excellent reason to be repelled by most physical contact, but she returned this hug with enthusiasm. Maybe she was getting better at the family thing.

Then she turned her smile on Ben and his daughter. "You must be Rachel. Thank you for coming. Ben talks about you all the time, you know. We've all been dying to meet you."

Sounded as if Ben was quite the buddy. Closer to Seth and Bailey than Eve was.

As she stepped inside, she made a face nobody else would see. There was her inner bitch. Her initial reaction to her adoptive sister's return had pretty well guaranteed both Bailey and Seth were wary around her. And, really, she was still ambivalent about how good a friend she *wanted* to be of theirs. Her tie with Bailey was more fictional than anything, considering they were "sisters" who had never met until last summer, when Eve was twenty-eight and Bailey twenty-nine. Why bother even pursuing a relationship so illusory?

Maybe because, despite herself, she *liked* Bailey? And because they had more in common with each other than either did with their parents?

Eve unwrapped her scarf and unbuttoned her coat. When she started to shrug out of it, she was startled to realize someone was helping. Ben Kemper was apparently a gentleman. He was free because Bailey already had Rachel's pink fleece gloves in one hand and was tugging on the sleeve of her pouffy purple parka. His fingers were cold, which had to be why a brief touch on her neck sent a shiver through her.

"Thank you. Your daughter's coat is prettier than mine," Eve teased.

He laughed, deepening creases in his lean face. Eve was embarrassed at how her body warmed and softened just looking at him. At maybe six feet, he was tall enough to tower over her five foot four—okay, five foot three and a half if she stretched. Classically handsome, Ben had been blessed with perfect bone structure, tousled blond hair that glinted gold in this light, and dark blue eyes.

"I don't know about that," he murmured. "I think red is your color."

Red was undeniably her color. With her dusky skin and black hair, she'd look ridiculous in petal pink or lilac. Admitting as much hadn't come easily. Like most little girls, she'd wanted everything pink. Which she'd been denied. Because *Hope* had loved pink, Eve had always believed. Her bedroom, the first she'd ever had all to herself, couldn't be painted pink, because that's what color Hope's was. The room with the closed door, the one kept exactly as it had been the day she disappeared. A shrine.

To this day, Eve didn't know whether her adoptive mother had steered her to buy clothes in other colors because only Hope was supposed to be able to wear pretty pink and purple, or because Eve really did look better in crimson and orange and yield-sign yellow. She'd seen distress on her mother's face and quit asking for the forbidden colors.

Mostly, she'd gotten over the desire to be blonde and blue-eyed, too, so she fit in her new family instead of being so obviously adopted.

"Hey." A couple of faint lines had appeared on Ben's forehead and she wondered how much he'd seen on her face. Not much, she hoped, unsure why his comment—maybe a compliment?—had sent her back in time. He laid a hand on the small of her back and gave her a gentle nudge toward the living room. With a glance down, she saw that he'd once again taken his daughter's hand with his free one.

She felt a small burst of pleasure at being part of the threesome, almost as if they were together, before her practical self squelched it. She'd just met these two, and was pretty obviously not Rachel's mother. Who might simply be tied up tonight, although Eve's surreptitious glance failed to find a wedding ring on Ben Kemper's finger.

Seated, neither of her parents seemed to have touched their glasses of wine, set on coasters on the coffee table. Both beamed upon seeing her. Her mother bounced to her feet and hugged her.

"Oh, this is so wonderful! All of us together! And Ben, too." She turned her happy smile on his daughter. "You must be Rachel. I'm so glad you could come. My, your hair looks pretty like that."

"Mommy did it." She cast a glance upward at her father. "Daddy can't. He says his fingers are too big."

Ben's face went particularly blank. Apparently she wasn't the only one to notice, though, because before Eve could think what to say to counteract what must feel like disparagement, Eve's father smiled at the little girl.

"I have two daughters, and I never learned to do fancy hairdos, either. Your daddy is right. His fingers probably are too thick." He waggled his own for her to see. Kirk Lawson's hands were not only shaped like a block, but oil tended to be embedded deep in any cracks. He owned an auto body shop.

Rachel leaned trustingly against her father. "That's okay. I like to wear my hair in a ponytail, too, and he can do that."

Seth, solidly built and brown-haired, appeared from the kitchen. "Hey, glad you could all make it. Rachel, nice to see you. I hear you're going sledding tomorrow."

She bounced. "Uh-huh. Daddy says so."

"That'll be fun."

Lucky girl, Eve couldn't help thinking. She hadn't had a daddy to do things like that with her until the Lawsons adopted her at nine years old. It had been a long time before she'd been comfortable with her new father, who seemed an alien creature to her. He was such a quiet man, he'd been hard for her to read. Patient, too, though. In a way, she had more faith now in his love than she did in her adoptive mother's. Karen might not have mourned any more deeply than her husband did for their lost daughter, but unlike him she'd never even tried to hide the ever-present grief. Since Hope's reappearance, the change in her had been stunning, making Eve doubt how adequately she'd filled the vacuum in that house— or her mother's heart. In contrast, Kirk's smiles for his real daughter didn't seem so different from the ones he gave Eve.

"The daughter we chose," he had told her last summer, after both their parents had overheard her saying things she shouldn't have to Bailey.

Before she knew it, she was seated in a rocker and had a glass of red wine in her hand. Ben Kemper sat on a rolling ottoman only a few feet away. Eve's mother had taken Rachel to the bathroom, and Seth and Bailey were both working on dinner, having turned down all offers to help.

Ben and her father discussed sports briefly, neither sounding all that interested. Then he looked at her. "Seth says you're a social worker."

"That's right. I'm with the Department of Social and Health Services. I supervise kids who are wards of the court."

He nodded; as a police officer, he'd interacted with social workers on a regular basis. It was probably a surprise they'd never met before. He asked some questions that demonstrated how knowledgeable he was. Eve admitted to occasionally feeling like a hamster trapped on her wheel.

"I run and run and run." She made a face. "My greatest fear is letting a kid slip off my radar. I've heard enough horror stories of what can happen."

Ben nodded. "I used to worry that I'd missed something when I was trying to decide whether to make an arrest on domestic violence calls. She says she's fine, she whacked herself in the face when she slipped on the ice going out to her car, yes, she and her husband were arguing but of course he'd never hit her. I leave and think, what if she's scared to death of him? What if he kills her next time, because I was credulous enough to buy this story she tells me with him standing a few feet away listening?" He shook his head. "But what can you do?"

"Never enough," she said. "I tell myself I'm human and I will make mistakes, but—"

His crooked grin told her he understood. "But it's an excuse, and it doesn't cut it."

"Yes." She shrugged. "As it is, I get frustrated because of the limitations on what I can do at my best. Foster homes have to meet a minimum standard, but is that good enough? The people are feeding a girl, keeping her safe, but do they listen to her read? Pay attention to whether she's doing her homework? Do they even know how to encourage her to excel academically? Often not. The rate of high school graduation for foster kids lags well behind that of kids living with their own parents. Never mind college attendance! And then there are the extras that are often beyond these kids—dance lessons, the rent on a musical instrument, the cost of a prom dress, clothes or things like iPods that let them fit in, the fee required for college applications. Do they ever get to museums? See art house films or documentaries versus the latest blow-'em-up multiplex hit? These kids deserve everything other children take for granted." Almost hoarse with her passion by the time she finished, she grimaced an apology. "Sorry. I get carried away."

His blue eyes were unexpectedly warm. She

was also aware for the first time that those eyes were shadowed in a way she saw sometimes in her kids—and in her own mirror.

"Don't apologize. You're right. I see situations on the job where I wish I could do more, too, and can't. But what's the answer?"

She'd had ideas lately, but didn't have an opportunity to share them. Her mother and Rachel returned, and then they were all called to the dinner table, where conversation was general. Her parents were excited about going to California to see Bailey graduate from USC. Bailey had been plagued again recently by a persistent journalist who wanted to write a follow-up article about her. Seth was clearly pissed about it; probably it didn't sit well with him that he wouldn't be there to protect her. To lighten the atmosphere, Eve told a few funny stories from her job, and Ben did the same. Rachel got brave enough to tell them about her kindergarten teacher and this boy in her class who was so wild, he liked to climb up on the table and dance and sometimes he'd start to take his clothes off. Ben cringed at hearing that one. He said something in passing that told her he was divorced. This was obviously his weekend with his daughter.

Eve kept having a feeling of unreality. Why hadn't Bailey ever mentioned how absolutely gorgeous Seth's partner was? Surely she wasn't oblivious. And then there was the glint in his eyes that seemed to be only for her—Eve. As if he was attracted to her. The idea scared as much as tempted her. Men who looked like him were magnets for women. What were the odds he didn't have a girl-friend—or a woman for every night of the week? Eve had never been loaded with confidence, and knew the last thing she needed was to get involved with a man unlikely to stay interested in her for long.

Oh, and she couldn't forget he worked with Seth, her sister's fiancé, which could make the whole thing awkward.

And, wow, was she overthinking this, or what? She'd have rolled her eyes if she could have done it unseen. What was she, twelve years old and sign-ing her name "Eve Kemper" even though the boy hadn't even asked her to dance yet?

Even so, she couldn't take her gaze from the tall, sexy man currently smiling at his daughter as he tucked a napkin over her pretty pink shirt so she didn't spill lemon meringue pie on it.

He won't call.

But she wanted him to so much, the ache filled her chest. It didn't help that tomorrow was Valen-tine's Day. If he called tomorrow…that might be better than a bouquet.

Not until she was fastening her seat belt prepa-ratory to leaving did it occur to her that she had scarcely noticed Seth tonight, and had felt not the slightest pang when she saw the way he looked at Bailey.

Heaven help her, she'd gotten over any remnants of her crush on Seth Chandler the moment she set eyes on his partner.

CHAPTER TWO

RACHEL HAD FUN sledding the next day—for all
of about five minutes. No, that was an exaggera-
tion, but not by much. She got cold and whined.
She insisted on trying to go down a short hill on
her own and fell off the sled, landing face-first
in a snowbank. She cried so hard Ben was frantic, sure she'd broken a bone at least. God! Nicole
would never let him hear the last of it.

Eventually, Rach settled down enough to admit
she'd just been scared, and her mittens were
soaked and she'd gotten snow in her boots so her
toes were cold, and couldn't they go home?

Disappointed, Ben said, "Sure," then struggled
with incredulity when not ten minutes down the
highway, Rachel declared, "That was fun, Daddy!
Can we go again?"

What was he supposed to say? You've got to be
kidding? An hour's round-trip drive for five minutes of fun and ten minutes of squalling? Maybe
Nicole was right and he didn't have what it took
to be an adequate parent.

But he remembered being a lot more patient
than Nicole was the first months of Rachel's life,

when she'd been colicky and content only when being carried against a shoulder. He'd walked miles those nights, gone into work feeling hollow with his eyes burning.

He was just…getting out of practice, that was all. It scared him sometimes, wondering whether his relationship with his daughter would grow increasingly distant with him such a small part of her life.

And what if Nicole remarried, giving Rach a resident daddy? Forcing him to see the woman he'd loved since they were in high school leaning against another man, her smile showing how happy *he* was making her.

Ben's stomach clenched at the picture in his head. He knew she was dating; Rachel had said things, and it didn't seem to occur to Nic that he'd mind. Or that he sometimes imagined—

He cut himself off. He was being stupid. He'd had her, and lost her. He had to get over thinking she'd ever give him another chance.

Since the divorce, he'd taken other women out, even slept with a couple of them. He'd half hoped Nic would hear through the grapevine. If she had, she didn't care. The past few months, Ben had quit bothering with other women. If she knew that, Nicole didn't react.

Maybe it was time he asked a woman out because he wanted to. Because he thought he might enjoy her. And, yeah, because his body stirred at the idea of getting naked with her.

By the time he dropped Rachel off on Sunday, he was cursing himself for not finding an opportunity to have asked Eve for her phone number. He called information from his cell phone and was told there was no listing for an Eve Lawson. Probably not a surprise, given her profession— and she likely didn't even have a landline. He kept his number and address unlisted, too, as did most cops. Of course, he had better resources on the job—but getting a date wasn't an acceptable reason to use them.

He could call her parents or ask Seth, but didn't like the idea of setting himself up for humiliation if she turned him down. She'd have voice mail at the local DSHS office...but, man, that wasn't any way to ask a woman out.

Ben usually carried his own cell phone all the time, but Seth had a tendency to lay his on his desk and leave it when he got coffee or used the john. Monday, Ben bided his time.

"Damn, too much coffee," Seth grumbled at last, and ambled out.

Ben went to his partner's desk and half sat on it, waiting until nobody in the bull pen was watching him, then casually reached for the phone, hoping it wasn't password-protected. *Quick, quick.* Contacts...what if Seth hadn't kept Eve's listing? But why wouldn't he, when she was Bailey's sister?

Yes! There it was. Ben committed the number to memory and set the phone down as casually as he'd picked it up, then wandered over to refill his own coffee cup.

Should he call her in the middle of the day, or wait until evening? *Evening*, he decided. He didn't want to catch her at a bad moment.

His apartment always felt especially empty and cheerless after he'd had Rachel. He kept thinking he should do something to make the spare bedroom more hers, but he occasionally considered buying a house and hated to waste a lot of effort on a cookie-cutter apartment. After walking in the door at almost seven that evening, he went straight to the kitchen and turned on the oven, then took a pizza from the freezer. He ought to add a vegetable, but decided "ought to" wasn't enough motivation.

Finally, he took out his phone. Called up Eve's number, waited as it rang. Once, twice, three times. His tension rose. Why hadn't he thought to ask Seth if she had a boyfriend? Four.

On the fifth ring, she answered. Her "Hello?" sounded breathless.

"Eve? This is Ben Kemper. We met at Seth's the other day."

Silence was his immediate answer. "Ben," she said finally, sounding cautious. "With the cute little girl. Did she have fun sledding?"

"She got cold really fast. She claimed to have fun, but I don't know."

"That's too bad. I remember the first time I had a chance to go. It was the most fun I'd ever had."

"Was it the Lawsons who took you?"

"Yes. I mean, before that I tried sliding on cardboard a few times—" She broke off. "I was older than your daughter, though. I mean, when Mom and Dad took me."

She was adopted. He knew that much, but nothing about the years that came before. Years that might explain why she'd chosen the work she did.

"I'll try again," he said. "With Rachel, that is. Maybe buy her some better winter boots and mittens she can leave here."

"Good idea, except she'll outgrow them fast."

Time for a segue into the reason for his call. "Eve, I'm hoping you'll let me take you to dinner one of these nights."

Waiting through the ensuing silence, Ben felt about sixteen, asking out the girl he'd had a crush on for the past year. No, longer than that—since middle school. He felt light-headed and realized he was holding his breath. Stupid. It wasn't as if this mattered so much. It was maybe a little more awkward than usual, because of Eve's relationship to Seth and Bailey, but—

"I'd like that," she said simply.

Yes! "I'm free any night," he admitted. That was

him, man about town. "But we can wait until the weekend if that would be better for you."

"No, as long as I don't stay out late, a week-night is fine."

He wished it wasn't too late for tonight. "To-morrow?"

"Tomorrow is good." Did she sound bemused?

Stimson didn't have a lot of fine dining, but he didn't want to suggest they drive any distance given that they both probably had to get up early the next morning. "Any chance you like Thai?" he asked.

She did. There might not be a decent Italian restaurant in town, but the Thai one was good. She gave him her address, and they agreed on six. "Just give me a call if you have to be late," she said, surprising him with her understanding until he remembered she'd dated Seth.

Damn it, had she *slept* with Seth? Man, he hoped not. Not only for his sake, he realized, but also for Eve's and Bailey's.

He leaned back in his chair, suppressing a grin. He had a date.

"I ALMOST CALLED you today," Eve confessed the next evening to Ben. The host, whose English was poor to nonexistent, had seated them in a booth, handed them menus and backed away. Eve didn't reach for hers.

Neither did Ben. His mouth kicked up at one corner. "Because you couldn't wait for this evening?"

She huffed, which had him smiling. "Seriously. Something happened today involving one of my kids."

"Your kids?" He looked startled.

Despite her worry about Joel, Eve giggled at Ben's expression. "Not literally! I'm sorry. I think of them that way. The kids I supervise."

"I had this sudden picture of children packed into bunk beds behind closed doors in your apartment." Amusement laced that slightly gritty voice. "You sternly telling them to hush until you and the nice man were gone."

"Are you a nice man?" Lord, she was flirting. Where had her ambivalence gone?

"Of course I am." Giving her a lazy, sexy grin, he nodded at her menu and picked up his own. "We should probably order before we delve into why you needed to call a detective about one of your kids."

They both decided on jasmine tea and to share an order of spring rolls. He ordered a green curry with chicken, Eve a spicy eggplant in a chili paste.

"Trying to scare me off?" Ben asked drolly.

She blinked, and probably blushed. "Oh, dear. I didn't think. It probably will, um, give me interesting breath."

He only laughed, although his eyes were heavy-lidded. "Curry might not taste so good second-hand, either."

Eve knew she was blushing now. He intended to kiss her. Thank heavens the lighting in here was dim and her skin didn't show the warmth as obviously as someone much paler would.

"Your kid," he prompted.

Kid? Then, embarrassed by what must be a blank expression, she said hurriedly, "His name is Joel Kekoa. His dad is Hawaiian and Joel looks it, too."

"Wait. Does he play football?"

"Yes. You go to games?"

"Sometimes. He's good."

"So I'm told. I mean, I've seen him play, but I'm not a connoisseur. He's a senior, and had the fun of being recruited by half a dozen major college programs."

"Yeah? Which one did he pick?"

"The University of Oregon."

Ben nodded, then waited for her to continue. He must know that grades weren't the problem; she wouldn't have been tempted to call him about anything like that.

So she explained about the grumpy old man next door to Joel's foster home, and about the smashed rose canes. She surprised herself by also sharing her unease with the new foster mother and her son.

"Then I had a call in the middle of the night from a Deputy Pruitt."

Ben nodded.

"Somebody threw a rock through the guy's bedroom window. I guess it just missed him. It was big enough, it could have done some real damage. The deputy says it was thrown hard. It skipped off the bed and smashed into the closet door, scarring it. Mr. Rowe—that's the neighbor—insists it had to be Joel who threw it. He's big, athletic, has a good arm, and supposedly was mad because Mr. Rowe complained to the foster parents about the damage to his roses."

"Was he?"

"No. He was more upset that the stepmom seemed to doubt him when he said he didn't have anything to do with it."

She felt—and sounded—troubled. She'd only talked to the deputy on the phone, not in person, but from his tone she'd suspected he was rolling his eyes at her defense of Joel, the obvious culprit.

Their spring rolls arrived, and she spooned dipping sauce to her small plate and took a roll, mumbling, "Ouch," when she discovered how hot it still was.

Ignoring the food, Ben asked, "Did the kid get arrested?"

She gaped at him. "No! How could anybody prove he'd thrown the rock? There were no witnesses."

Expression inscrutable, he didn't say anything

for a moment. Then, "Why me? This doesn't sound like anything that would normally be referred to a detective."

Was she imagining his restraint? Or was it that she'd imagined his sympathy the other night when she talked about the plight of foster children?

"Just...to get your take." She shrugged. "I had the feeling the deputy instantly agreed Joel was guilty. Foster kid, minor feud going on between him and the neighbor."

"Who do you think threw the rock?"

Annoyed now at his measured tone, she raised her eyebrows. "How would I know? From what Joel said about the neighbor, he's been at war with every kid that ever walked past his place. Never mind the adults. The last time I was over there, Joel and I were talking at my car, and Mr. Rowe was watching us out the window the whole time. Just a slit between drapes. You know." For some reason, she didn't tell him that Gavin had been doing the same, and more openly. She'd begun to regret ever mentioning the incident to Ben.

"Okay," he said mildly. "I'd have thought you'd go to Seth. You've known him longer, and he's going to be your brother-in-law."

She made sure her tone was light. "It was impulse, that's all." Crazy to feel let down, disappointed because Ben didn't jump immediately in on her side. "Don't worry about it," she added. "It was just that I had you on my mind after you called. If the impulse strikes again, I'll call Seth. Family discount, right?"

"No." Ben's gaze held hers. "Call me, not Seth. Anytime. I mean that."

Well. Eve had not a clue how to take this.

"You're right. I probably am more sympathetic than Seth is. He's good with kids but doesn't have any of his own, and until Bailey had probably never given a thought to issues foster kids have."

"And you have?"

"My ex was in foster care by the time I knew her."

"A good one, I hope."

"Her last one seemed like it. But sometimes I wondered—" He cut himself off, alarm flashing in those shadowed eyes. "Doesn't matter," he said after a minute.

Eve didn't have any choice but to squelch her curiosity. Pretending she didn't wish he'd finish that last thought, she said, "So you married your high school girlfriend?"

He seemed almost embarrassed to admit he had. They'd gone their separate ways after his first few months of college, but Eve had the impression that might not have been by his choice. He'd initially taken a job with the busier and more urban King County Sheriff's Department, which surrounded Seattle, but had run into Nicole again at a party and immediately applied for a job locally.

"Ancient history," he said then. "What about you? How'd you end up back in Stimson?"

"Oh, once I went to work for DSHS, I asked to be assigned here. I thought my parents needed to have me close. You know their history."

He nodded. "Hope."

Always Hope. "They never quit grieving. I think I...softened their grief."

"I bet you did more than that," he said gently. "I saw their faces when you walked into the living room the other night. You can't tell me they don't love you."

"No, I'm sure they do. I was really lucky that they took me in. I needed them, and they needed me."

She let him be satisfied by a simple truth that wasn't the entire truth. Something way more complex almost always underlay simple, in her experience. But Eve was too ashamed of her unfulfilled longings to air them for him anyway.

No, she told him, she'd never come close to anything as serious as marriage. "Just hasn't happened," she said, going for unconcerned.

"What about Seth?"

Surprised by his blunt question, she hesitated. It was good he felt compelled to ask, wasn't it? Surely the implication was that he wanted to pursue a relationship with her. And, despite her hesitations, she couldn't remember being as attracted to a man as she was to Ben.

"I liked Seth," she admitted. "I was more interested than he was, I suspect, but, honestly, we never got past a few casual dinners. A couple of movies." She lifted one shoulder. "I didn't take it very well when he dropped me, but I'll bet you can guess why."

"Hope. Bailey," Ben corrected himself.

"Right. It took me a while to realize that what really hurt was being thrown over for her. I guess you can tell I have some unresolved jealousy going on here."

"I'd be surprised if you didn't." The smile in his eyes reassured her. "I saw your mother when she came to see Seth every week. The hurt and hope on her face—" He grimaced. "Poor choice of words. You had to have been left wondering..."

When he didn't finish, she did. "Whether I came close to filling the hole in their lives left by her disappearance? I didn't wonder. I knew."

"You're sure it wasn't in your head? Even if the two of you had really been sisters, they'd have mourned for her as much. The one doesn't necessarily have anything to do with the other."

"I do know that." She averted her face. This wasn't something she usually shared with anyone. And...she'd been lucky. How many times had she had to remind herself? The Lawsons loved her. They'd given her so much. "I was nine when they adopted me. When your own parents don't want you, and then you get passed around in foster care, it can't help but make you doubt yourself. How… lovable you really are." She hated seeing what might be only sympathy in his expression, but looked a lot like pity. "So my rational self knows you're right. Doesn't mean that somewhere deep inside I don't still wonder."

"I understand."

His forehead had crinkled and a momentarily distant look in his eyes made her speculate whether he had better reason to understand than he'd said. There had to be a cause for those shadows she'd noticed.

Instinct told her not to ask, though. Feeling as if she'd bared enough of herself, too, she asked a question about how the detective division worked, and from that point on their conversation avoided anything too personal.

During the mostly quiet drive to her apartment house, Eve regretted saying as much as she had. She hadn't much liked herself lately. She needed to put the jealousy and resentment and self-doubt behind herself. Telling a guy she liked how petty she could be—and on a first date—should be on her list of top ten don'ts.

Thinking about why she'd shot her big mouth off had to be the reason she felt tense. Although she couldn't stop herself from thinking about the good-night kiss. The one that would be a peck if Ben had changed his mind about her.

He parked in a visitor's slot at her complex and

walked her up, waiting while she unlocked her door. She dropped her handbag on the small table just inside and turned to smile at him.

"I'm glad you suggested this. I had a good time, Ben. Thank you for dinner."

"I enjoyed myself, too. I should have asked for your phone number six months ago."

Eve blinked. "But...we hadn't met."

"I saw you on TV. The press conference. I...commented to Seth on what a beauty Bailey's sister was. I kind of wonder now if the Thanksgiving and Christmas get-togethers weren't engineered for us to meet."

"That never occurred to me." Was it possible he liked her looks better than Bailey's? Because of his daughter, she'd assumed his ex-wife was another blue-eyed blonde, but...maybe not. Rachel could have taken after him.

"Better late than never," he murmured, and stepped closer. He tipped her chin up with one big hand, bent, and brushed his lips over hers.

The soft contact was tantalizing enough to have her rising on tiptoe to try to sustain it.

"I've been thinking about this all evening," he said huskily, and nipped her bottom lip before stroking it with his tongue.

Eve wrapped her arms around his neck and let her lips part, astonished by her instant, powerful response. His tongue slid over hers, teasing more than commanding. The lighter he kept the kiss, the more she wanted deeper, hotter.

He groaned suddenly and banded his arms around her to lift her. It was as if he'd abruptly lost patience. Her breasts were flattened against his broad chest and she felt his erection. The thrust of his tongue became rhythmic before he broke away to kiss her jaw, then her throat. Eve let her head fall back, savoring the warm tension of his mouth, the way he rocked his hips as if he couldn't help himself.

But when he reached her collarbone, he went still before releasing a ragged exhalation and letting her slide down his body. She hadn't realized he'd lifted her off her feet until they made contact again with the floor. It was lucky his arms stayed around her for a minute; her legs felt shaky, weak. Warmth pooled down low, shocking her with her readiness. She was rarely to never this enthusiastic.

Ben nuzzled her cheek. "I got carried away."

"I think I did, too," she said tremulously.

"Good." He lifted his head to look down at her, his eyes narrowed, the blue deepened. His hair, a dull gold in the subdued light of the hall, was ruffled. By her fingers. "I want to see you again."

Her teeth closed on her lip to steady it. That made a light flare in his eyes. "Yes," she whispered.

"I'll call you." His voice was pure gravel.

"Okay." Meek woman, and she didn't even care.

He gave something like a laugh, said, "I don't think I dare kiss you again," and released her slowly enough to suggest the same reluctance she felt. He backed into the hall and ordered, "Lock behind me."

"Yes, Detective."

He grinned at her teasing, let his gaze run over her one more time and made another inarticulate sound that had her almost unbearably tempted to do the unthinkable—invite him in. After a first date.

But he kept backing up, and she found the strength to say good-night and close her door, turn the dead bolt and put on the chain.

After which she slumped against the door, let out a soft moan and began to smile.

BEN FROWNED AT his rearview mirror. A logging truck was careening along the highway behind him, closing the distance fast. The narrow, two-lane road wouldn't allow an opportunity to pass for several more miles. The driver had better not crowd his bumper.

"So." His passenger cleared his throat. "Looked like you and Eve hit it off."

Ben flicked a glance at Seth. They were returning from an unproductive interview in the far corner of the county. Ben would have liked to lean on the guy a little harder, but knew they didn't have enough justification yet.

"Bailey put you up to getting the scoop?" he asked.

"No, she'd have no reason not to go straight to the source herself."

Eve, he meant.

"Do they talk?"

"They seem to be getting better at it."

The warmth Ben had seen between the two women had seemed genuine, enough so he'd been a little surprised last night when Eve admitted to also feeling jealousy.

"Eve came across as welcoming at the press conference last year."

"For her parents' benefit."

The remark made Ben feel conflicted. To give himself a moment, he checked the rearview mirror again. The truck loomed, still not slowing down. A sonorous horn sounded. "Son of a bitch," he muttered.

"What?" Seth turned. "If he rides our tail, let's ticket him."

"Works for me." Ben moved his shoulders in an effort to relax tension that had come out of nowhere. "Eve and I had dinner last night," he said abruptly.

"Hey." Seth sounded pleased. "Why didn't you say something?"

The driver of the logging truck either surrendered to common sense or noticed that he was closing on a police car, because he slowed and dropped back.

"Seemed a little awkward when you were seeing her not that long ago."

"I've told you before, there wasn't much to it." Seth seemed to brood for a minute. "I'd have probably quit calling her a lot sooner if not for Karen."

Ben raised his eyebrows.

"Seemed like every damn week when she came in, she'd say something about Eve. I'd think, yeah, she was fun, why not?"

"Then why not?" Ben asked.

"No chemistry. It's either there or it's not."

Ben grunted his agreement. He'd met beautiful women who left him cold.

"I kissed her good-night politely. Never got past that," his partner added.

Ben relaxed a little more. Eve had implied as much, but he wasn't sure she'd have told him if she'd slept with Seth. Good God! Imagine if she had, and then he'd fallen for her adoptive sister. Things were bad enough as it was.

His partner nodded acknowledgment, and, men being men, they let the subject drop, reverting instead to the current investigation of an unnecessarily brutal jewelry store holdup. Fortunately, no customers had been in the store. The owner had tried to flee out the back to get help, leaving his assistant behind the counter, but one of the two masked men had caught him and beaten the shit out of him while the other pepper-sprayed the assistant. They'd smashed glass cases and left with sackfuls of gold pieces set with diamonds and other precious stones.

The store was new this last year, in a strip mall of businesses that were higher end than usual for Stimson and environs. Some years back, the city had annexed a whole lot of land, but opposition from an organized group of homeowners had kept them from including an area that had since seen extensive development including half a dozen condominium complexes. Lots of new people and businesses meant a swell in crime and a headache for county law enforcement.

A jewelry store heist, though, that was unexpected. Jewelry could be hard to unload for anything close to value. The men had worn heavy boots, dirty jeans and hooded sweatshirts as well as black ski masks, which didn't sound like members of a sophisticated ring. Even more telling, they had fled in a white van that belonged to a local electrical company. Reported stolen that morning, it was found abandoned half an hour after the heist beside an often deserted road leading to the county's solid waste transfer station. Interestingly, the thieves had left the key in the ignition, which Ben thought was remarkably considerate.

It also happened that Ramstad Electrical Inc.

had recently fired an employee named Ken Hardison who was reportedly disgruntled. He'd been assigned that particular van and could easily have copied or even kept a key.

Ken Hardison had been home when Ben and Seth came knocking on his door, but had proved to be surly and unwilling to say much more than, "If you found my fingerprints, it's because I did the wiring on that store."

"Is that why you think we're here?" Seth had asked blandly.

"Why else would you be?" He'd glowered at them. "I never stole anything in my life."

His girlfriend had left him after he'd apparently taken his rage at being fired out on her, following a couple of previous accusations of domestic violence. Sweet-natured, he was not.

Ben really wanted to talk to the girlfriend, but they had as yet failed to locate her. Who could blame her for going into hiding? He just hoped she hadn't left the area.

Ben parked outside the sheriff's department headquarters and was reaching for his door handle when he thought of something. "You ever deal with Eve on the job?"

Seth already had his door open, but didn't get out. "Sure, that's how we met. Don't let her fool you. Some of her 'kids' are juvenile delinquents. I arrested one of them for setting a fire at the high school."

"I remember that. Eve was his caseworker?"

"Yep. She was disappointed in him, but also way more understanding than I was." He grinned. "We had some spirited debates. I was actually kind of surprised she agreed to go out with me after that. Why'd you ask?"

Ben waited until they were walking across the parking lot to answer. "She's having some issues with another of her kids. Thinks he's good as gold."

"Sounds like Eve," Seth said tolerantly. "She's deeply committed to those kids."

"She has the right background for her job."

"I'd say so. Gives her a bias, too, though."

"She admitted the arsonist was guilty, though?"

"Yeah, that wasn't the issue. Her goal was to see him get help instead of time in lockup."

"Did she win?"

Ben thought the other detective looked embarrassed.

"Pretty much. He did thirty days in juvie, then went to a group home for intensive counseling. When I asked, she told me Friday that he's doing really well. So, hell, maybe she was right and I was wrong. Kid was only fourteen."

Ben laughed. He had no trouble picturing Eve Lawson firing up in defense of a troubled boy. He'd seen a hint of that passion when she talked about how inadequate the foster care system was despite the best efforts of everyone who worked in it.

And, damn, he'd felt her passion when he kissed her. His intention had been to keep it light, but when his touch seemed to ignite her, he'd had a hell of a time making himself back off and leave.

The chemistry was there, no question. She intrigued him, too. That was one complicated woman. He'd thought about her all day and had every intention of calling her as he'd said.

He was still bothered by her ties to Seth, however. With Eve being Bailey's sister, Ben had a feeling Seth wouldn't like anyone hurting her.

Ben mulled over the idea of sounding her out on whether she had her eye out for an engagement ring or was open to something less serious. He could do it subtly. The idea of screwing up a solid partnership on the job because of a woman didn't sit well with him.

Back when he was with Nicole…well, that would have been different.

Might still be, he admitted, if she needed him.

He let out a harsh breath. Nic wouldn't turn to him if she was facing life imprisonment. Far as he could tell, what she mostly felt was resentment because she was stuck dealing with him where Rachel was concerned. He was clearly alone in feeling any lingering…he didn't want to call it love. Okay, then: fondness. Memory of what they'd shared. Regret.

A year and a half had passed since their split, and all he seemed to awaken in her these days was annoyance. No more delusions, he told himself.

It was good he had Eve on his mind. Complications or not, he'd definitely call her tonight.

CHAPTER THREE

HAVING SPOTTED BEN alone at a booth at the back of the diner, Eve waved off the hostess and hurried to join him. He had seen her immediately, and before she reached him slid out of the booth to stand. He'd probably put in as long a day as she had, but that didn't keep him from looking sexy. The badge and weapon he wore added an element of danger to the rangy, broad-shouldered physique and fallen-angel face. She wasn't the only one who noticed. Several women diners had turned their heads to stare.

"Eve." It was as if no one else was there. "You're wet."

She surveyed him. "You're not."

"It wasn't raining when I got here."

"Well, it is now," she said unnecessarily. She shed her raincoat with his help and laid it and her handbag on the bench seat, sliding in after them.

Ben resumed his seat, facing her. It wasn't a surprise that he'd requested the booth in the back corner; Seth had always done that, too. Nor that Ben preferred to have his back to the wall and be able to sweep the entire room with an assessing gaze. It must be a cop thing, and was fine by her. *She* didn't want to see anyone, and would be just as happy at the moment if no one she knew spotted her.

"Thank you for suggesting this. What a day."

"Bad?" he asked. Although she suspected he remained aware on some level of every single person in the café, his gaze stayed intent on her alone. Did he know how seductive that was?

"No, just long." Distressing, too. She hadn't liked what she'd read between the lines at her last home visit and would need to reassess that placement. Sad to say, things like that weren't out of the ordinary. She didn't need to talk about it. "I hope you didn't mind eating so late," Eve added. She'd had to call him this afternoon and ask to push dinner back a couple of hours or do it another night.

"I had plenty to do." This smile was humorless. "Filling a couple of hours is never a problem."

"No, I don't suppose it is. Bailey said you and Seth are working on that jewelry store robbery."

"We are," he agreed.

"But no arrests?"

"Unfortunately." He hesitated. "Between you and me, we're pretty sure we know who did it. Backing up our suspicions isn't going as well."

"I'm amazed you got that far," she admitted. "With them wearing ski masks—" Seeing the way his gaze flicked past her, she turned her head to see the waitress approaching. "Oh, dear. I should decide what I want to eat, shouldn't I?"

Having eaten here a few hundred times before, Eve barely had to open the menu. The salads were tasteless, so she mentally shrugged and went with a teriyaki chicken sandwich and fries. Ben ordered a burger and fries.

Once they were alone again, he told her a little more about the investigation and the people they'd talked to, mentioning the domestic abuse police reports and the missing girlfriend.

"She has a kid, too, so I can't blame her for doing her best to disappear. It's more of a surprise that women stick so long with a creep like that, especially when they have a child to think about."

"Has Child Protective Services been involved?" Eve asked. "After a couple police visits, they might have been called to evaluate the safety of the child. If so, she may have thought she had to keep them informed about where she is."

Expression arrested, Ben said, "I didn't think of that. Good idea."

Pleased, she nonetheless wrinkled her nose. "CPS, now, that's a job I wouldn't want. If I'm afraid of something bad happening because I let a child slip through the cracks, it's a thousand times worse for them. Too often, they're investigating really horrific situations. You know how hard it is to be sure you're making the right call. More often than not, kids will deny abuse."

"Because whatever family they have feels safer than unknown alternatives."

She nodded, then smiled her thanks when the waitress brought drinks. "I'm glad you suggested this," she said. "I don't think I'd have been up to fine dining tonight." She should have detoured to the restroom to brush her hair and fix her makeup, but there wasn't a lot of point since she'd have had to walk right past him first, and he'd have gotten a good look at the real end-of-day Eve.

"You ever think about having a family of your own?" he asked. "It would be tough, putting in these kind of hours."

The question sounded casual, but surprised her anyway. And—okay—made her feel a little giddy even though this was only a second date. Was he really asking whether she intended to have children?

No—wait. He might just be concerned about his daughter, assuming they were to get any more involved. Even so, that suggested he was thinking ahead, which was a good sign.

"Eventually, I would like to have a family," she said. "And you're right. When—if—that happens, I'd want to cut back to part-time or find an alternative. I know what it's like not to be important to your own parents." Hating the suddenly raw sound to her voice, seeing a shift in his expression, she gave a small shrug. "I think your Rachel is lucky. She seems so confident, and you're good with her."

His jaw tightened. "The divorce hit her hard."

"Probably, but once she's sure she can still count on both you and her mother, she'll be fine."

He looked hard at her. Didn't he believe her? No—probably all he wanted to know was whether she was being sincere or was only trying to allay his worries.

Eve was glad that their food arrived before she felt compelled to start babbling. After spreading the napkin on her lap, she was tempted to change the subject altogether, but reminded herself he was the one to start talking about family and children.

"Do you miss her?" she asked.

His startled gaze flew to hers. "Nicole?" Then his expression was shuttered. "You mean Rachel. Yeah, I do. Every day. And Nicole…" He frowned and didn't finish.

Eve knew better than to say anything.

"She keeps making plans on my weekend, figuring it won't matter to anyone if we do a switch."

"But it does." A lump rose in Eve's throat. "To you and Rachel both."

Again he studied her with that unnerving intensity. "Why do you include Rachel? It's always something fun Nicole has come up with. Another kid's birthday party—and, no, I know she has no control over when Rachel's friends schedule their parties. A play, a chance to go roller-skating. I sound like a jerk if I say no."

"In the short term, Rachel wants to do something fun. But she also needs consistency. To be able to count on her time with you. Consistency, rules and routine form a...a foundation for kids. They need their parents to say, 'This is how things will go,' and stick to it." She made a face. "And here's the woman with no parenting experience lecturing you. I'm sorry."

He shook his head. "You do know what happens when things go wrong and how to turn them around for a kid. In comparison, I suspect most parents do nothing but bumble along, hoping they aren't screwing up."

Eve laughed. "That's mostly what social workers do, too, you know."

His swift grin chased the shadows from his eyes and made her heart squeeze. "Don't disillusion me."

"Okay."

He took a big bite, and she followed suit. A minute later, he said, "It was the hours that did my marriage in."

Eve frowned and set down her sandwich. "Really?"

"You sound surprised. You must have read that cops have a really high divorce rate."

"Well, sure I have, but I doubt the hours you put in are the main reason."

"Women get tired of not being able to count on their husband being home for dinner or special occasions. Nicole claimed she felt like a single parent anyway. I think it's not so much the long hours as that they're erratic."

"So are mine!"

"And you've never had a guy you were seeing think you ought to put him first?"

"If a man so much as suggested I should ditch some child's problem to be on time for our dinner date, *I'm* the one who'd lose interest," she said with spirit. "The kids I was dealing with at the end of the day today—they *had* to come first, if only temporarily."

"People don't always get that."

He meant his wife didn't get that. "You were a deputy when you got married."

Ben looked wary. "I was."

"You must have dated for a while first. Maybe lived together?"

This so wasn't her business, Eve realized belatedly, but the whole idea made her mad. Love shouldn't be conditional. What good would it be, then? All too often, she saw the damage done to children because parents or teachers or foster parents couldn't love or accept them with their flaws. And wasn't this the same thing, in a way? Ben's ex-wife had loved him…until an aspect of who he was irritated her.

"We might have gotten married too soon," Ben

said, sounding constrained. "I was the one to push for it. Once I saw her again…" He shrugged.

He didn't have to finish. He'd known his Nicole was the one. That's what he was thinking.

And Eve was painfully jealous. Her fault for pursuing the subject of his ex-wife, but maybe it was just as well to know up front how things stood. What were the odds he'd ever feel so much for another woman?

Bailey didn't have to wonder; she'd seen the difference. For Seth, Bailey would be the one-and-only instead of the fill-in Ben was probably looking for.

Ignoring the tight feeling in her chest, as if her rib cage had shrunk, Eve made herself say, "What from I've read, cops have other issues that affect their marriages. Alcoholism, chronic anger that may have to do with PTSD, a controlling nature to start with, a tendency to shut down around anyone but coworkers, the necessity of living with the awful things you see."

He let out a sound that he might have intended as a laugh, but lacked all humor. "Gee, thanks. I feel like a real prize now."

Eve made an impatient gesture. "I'm not talking about you. At least, not from what I've seen so far. You have talked to me about what you're working on. A little bit about frustrations and doubts. You listen to me. You don't seem to be a heavy drinker—"

"I'm not."

She nodded. "My point is, the fact that you work lousy hours shouldn't be enough to end a marriage. You do an important job, one I assume you find fulfilling. What were you supposed to do, quit that job and start doing something you hate just so you could sit down for dinner at six o'clock every night?"

There was a silence long enough to give Eve the idea she'd gone somewhere she shouldn't have. Oh, God. What was she *thinking*? Listening when a guy criticized his ex was fine if tiresome; jumping in feetfirst herself, not so smart.

"You're saying that Nic drawing a line in the sand over the hours I worked was...a diversion." Ben's tone was flat. "No, an excuse."

"I don't know her at all." Her embarrassment came out in awkwardness. Eve couldn't make herself meet his eyes. "So, no, I'm not saying that. There's no reason you'd tell me the problems you had in your marriage. It's just..." Oh, great, she couldn't stop while she was ahead! Now what?

"It's just?" He had plainly lost interest in his dinner. And probably her, too.

Well, so be it, she thought in defiance.

So she finished what she'd meant to say. "If a couple isn't going to stick together, especially when they have kids, the problems should be deep and wide, not...not something trivial."

"Trivial," he repeated.

What was that saying? In for a penny?

"Marriages succeed even when one spouse is deployed for six months out of every year. Being late to dinner on a regular basis because you're dealing with the tragedies other people suffer? That's nothing."

His face had become unreadable. She couldn't remember the last time he'd moved. He didn't want to give anything away, which most likely meant she'd hurt him.

And, gee, why would that be? Because, knowing absolutely nothing about his marriage beyond his casual mention that the hours he'd worked had been a problem, she'd decided—and told him—his wife must not really have loved him. Alternative: he'd taken her little speech to mean he must have problems that had impacted his marriage.

Way to go, Eve. She'd become a self-righteous know-it-all. What a shock no guy had yet fallen to his knees in front of her to declare she was the one for him!

She stared down at her plate, uncomfortably aware she probably looked like a turtle trying to shrink into its shell. Her cheeks heated until they must be flaming red. Ben didn't say a word.

Finally she couldn't let the silence go on. She took a deep breath and raised her chin, to find him still inspecting her, as if deciding whether she was a poisonous kind of spider he should crush or a garden-variety kind he might let crawl off and hide in a crack.

"I need to go," she said, snatching up her napkin and dropping it on the table and then grabbing coat and handbag. Even as she slid out of the booth, she added, "I'm sorry. I should have kept my mouth shut."

At last, his expression changed. "Eve. What are you...?"

"Good night." And she fled, walking faster and faster until she was nearly running once she made it outside.

For no reason. When she reached her car, parked half a block away, and looked back, she saw that Ben hadn't followed her.

And why would he?

WHAT THE HELL?

Stunned, Ben watched Eve hurry away without once looking back. He'd reacted slowly enough, he had barely gotten to his feet when the restaurant door swung closed behind her. Even if he thought he could catch her, he couldn't leave without paying since the bill Eve had dropped on the table wouldn't cover the total.

At last he slid back into the booth, where his remaining French fries didn't look all that appealing anymore. Eve had hardly touched her meal.

How had their dinner date blown up in his face

so fast? So, okay, he hadn't liked Eve's analysis of his breakup with Nicole, even if she'd been coming out strongly in his favor. Maybe it was habit, too many years of leaping automatically to defend Nic, but at least he hadn't argued. In fact, he'd have sworn he'd locked down his emotions. On the job, he had plenty of practice at that. But, obviously, Eve had seen enough on his face to send her running. That made him feel like shit, even if he was still roiling inside over what she'd had to say.

Your wife didn't love you or she'd have understood you're doing the job you need to do. That's what Eve had been trying to make him see.

Great guy that he was, he'd wanted to slam her for it.

Frowning into space, he brooded over his own irrationality. A beautiful woman had tried to tell him the divorce wasn't his fault. She'd even made it sound as if she thought law enforcement was a calling, that he accomplished something noble. And him, he'd been furious because she implied that Nicole had been—was—shallow.

Or did this tightness in his chest have another cause? Maybe he couldn't deal with the possibility that Nic never really *had* loved him.

No point in wasting time thinking about that anyway. What difference did it make now? The divorce had been signed, sealed and delivered over a year ago.

Except, if it didn't matter, why was he so bothered? Ben rubbed his breastbone with the heel of his hand. Easy answer: no man liked thinking he'd been a fool.

Maybe his hesitation where Eve was concerned had been right on. He could call, apologize for whatever he'd done that had upset her and consider himself lucky they hadn't gotten in any deeper before the crash. Because, damn, did he want to be psychoanalyzed every time they went out?

He made a sound. Yep, like Eve would agree to another fun evening with him.

Troubled, he signaled the waitress for the bill, lied and said Eve had been called away to explain their mostly uneaten meals, and went home.

There, he decided to call her right away and get it over with. No surprise, she didn't answer.

"Eve, I don't know what you thought, but I wasn't mad. You had nothing to apologize for. I'm, uh, still a little touchy where the divorce is concerned. I guess you could tell. It's my fault for bringing it up, though. I appreciate what you were trying to do—" Did he? "—and I don't want you to feel bad about it. I'm the one who feels like a jerk because you didn't get a chance to eat dinner, and after a tough day." He hesitated, knowing he'd be cut off soon, unable to think of the right way to end this. "I'll call you tomorrow," he finished hastily, and was left standing there holding his phone thinking, *Wait. Call her?*

EVE WAS TOO chagrined to answer when Ben's number came up on her phone. Her behavior was inexcusable.

At home, she took a long hot shower and changed into sweats and fuzzy socks before making herself a cup of tea and sitting down to stare at her phone as if it was a crystal ball.

With a sigh, she called voice mail, put in her password and braced herself for Ben's voice.

Eve, I don't know what you thought, but I wasn't mad.

Uh-huh. Sure.

By the end of his message, *bewildered* was a really good description of her state of mind. *He* felt bad? He was going to call her tomorrow?

She listened a second time, paying attention to his intonation, to that hesitation near the end.

Oh, God—what if he did call? Her stern inner voice told her: *Be a grown-up, even if you haven't been acting like one lately, that's what. Smooth things over so it won't be awkward if you run into him at Bailey's in the future.*

Eve made a face. Okay, it was good advice. And yes, that's what she'd do. If nothing else, it was entirely possible she'd end up encountering him through work, the way she had met Seth in the first place.

What she'd say if Ben asked her out again remained undecided when she went to bed with a book.

Her morning was devoted to figuring out where to put the two kids she'd decided urgently had to be moved, then making the calls so it could happen. She drove nearly half an hour out to the tiny town of Lowell so that she could talk to the foster mom who'd been angry enough at a five-year-old and an eight-year-old to feed them nothing but bread and water for several days even as the rest of the family sat down to their usual meals. Eve packed the poor kids' minimal possessions and called the school to let them know she would be picking the children up at the end of the day. She let the social worker who'd assessed the foster home know what had happened, making sure she didn't sound critical. They all made mistakes. The home had looked decent, the kids had been well dressed, and if Eve hadn't discovered what happened, she wouldn't have seen any red flags, either. She was still bemused at how the idea her version of discipline might be inappropriate had shocked the foster mom, although she'd flushed when Eve asked if she had ever put her own children on a diet of bread and water. Clearly, the answer was no.

Whether the kids would be able to stay more than temporarily in the new foster home was an open question. Constant changes were really damaging to children's sense of security, but there was no way Eve would have been able to leave them where they were.

She was briefly back at her desk in a cubicle at the DSHS offices when her mobile phone rang and she saw Ben's name. Oh, boy.

I'm going to demonstrate my maturity, remember?

"Ben," she said pleasantly. "Thank you for calling."

The little silence told her she'd taken him aback. "Did you get my message?"

"Yes, it was nice of you to call. I really am sorry I behaved so poorly. I don't know what got into me, lecturing you as if I know anything at all about your marriage. You just…touched a hot button of mine, I'm afraid, and I was tired enough to let loose. And then what did I do but flee the scene of my crime." She tried to inject a note of humor into her voice. "So you're definitely not the one who should be apologizing. I am."

"No," he said, a little extra gravel in his voice. "I meant that apology. I guess I'm a typical man, blanking out emotions. What you said made sense. It left me feeling a lot of contradictory things I had trouble working through."

Eve bowed her head and massaged her forehead. "I am sorry," she said softly. "I swear I'll keep my mouth shut the next time we run into each other at Seth and Bailey's, if we do. Okay?"

Another silence had her going still.

"I was kind of hoping we could put this behind

us and try again," Ben said, just enough uncertainty in his voice to bring her head up.

"You must have women circling all the time," she said. "I'm beginning to think I'm pretty messed up. I guess I don't understand why you'd want to bother."

"I'm not who you think I am," Ben said. "Most women react to who I am on the outside. I kind of had the sense you saw a little deeper."

Once again, he'd made her feel ashamed of herself. He was right. The truth was, she wouldn't have been interested in him at all if his head-turning looks said all that much about his character. Gorgeous men tended to be full of themselves. For whatever reason, Ben wasn't.

"You're right," she said. "I'm…making assumptions."

"Damn it, *you're* a beautiful woman! You must know that."

People had told her so, but when she looked in the mirror, filters kept her from seeing herself the way other people claimed to.

"Is that why you asked me out?" she had to ask.

Each pause left her wishing she could see his face.

"Partly. Sure. I reacted to your looks. But I reacted to your looks when I saw you on TV last summer, too, and I didn't do anything about it because I didn't know you. It was meeting you, seeing—" He stopped.

"Seeing what?" Eve whispered.

"Self-doubt. Kindness. The way you move, your smile, your laugh."

Self-doubt was first on his list? she thought incredulously. How ironic that she'd been drawn to the same quality in him. Or maybe that wasn't quite right to describe what she'd seen in him. She'd thought of it as the shadows in his eyes. Buried pain, hurt, a constraint that didn't match his outward perfection. And...the gentle way he touched his daughter, the love in his eyes when he looked at her.

"That...might be the nicest thing anyone has ever said to me," she told him, in a voice that didn't sound quite like hers.

"Does that mean you're willing to give it another shot?"

Her sinuses burned and a smile trembled on her lips. "Yes. I'd love to give it another shot. If...if you mean it."

He cleared his throat, and his voice still came out husky. "I do."

The brief discussion about when and where they'd see each other again felt mundane compared to what had come before.

Friday night, they agreed finally. Dinner again. Possibly a movie, depending on what was playing at the four-screen theater in town.

Of course, all she did in the intervening day was get more and more nervous about seeing him again. She wished they could have had lunch that day. Or at least dinner. She hadn't suggested it, though, and neither had he.

They ended up driving to Mount Vernon, a county over, and eating at an Italian restaurant on the main street that paralleled the Skagit River, then walking the block to the restored Lincoln Theatre with its single screen to see a foreign film that had been recommended to Eve.

Dinner was pleasant, but she thought they were both being so careful with each other, neither said anything important. At the theater, they chose seats on the aisle. He helped with her coat before shrugging out of his own parka.

At least, sitting side by side, their shoulders touched. Making yet more careful conversation, Eve focused on his big hands resting on his thighs. With his long fingers, they could have been a pianist's hands, or an artist's. Her heart gave a bump as she wondered what they'd feel like on *her*. As if reacting to her thought, his right hand flexed, curling into a fist before straightening. She looked up to see he was watching her. Reading her mind?

They stared at each other, Eve caught feeling unguarded. She couldn't remember ever having such an intense physical reaction to a man.

"Excuse me," a voice said, and she jerked to see a couple laden with popcorn and drinks waiting to get by to empty seats.

The moment broken, Ben murmured an apology and he and Eve both stood to let them by. Eve straightened her coat on the back of the seat and sat down again, then sneaked a glance at Ben. This time, his expression was wry.

"Guess this isn't the place to say I like the way you look at me."

Oh, boy. "Um, probably not," she managed.

He laughed, lifted his arm and draped it around her. "So, how do you feel about cuddling at the movies?"

Smiling, Eve shifted closer. "Definitely positive."

His breath warm on her ear, he murmured, "Good." And then, as the lights dimmed, "Ah. Here we go."

Now, if only she could concentrate well enough to read the subtitles.

CHAPTER FOUR

"So we're going to rerun this dinner, huh?" Eve teased, as she slid into the booth across from Ben at the diner.

He had hesitated to suggest eating here, but, damn it, there weren't that many decent choices in town that didn't have white tablecloths and require more time and effort than he and Eve could spare on a working night. Monday night they'd gone out for pizza and a couple games of pool. Turned out she knew how to wield a cue and had a good eye for trajectory. Her chortle of satisfaction had compensated his male ego after he lost two out of three games. When he'd called her at work Tuesday to ask if they could have dinner again Wednesday, his options were limited.

So he'd crossed his fingers and said, "What about the café?" and she'd agreed, but sounded distracted enough he hadn't been sure she'd thought it through.

Now he agreed, tongue in cheek, "There's that saying about getting back in the saddle right away."

Eve wriggled a little and wrinkled her nose at

him. "Now that you mention it, the seats do feel a little like a saddle, and they're not padded much better, either."

"The place could do with some updating," he conceded. "Ah…maybe this wasn't such a good idea."

"Don't be silly," she retorted. "The food's good, it's quiet enough to talk and nine times out of ten you can snag the back booth."

Ben gave a crooked smile. "You noticed, huh?"

"You and Seth," she said, and bent to study the menu.

Did she have to remind him she'd dated his partner? Then he had an unwelcome thought. Was she a cop groupie?

"You gone out with a cop before?" he asked casually.

"Hmm?" She glanced up. "Oh. No." An impish grin flashed. "And I was so annoyed at Seth by the time he asked, I couldn't figure out why I'd agreed."

Ben relaxed and laid one arm along the padded back. "He said something about that. Admitted he might have been wrong and you were right about that kid, too."

"Did he?" Humor gave her a tiny dimple in one cheek even when she was suppressing a smile, like now. "Funny thing, he never told *me* that."

Ben couldn't help grinning. "What man likes to admit he's wrong?"

Her gaze became more searching. "You don't, either?"

"Not my favorite thing to do." For some reason, he flashed to his divorce. Was that why he couldn't let go? Because admitting he'd been wrong really meant admitting he and Nicole shouldn't have gotten married in the first place, and he wasn't willing to do that?

He flicked the thought away. "Here comes our waitress. You made up your mind?"

Eve closed the menu. "I'm going to try again with the same meal."

"Since you didn't get to eat it last time," he said slowly.

"Since I was an idiot." She smiled at the middle-aged waitress and gave her order. Ben did the same.

When they were alone again, he asked about her day. It sounded a lot like his, the way she described it. Apparently reports figured as largely in her job as they did in his. That and driving from one end of the county to the other, too often finding the person he'd gone to talk to had forgotten he was coming or decided to dodge him. He mentioned a couple of obscure back roads, and she knew them both, laughingly telling him one was a speed trap and she was too smart for it.

"Yeah, that dip makes a good place to tuck a patrol car out of sight, plus teenagers love to build up speed and try for some air there." He cocked an eyebrow. "Tell me you don't speed."

"I don't speed," she said obediently. Rolled her eyes and added, "Anymore."

"There've been a couple of ugly accidents on that same road in just the past year or so."

"I know. And really I don't. I was as stupid as any other teenager, but I've outgrown that kind of defiance."

Their food came and they kept talking, sharing more tidbits from their jobs, likes and dislikes, a book he'd recently read, foods they detested, the concept of diving in the cold waters around the San Juan Islands, something he'd done a few weeks back with friends.

"In the middle of the winter?"

Laughing at her horror, he said, "You don't get cold when you're wearing a wet suit. The only kinda miserable moment is when you have to peel it off on deck."

"Ugh," was her conclusion. "Now, snorkeling in the Caribbean I could go for."

He'd done that, too—on his honeymoon. He figured it was just as well not to say so.

And, wouldn't you know, that was when his phone buzzed and he glanced to see he had a text from Nicole asking him to call when he had a minute. That sounded tentative for her, which had him on edge. Was something wrong? She'd have said if it was an emergency, he told himself, and put his phone away without comment. Eve's gaze had followed it, though, and her expression was enigmatic.

For something to say, he asked her whether anything had come of the grumpy neighbor's complaints about the Kekoa boy.

"Unfortunately, there's been another incident," Eve said, expression perturbed. "The foster dad called today. Mr. Rowe's car was keyed. Apparently he usually parks in the garage, but he'd intended to go out later, so... Whoever did it was smart enough to stop with one side—the side Mr. Rowe couldn't see from his front window."

"Calculated."

"What crossed my mind was malice aforethought."

"The definition of first degree."

She shivered. "It happened about when the boys got home after school. Gavin drove—he has his own car—and Joel took the school bus."

"Not a real friendly relationship there," Ben mused.

"No. Not outwardly hostile, either, but—" She chose not to finish.

"The neighbor call the police?"

"Yes." Eve looked even unhappier. "Officer Pruitt again. He confronted Joel instead of making any effort to knock on doors and find out whether anybody else had seen it happen."

As far as Ben knew, Ed Pruitt was a competent police officer. Either he wasn't ambitious, had scored poorly on the tests that led to advancement or liked being first responder. Whatever the reason, he had stayed in uniform through his career and had just passed his twenty-fifth year on the job.

"You sure he didn't?" Ben asked. "Or is that what the boy told you?"

"Well…" She frowned at him. "You're right. Pruitt is leaning hard on Joel for no other reason than because Mr. Rowe doesn't like him, though."

"Cops do get tunnel vision sometimes, just like anyone else," Ben said mildly.

"Are you implying I have, too?"

He didn't think she'd appreciate being told she looked cute when she bristled.

"Nope. Just saying we're not perfect, hard as we try." One side of his mouth quirked up. "Well, I might have achieved that exalted state, but…"

Eve's laugh erased her wariness. "Right. A *perfect* detective would have arrested the guys who hit that jewelry store, wouldn't he have?"

His smile turned into a grimace. "That's a low blow."

She laughed again. He liked the sound, a merry ripple that was almost a giggle.

He picked up the dessert menu, tucked behind the catsup and salt and pepper shakers. "Pie?" he asked, even though he also felt an itch to call Nic and find out what was up. He could make an excuse and go to the john....

"I couldn't." Eve looked down at her empty plate ruefully. "I missed lunch, so I was starved, but I still don't know how I stuffed all that in."

He'd kind of wondered that himself, but he'd noticed that Eve rarely completely relaxed. She fidgeted, she tapped her foot, she paid attention to everything going on around her. Energy hummed through her. He'd be willing to bet she burned more calories than average for her size and weight.

He'd also really like to find out how it felt to go to bed with a woman whose engine never idled. He doubted she'd be passive. The thought was enough to make him shift a little uncomfortably.

She noticed, but only said, "I'd love a cup of coffee, though. I'll watch you eat. And maybe steal a bite or two, depending on what you order."

Damn it, Nicole could wait.

Ben went for cherry pie a la mode, and she stole more than a couple of bites. Sharing with her was fun, and it gave him an excuse to prolong the evening. Since they'd met here, like last time, and Eve would be driving herself home, her inviting him in wasn't going to happen. A good-night kiss would have to be hasty, given that it was raining, weather that was more common than not in western Washington at this time of year.

While they waited for the waitress to return with change, Ben braced himself for Eve to take offense, but had to say, "This is my weekend with Rachel." That sounded kind of bald, so he added, "If you want to think about Sunday night after she's gone…"

If her expression changed, he couldn't tell. "Oh, I usually have Sunday dinner with Mom and Dad." Her tone was pleasant. "Do you have any special plans?"

"Maybe a movie Saturday." Rachel liked to bake, too, so he'd bought some shaped cookie cutters and sprinkles and what have you so they could have some fun with sugar cookies. He was a little embarrassed to admit that. Plus…damn it, he couldn't help picturing Eve with them, that rippling laugh delighting Rachel as much as it did him.

But letting her get to know Rachel better implied something he didn't intend. He didn't want his daughter to become attached to one after another of the women in his life.

As Eve walked out of the café ahead of him, he tried to decide if she'd understood the signal he'd sent by not suggesting she join him and Rachel this weekend, or whether she just thought he was being cautious about jumping in too quickly.

If he were smart, he'd come right out and say, "I'm not looking for anything long-term," but he couldn't seem to make himself do that, and he knew why: he wanted Eve, and he'd never have her if he was that blunt.

What if he hurt her, a woman who'd been hurt by too many people?

The worry made shame curl in his belly.

He kissed her good-night anyway, even though cold rain ran down his neck while he was doing it.

But he dialed Nic's number even as he walked to his own car.

"YOU THINK THEIR haul is stashed under one of their beds?" Seth asked, frustration adding an edge to his tone.

Frustration Ben shared. Neither of them knew where to go next with this, and new crimes were pulling them away. The amount of time they could give to investigating the jewelry store heist was diminishing.

"Why not?" he said. "They must know we're not even close to getting a warrant."

The frustration still simmering, he ran a background search on a guy he liked for a more conventional holdup at a corner grocery store and gas station. The perpetrator had kept his head down and his face shielded by a hoodie, but watching the footage from the surveillance camera, Ben kept thinking, *I've seen this guy before.* His stature, the way he moved, the dart of his hand as he snatched the money… The name had come to Ben in the middle of the night, a lightbulb bursting on.

"Oh, yeah," he murmured now, when he saw that Henry James Whitmore—otherwise known as Whit—had been picked up a couple more times since Ben had last collared him. In fact, Whit had been released from a six-month lockup three weeks ago.

Ben shook his head. Some people never learned.

His phone rang and he reached for it absently. The number looked familiar, but didn't belong to anyone he knew well.

"Detective Kemper, this is Julie Silveira from Child Protective Services. I heard from Michelle Baker."

"Did you?" he said softly. Something in his voice had Seth swiveling his chair to look at him. "Thank you for calling."

A minute later, he hung up, his grin triumphant. "Ken Hardison's girlfriend just surfaced. She says she'll talk to us."

Seth was already rising to his feet. "Now?"

"Sounds like. I have an address."

She'd been hiding out at a friend's house in Everett, an hour's drive away.

Michelle Baker turned out to be painfully thin, with lanky, dull hair and the physical mannerisms of someone who had become conditioned to try to appear deferential—or maybe she was going for invisible, if only subconsciously.

"He always said he'd never let me go," she said after she'd looked nervously up and down the street before letting them in the front door of the run-down place a few blocks from the community college. "I'd have liked to stay with my sister, but—" her shrug had a defeated quality "—he's been knocking on her door every day or two since I took off. I told her to be careful."

He asked about her child, and Michelle said she was napping. "He never hit Courtney," she said, "but that last time, she saw what he did to me and I just didn't know what to tell her."

They refused coffee and talked briefly about measures she could take to protect herself, but Ben could tell she wasn't convinced, and he couldn't blame her. Hardison's history suggested he was just the kind of guy to be enraged by a restraining order.

She looked from Seth to Ben, her confusion apparent. "Is that what you wanted to talk to me about? 'Cause I never got two detectives before when I complained."

"No. I'm sorry." Ben cleared his throat. She seemed more comfortable talking to him than to Seth, which wasn't unusual. Seth's rougher face and bulkier build were intimidating to a certain kind of witness. "We're not usually involved in domestic violence calls." Until they escalated into homicide, of course, but he wasn't about to say that. He explained that Ken's name had come up in the course of their investigation into a recent robbery, and they were hoping she'd be willing to tell them if she'd heard him making plans.

"Um... I heard some stuff." She ducked her head, hiding her face behind her hair. "I shoulda told somebody," she said softly. "I felt bad when I saw about it on TV. I mean, them hurting that guy." She looked up. "He didn't die, did he?"

"Why don't you tell us what you heard before I answer any questions," Ben said gently.

"That jewelry store," she said, looking surprised. "That's what you're here about, isn't it?"

He smiled at her. "Yes, it is."

After agreeing to be recorded, she began, "See, he was real mad about getting fired."

At the end, Ben asked if she'd be willing to testify in court as to what she'd heard. When she hesitated, he told her honestly he couldn't guarantee Hardison would be convicted, but if he was, he'd be put away for a good, long time given how brutal the assault had been on the store owner and how serious his injuries.

Her face firmed and she squared her shoulders. "I'll do that. After he hurt me so many times, he don't deserve any loyalty from me."

"No, he doesn't." Ben smiled at her as he rose to his feet. "You've been an excellent witness, Ms. Baker." He extracted a promise from her to inform him of any moves, and told her he'd keep her informed. Seth thanked her, too, then grinned at Ben as they walked to their car.

"I have Dietz on speed dial," he said.

Jennifer Dietz was the Deputy Prosecuting Attorney they'd been working with on this investigation.

"Call her," Ben agreed.

NICOLE CROSSED HER arms and adopted a combative stance as she waited with Ben for Rachel to rush to her room to grab her rolling pink suitcase. "What if you get called in to work?" she asked. "Tell me you have somebody *responsible* to watch over Rach until I can pick her up."

They'd only had this same conversation twenty or thirty times. Had she dredged it up again because he'd been incautious enough during their phone conversation Wednesday to mention being out for dinner? Dumb to let it slip, given that Nic had been friendly, wanting to talk about an issue she had with Rachel's teacher.

Now he unclenched his jaw enough to allow him to speak. "You've met Mrs. Chaffee. She's watched Rachel a couple times before. Rachel likes her."

"What if *she's* not home?"

He kept his voice low, but wasn't able to strip it entirely of anger. "I haven't yet left my daughter alone, and I won't. She's as safe with me as she is with you."

"Daddy?" Speaking from right behind her mother, Rachel sounded uncertain. He hadn't heard her returning.

"Hey, kiddo." Tilting his head to see past Nicole, he smiled at his little girl. "You sure you have everything?"

"Uh-huh. Bye, Mommy." She submitted to a hug from her mother, then took Ben's hand and trotted down the porch steps happily with him.

His last glimpse was of Nicole still standing in the doorway, even from a distance radiating hostility.

He tried to call up a recollection of the last time there'd been warmth between them and failed. Passion, yes, but it had been forever since he and Nicole had had fun talking over dinner, or since she'd asked about his day and seemed to care. And, yeah, he *had* asked about her day, and cared.

He heard his own voice. *You're saying that Nic drawing a line in the sand over the hours I worked was...a diversion.* He rejected the thought between one blink and the next. No, there'd been love, all right. He just wished he knew what had killed her love for him.

"So, pumpkin, how was school?" he asked, looking in the rearview mirror to see Rach, and listened to her chatter.

She worked her way around to negotiating mode. "Can we have pizza, Daddy? You said—"

"We're not going out tonight," he told her firmly. "If you want pizza tomorrow after the movie, that's what we'll have. Tonight, I'm making tacos, which I *know* you like."

She giggled. Which made him remember Eve's laugh, but, no, he wasn't going there.

"And for dessert," he added, "we're making cookies."

"Can we make chocolate chip?" she begged.

"Nope, we're doing cutout cookies like people make for Christmas, except we can make hearts and trees and unicorns and all kinds of shapes instead of reindeer and stars."

Her face brightened. "With frosting?"

"And sprinkles."

"That will be fun," she decided, and bounced in her booster seat.

Unfortunately, he'd overestimated her attention span. She happily cut out enough cookies to fill one cookie sheet, "helped" him spread frosting once they'd come out of the oven and decorated about two cookies before asking if she could watch a movie now.

If she'd chosen *How to Train Your Dragon 1* or *2*, or even *The Lego Movie*, he might have joined her. But *Frozen*? He swore she watched it every time she came, and he knew she had it at home, too.

So he put the DVD in for her, poured her a glass of milk, gave her a couple of cookies and set himself to cutting out, baking and decorating a couple of dozen more. Slapping on frosting, he wondered how different it might have gone if Eve had been here. He bet *she* could have made decorating cookies fun.

ROD CARTER FINALLY agreed to meet with Eve on Saturday morning. It wasn't as if she'd had any more interesting offers for the weekend. So why not work? she thought wryly. In an attempt *not* to think about Ben and Rachel and what they were doing, she turned her mind to Joel, who had sounded scared the last time they talked.

She had suggested a coffee shop, wanting to separate Rod from his wife and also be able to talk without either Joel or Gavin overhearing. She was already seated in a comfortable, upholstered chair with her chai, staking out a reasonably private corner, when he arrived ten minutes late.

"Sorry," he said, when he joined her after getting his coffee. "Ah, Lynne wanted me to say how sorry she is that things aren't so good with Joel. She's really trying, you know."

His discomfiture suggested he didn't believe that, but Eve decided to steer away from challenging the statement right away.

"I'm sorry you weren't there to talk the last couple times I've come out. You know Joel a lot better than your wife does."

Lines deepened in his forehead. "I thought I did."

"I gather Mr. Rowe is a difficult neighbor." Eve sipped her tea.

Rod grunted. "You could say that."

"Do you know who besides Joel has annoyed him?"

"Who hasn't?" he muttered. "He reamed me

out a month or so ago when some dog knocked over my garbage can and I wasn't out there early enough in the morning to pick up all the crap."

"Gavin?"

"Oh, Gavin has his car souped up and Rowe bitches about the racket." He brooded briefly. "There's no pleasing him. Guess he was never young."

"I don't suppose there's a teenager in the neighborhood he likes."

"Or a kid of any size. Trick-or-treaters don't knock on his door, I can tell you that," Rod said with feeling.

Time to lay it out. "Do you have any reason to believe Joel would be pulling these tricks on Mr. Rowe?"

He tried to meet her eyes and couldn't. "It's not me who is accusing Joel! It's that son of a bitch next door."

"Your wife seemed to be taking the accusations as fact."

"She's just pacifying the old man. Letting him think we're dealing with it."

"So you *don't* believe Joel retaliated against him?"

He hesitated. "I don't want to. Lynne…"

Eve waited him out.

"I've been working long hours lately." He was a PUD lineman, and during winter in a wooded county, outages occurred with every windstorm.

Eve nodded her understanding.

"Lynne sees more of the boys than I do. Joel… he seems to resent her some, or at least she thinks so. He's been a lot quieter lately. Kinda withdrawn. I thought he and Gavin would hit it off, but Joel hasn't acted interested."

Eve let herself look surprised. "He didn't say anything like that to me."

At last Rod met her eyes. "Would he?"

"Yes," she said slowly. "I think he would. He's been pretty open with me."

Rod looked away again. Wondering what Joel *had* told her?

"It's just teenage pranks." Once again, he didn't sound as if he quite believed what he was saying.

"Mr. Rowe could have been badly hurt by the rock through the window. That showed a degree of malice."

Aforethought, she added silently.

He shifted in his chair, took a drink of his coffee, twitched a little. "Eve, I don't know what I can tell you."

They discussed Joel's school performance, which was still excellent, his decision to go with the University of Oregon, Gavin's adjustment to a new high school.

"He already has a girlfriend," he said with a chuckle. "One of the cheerleaders, wouldn't you know. Cute little thing."

Eve hoped Joel hadn't had his eye on that same

cute little thing. She wouldn't put it past Gavin to target a girl just because Joel liked her. Then she felt the smallest bit guilty about the antipathy she felt for a sixteen-year-old boy she really didn't know that well.

She gave up shortly thereafter and let Rod make a hasty escape. Although she'd finished her tea, she sat where she was for a few more minutes, thinking. No great ideas came to mind. Her best hope was that the tricks had come to an end. As annoyed as she was at Officer Pruitt, his interest must surely be making the perpetrator nervous. He—and she couldn't help seeing Gavin's smug face—might not have believed Clement Rowe would call the police. Nothing had happened since Tuesday. Five days. That was good, right?

"Is something up?" Eve's mother asked after passing her the butter. "We haven't heard much from you lately. Or seen you."

Her dad didn't comment. A quiet man, he only continued eating, although Eve had no doubt he was paying attention.

She cast her mind back. In fact, the last time she'd seen her parents had been the Friday night at Seth's when she'd met Ben for the first time.

"Just busy," she said, and told them a little about Joel's troubles. She'd bragged about him before, so they looked surprised.

"But he sounds like such a nice boy!" her

mother exclaimed. "Surely no one really believes he'd try to hurt an old man."

"*I* don't. His foster father isn't being as supportive as I'd like, though."

"Boy has a lot to lose," her dad remarked.

"I keep thinking that, too," she agreed. "A few months from now, he'll be gone. Doing something like this, he'd be risking his full ride to college. He's too smart to do that, even if he had a nasty streak, which I swear he doesn't."

Eve talked a little more about her work, hoping to divert her mother from her curiosity about what had been occupying Eve's time. For some reason, she didn't want to talk about Ben. Maybe she was afraid to jinx the tentative beginning they'd made.

But she should have known Mom better than that. Into the first pause, she said, "You're surely not working twenty-four hours a day."

"Well, not quite. I actually did work yesterday." She hesitated, conceding defeat. "I've started seeing someone. A guy, I mean. We've had dinner four or five times, seen a movie." She shrugged. Silence answered her.

"Goodness," her mother finally said. "Is this anyone we know?"

Damn. They did know Ben. No way she could lie.

"Ben Kemper, Seth's partner. The man who came to Seth's for dinner that night, with his little girl. That's where we met."

Her mother had gone very still. "Yes, of course I remember meeting him."

"His little girl is so cute."

"Yes."

Dad watched Eve with a somber expression.

"Is something wrong?" she finally asked. "Did you not like him? Or you've heard something about him—?"

"Not at all. I'm just wondering why you didn't mention him. You must have known we'd be interested."

Oh, wonderful. She'd hurt their feelings. These days, her specialty.

She looked down at her plate, fumbling for an explanation she already knew would be inadequate. "It's so…new. I wasn't sure it would go anywhere."

"But it sounds as if you've gotten together with him several times a week."

"Yes. I just…" *Oh, give it up.* "I don't know if he's serious at all. He's so handsome, I suppose I'm a little intimidated. Plus, there's the fact I dated Seth last year. That makes it awkward."

"I don't know why it would," her mother said. "With Seth engaged now, he's not likely to mind."

Oh, please, she thought. Seth wouldn't have minded while they *were* dating if at any time she'd said, *Sorry,* and switched her attention to Ben. Because, face it, Seth had never worked up much interest in her.

She waited for the familiar burning sensation, but it never came.

I really don't mind.

Because of Ben. And because she'd never been in love with Seth anyway.

Relief filled her. Oh, thank goodness, she was done with that silliness. Her pride had been bruised, that's all. She pictured her adoptive sister's approaching wedding and felt nothing but pleasure for Bailey, whose life hadn't been easy. Falling in love, believing in a man, had been no cakewalk for her, either.

And *she* had more excuse than Eve did.

"I'm sorry you didn't feel you could talk to me," Eve's mother said stiffly. "I thought we were closer than that."

Kirk Lawson touched his wife's hand. Eve had seen him do that so many times, sending an unspoken message that his wife always heeded.

Mom's smile looked only a tiny bit forced. "Oh, don't listen to me! I know you have friends to talk to. I miss you when we don't see you, that's all."

Guilt, guilt. Resentment tangled in Eve's chest along with regret that she *hadn't* called and girlishly confided in her mother that she was seeing an amazing man who she thought could be the one.

As if she'd smacked into a solid wall, she knew why she hadn't wanted anyone, and especially her parents, to know about Ben: because she *didn't* believe anything would come of their relationship. It was too good to be true. *He* was too good for her.

And she was very afraid more than her pride would be hurt this time.

"We've had a good time talking," she told her parents, "but the thing with Ben has been totally casual so far." Except for his kisses, but no way was she talking about that. "I promise I'll tell you if we get the least bit serious."

Her mother shook her head. "I don't know why I'm grumbling about you not calling. It's not as if I couldn't have called you." She looked at Eve's plate. "Eat, eat!"

Tension might be pasted over, but that didn't mean Eve hadn't hurt her mother's feelings. Something she'd done often since Hope aka Bailey had made her wondrous reappearance.

What Mom didn't get was that she hurt Eve's feelings every time she rhapsodized about how happy she was because Hope was home. And Eve *knew* she was being petty, but, oh, it was hard not to be.

So she chattered gaily about a lengthy email from her college roommate, and knew from her father's sidelong glance that she wasn't fooling either of them.

CHAPTER FIVE

EVE DIDN'T RETURN the voice mail message Ben had left Sunday evening until lunchtime the next day. Her call caught him as he was walking into headquarters, carrying a deli lunch to be eaten at his desk.

"I put my phone on Silent while I was at my parents'" was her explanation.

Given her job, he didn't believe for a minute she hadn't checked messages. But, okay, she might just not have been in the mood to talk. Or maybe Sunday dinner at her parents was midafternoon and she'd gone out with friends later.

"Good weekend?" he asked.

"It was okay. How about yours? Was the movie a success?"

"Rachel enjoyed it. I thought it was a snoozer." Ben had kept thinking that if Eve had been with them, he could have laid a casual arm around her, shared a few amused glances. He'd had to remind himself irritably that they weren't going to play happy family. "Thank God it was short," he added.

Eve laughed. "There are some entertaining animated movies."

"I won't argue. This wasn't one of them." He leaned a shoulder against the wall outside the detective bull pen. "Can we do something one of the next couple of nights?"

"Hmm? Oh, sure." A murmur of voices told him she'd been distracted. A moment later, she came back on. "Not tonight. There are some families I can only catch at home during the evening, so I schedule at least one a week."

More disappointed than he would have wanted to admit, he said, "Tomorrow night? Maybe Thai again? Or how about Mexican?"

"Let's do Mexican." She suggested a favorite restaurant, they set a tentative time and she was gone, leaving Ben feeling…dissatisfied.

What would she say if he offered to cook dinner for her Friday night, assuming she didn't make the same offer to him first? Damn it, they were adults! He wanted her, and was pretty sure she wanted him. They'd been dancing around each other for a couple of weeks now, mostly able to exchange only relatively chaste kisses when he walked her to her car in a parking lot with other people coming and going. Neither had commitments elsewhere, except his to his daughter. Why not move on to the good part?

But he'd seen Eve's wariness and knew why not: she wasn't ready. Plus, he couldn't help won-

dering how much him closing her out this weekend had to do with the vague way she'd responded
on the phone, as if he were a distant acquaintance
she'd been surprised to hear from.

Yeah, well, tough shit, Ben thought.

If happy family was what she wanted from him,
she was going to be disappointed.

He grimaced, knowing she wouldn't be the only
one who'd be disappointed.

Maybe he needed a new strategy. And speaking
of dancing…it actually wasn't a bad idea.

THE MUSIC PUMMELED Eve's ears, reducing her to
lip-reading and occasionally shouting a comment
to Ben.

She was enjoying herself anyway. For Friday
night, he'd suggested they go dancing at one of the
Indian casinos. She'd never been to this one, but
so far, the food and band were both good. Maybe
it was just as well to do something fun and not
be able to talk. She'd gotten a little frustrated this
week because there was so much Ben didn't want
to talk about. His daughter, for one. His ex-wife…
well. Eve made a face she hoped he wouldn't notice with the dim lighting. Given the way she'd
blown it the one time, any mention of Ben's ex-
wife was definitely off the table.

And, yes, she should probably be relieved that
he *didn't* want to talk endlessly about his ex. All

she had to do was remember the tedium of an evening out with a guy who did exactly that.

"Dance?" Ben mouthed.

They'd sat the last two out. Ben only wanted to take the floor for the slow dances, which was okay by Eve. She liked swaying in his arms, her own wrapped around his waist or his neck, her body plastered against his lean, powerful length.

Even so, when she stepped close, she rose on tiptoe to tease him, her mouth next to his ear. "Big tough detective afraid he'll look foolish gyrating to nineties' rock?"

His hand settled on her lower back. "Afraid?" His breath tickled her ear and neck. "Big tough detective *will* look foolish. Trust me, you're safer sticking to the slow dances."

She laughed but felt her cheeks heat at the glint in his eyes. With his erection pressed against her belly, she felt anything but safe.

Tempted was more like it. She knew Ben was hoping she'd invite him in tonight instead of kissing him goodbye at the door. She wanted to. She did.

But she also didn't.

She'd never been quick to jump into bed with a guy, not even in college. She craved at least the illusion of something besides down-and-dirty sex. But she also knew she was dragging her feet even more than usual with Ben, and she knew why, too. She wanted more than an illusion from him.

And this week, she'd begun to suspect he didn't have any intention of letting her get to know him on any very deep level. He might tell a story about playing football in high school, but he didn't talk about his parents, his marriage, his daughter. Any nonpersonal subject was fine; they had spirited debates about politics, movies, books, ethics. Any topic edging into what made him who he was, a door visibly closed.

Having her own sore places, Eve understood. She guessed that part of her discomfort came from the fact that he knew a whole lot more about her than she did about him. The other part came from her slow realization that he wasn't asking her the kind of questions that would make her think he was really curious about her, either.

Maybe she was expecting too much too fast. Or maybe she'd been right when she told him she was too messed up to have a serious relationship.

Of course, that hadn't seemed to give him pause, possibly because he didn't want serious.

Although his wandering hand felt quite serious. It had left her butt, moved up the curve of her waist, and come to rest beneath her armpit, very, very close to her breast. Brooding hadn't stopped her from tingling as that hand advanced.

She sighed, and felt Ben tip his head to try to see her face, tucked on his chest. She had a very nice view into the V of his shirt where he'd left the top couple buttons undone, exposing a hint of sleek skin stretched over impressive muscles.

"Want to sit down?" he asked.

Eve shook her head. "No. Just…" She didn't finish, and he didn't ask.

That big hand roved downward again, leaving her breasts aching with a desire to be touched.

I could invite him in.

Maybe sex with him would be nothing special. She knew him better than to think he'd be a completely selfish lover, but that didn't mean she wouldn't be left feeling…let down.

If so, she could get over what was probably just a crush. So going to bed with him was probably the smart thing to do, right?

Eve grimaced. It was like persuading herself that a pint of chocolate mint ice cream would rev her up, help her get more work done, make her boobs bigger, whatever. Amazing how the mind could justify something unhealthy that you really, really wanted anyway.

The music slowed to a whisper, then ended. For a moment, neither she nor Ben moved. She let herself relax against him and feel the security of the arm that still held her close. He was nuzzling his cheek against the top of her head. The hard ridge against her stomach did not subside.

But, at last, his chest rose and fell on a deep breath that vibrated against her breasts as if he'd stifled a groan, and his hold on her loosened. Eve made herself straighten and step back, then turn to walk back to their table.

In the lull before the band launched into another song, Ben murmured, "Maybe we should call it a night."

She nodded. "This was fun, but I think I'm ready to go."

He signed to pay for their dinner, pocketed his card and half encircled her with his arm again to keep her close to him as they made their way out. That entailed winding between blackjack tables and rows and rows of slot machines with people perched on stools in front of them.

She and Ben retrieved their coats and stepped outside, both pausing to breathe in the crisp air and, for her at least, to sag a little in relief at the relative silence. His fingers wrapped her upper arm, as if he thought she'd take a tumble without his support. The way he always touched her when they were walking made her feel protected and…feminine.

Ben gave her a gentle nudge to start her walking. "I liked dancing with you, but I've got to tell you, I'm not much for nightlife."

She pretended to gasp. "No! Really?" Then she chuckled. "Somehow I guessed that when you wouldn't jump around and pump your arms to the fast songs."

His grin flashed. "And you would have?"

Eve's mouth curved. "A few years ago. I actually haven't been dancing in ages. When you're the one watching and not doing, though… Um, people were clearly having a good time, but…"

"They looked ridiculous."

She laughed. "I guess so."

The smile still lingering on his face and deepening the crease in his cheek, Ben told her, "I was hot stuff in high school, you know. Jock, student body vice president—did I ever tell you that? Had the prettiest girlfriend in the school, too. But I guess I don't have any rhythm. I'd wham people in the chin, bump into them. Once I knocked Nicole down. Real romantic." He shook his head. "Haven't dared cut loose since."

There—he'd said his ex-wife's name. That meant something, didn't it?

He let her go to remove his keys from his pocket and point the remote at his SUV ahead to unlock. At the same moment, she heard a faint buzz. The remote…? But then she realized it was her phone, dropped in her coat pocket. She was right beneath one of the tall, glaringly white lights that illuminated the parking lot, so she stopped where she was and took her phone out.

Ben was a few steps ahead when he realized she was no longer with him. He turned. "Eve?"

"I think somebody just left me a message."

She'd missed two calls, both from Joel Kekoa,

and discovered she'd received a text, too. That was probably what she'd heard coming in.

She opened it.

Need u.

Oh, God.

She hurried toward Ben. "I'm sorry. This sounds urgent. I need to listen to my messages."

He only nodded and said, "Hop in." He started the engine and backed out, heading toward the exit as she put in her voice mail password.

Joel's first message was almost incoherent. "There's been a fire and that policeman's here again and, shit, I think he's going to arrest me! Where are you?"

The second one wasn't any better. "This is really bad, Ms. Lawson. There was a fire at Mr. Rowe's house, so of course everybody is sure *I* set it. *Please* will you call?"

She did, but he didn't answer and she ended up with his voice mail. "Joel, this is Eve Lawson. If you don't call me back, I'll come over there. I'll be, oh, about half an hour. Okay?"

Clutching the phone, she looked at Ben. "If you can take me home, I need to go out again."

"The same kid? The football player?"

"Yes. He sounds freaked. Evidently there was a fire at the grumpy neighbor's house, and Joel thinks he's being blamed for it."

"I could try to reach Pruitt."

She thought about it, but finally shook her head. "I need to go over there anyway, if only to talk to Joel. If it looks like it's all over and everybody has gone to bed, I'll go home."

"We can go straight there, if you'd like."

Eve hesitated, oh so tempted in a different way, because she really wanted Ben with her, but she knew she shouldn't drag him into something he couldn't do anything about.

"It sounds like Officer Pruitt is there again. I can't imagine he'd like having you show up."

"As long as I make it clear I'm there strictly as your friend, I can't see that it would matter."

"You wouldn't rather go home?"

He reached across the console to close his much larger hand over hers, still clenched around the phone. "No, Eve. It wouldn't sit real well with me to wave as you drive away in the middle of the night to what's probably an upsetting scene. Do you really think I'd go home and hit the sack without giving you another thought?" The edge of anger in his voice belied the comfort of his touch.

Her sinuses burned. Refusing to cry, she breathed in and out, in and out, calming herself by will alone. Finally she was able to say, almost steadily, "Thank you, Ben. If you'd take me, I'd really appreciate it."

He gave her hand a gentle squeeze before returning his to the steering wheel. "You go dashing out into the night like this very often?"

Eve's chuckle sounded a little tremulous to her ears. "Probably not as often as you do. I don't know, maybe every couple of months some crisis erupts in the middle of the night."

He was quiet for a minute. His hands flexed on the wheel, then loosened again. "I didn't realize."

"No. Um, Joel's foster home is in the one subdivision out past the high school that *isn't* brand-new. Right off Sanders Road. Do you know it?"

He lifted an eyebrow. "I know damn near every road in this county. I patrolled for a couple of years before I made detective."

"Oh. Right."

It turned out he did know what development she was talking about. They had almost reached it when a fire truck took a turn out of the development right in front of them. The lights were no longer flashing.

"If it was arson, you know a fire marshal will be called in," Ben said, interrupting what had been a prolonged silence.

"I've never had anything to do with the fire marshal's office."

Once in the neighborhood, Ben asked for directions.

There was no need to tell him the exact address. Lights blazed down the block on both sides of the street. A few neighbors still stood on porches, as if hoping for another burst of excitement. A sheriff's department sedan blocked the driveway at Joel's house.

Ben rolled to a stop behind it. He'd barely set the emergency brake when Eve leaped out. She inhaled the pungent smell of charred wood, although it was fainter than she'd anticipated. Relief almost made her sag when she saw that Mr. Rowe's house still stood, no obvious evidence of damage to be seen. She hurried toward the Carters' house, but Ben still caught up with her before she could ring the doorbell.

It was Lynne who came to the door, wearing a fluffy pink bathrobe and matching slippers. Her surprise showed at the sight of Eve. "How on earth—" Her "Oh" came out flat. "I suppose Joel called you."

"That's right," Eve said pleasantly. "May we come in?"

Remembering herself, Lynne said, "Of course," and beamed a warm smile at Ben. "And you are?"

"Detective Ben Kemper."

"Detective? Oh, I assumed you were with Eve."

"I am." He, too, sounded pleasant but not gushing with sympathy despite Lynne's charming smile.

Eve was more pleased than she should be. It was dumb, of course, but she wanted him on *her* side.

No, Joel's, she corrected herself quickly.

With their arrival, the living room immediately felt crowded. In fact, the only remaining place to sit was the middle cushion of the sofa. When Joel saw her, his face momentarily contorted and he scooted over so she could take the place at the end. Eve patted his arm and saw his throat work. Ben took up a bodyguard stance directly behind her, shaking his head when Pruitt began rising to his feet.

"I'm fine," he said. Looking over her shoulder, she saw him nod at Pruitt. "I'm not here in an official capacity. Eve and I had gone out to dinner when she got a message from Joel."

"I see." Not looking entirely reassured, Pruitt ran a hand over a head that was starting to bald, then transferred his gaze to Eve. "Ms. Lawson, I'm not sure why Joel dragged you out. We'll be investigating this incident further tomorrow, and I was about to take off and let everyone go back to bed."

She couldn't imagine Joel would be able to sleep. Everyone else… Eve let her gaze wander from face to face. Rod, typically a good-natured, open man, appeared disturbed. He wore sweats and a faded T-shirt. Lynne had the expression of a good hostess and had somehow managed to brush her hair, while Gavin, barefoot but in jeans and sweatshirt, lounged in a recliner with the footrest up, gaze roving just like Eve's. Their eyes met, and he held her gaze. The small smile he allowed to play on his mouth instantly sharpened her dislike. She looked away deliberately, dismissively.

Officer Pruitt began talking, giving a synopsis of events, theoretically for her benefit, but he looked at Ben more than he did at her. Of course, she thought, wanting to roll her eyes.

Mr. Rowe fortunately was not a heavy sleeper, Pruitt said. He had smelled smoke, and rushing through the house discovered a fire leaping up through his back deck. It had become fully engaged, the boards of the deck burning, flames licking against the house siding. He had called 911 then hurried out and turned his hose on the blaze. By the time firefighters arrived, it was mostly out. Although the damage was minor, because they were sure they smelled gasoline, the crew chief had notified the fire marshal's office. Mr. Rowe had insisted "that boy" next door had to be responsible, and indeed the firefighters had observed a gas can abandoned by the side door into the Carters' garage. Mr. Carter confirmed it was his, and was usually in the garage next to the lawn mower. Tonight, leather gardening gloves had been sitting atop it, which ensured there'd be no fingerprint evidence. Both boys, when summoned, had come out of their respective bedrooms. Joel claimed to have been asleep, Gavin to have been listening to music with his earbuds in. The screen on Joel's bedroom window was not fully clipped on. Except for Rowe's accusation, that seemed to be the sole indication he might be the culprit, although she could understand why he'd panicked. Rod said he hadn't walked around the house that way since the last time he'd mowed, in early November, so the screen could have been knocked askew weeks or months ago.

Pruitt continued, telling them he'd spoken to the nearest neighbors. All had either gone to bed or were watching TV. Nobody saw a thing.

"Fortunately, not a lot of harm done," he concluded. His glance settled meaningfully on Joel. "A couple more minutes, and it would have been a different story. This was no prank."

Eve stayed mute, unable to disagree. She looked back at Gavin, whose face was now creased in what to all appearances was real concern. Gut instinct told her he was acting for all he was worth. She hoped Ben had seen the earlier smile.

Eve rose. "Joel, is there someplace we can talk for a minute?"

"Uh…" His head turned. "I guess my bedroom."

Lynne spoke up. "Why don't you just go out to the kitchen?"

"That's fine," Eve said.

Joel followed her, Ben remaining behind. Eve heard Gavin saying, "There's no way Joel did anything like this," and she gritted her teeth. Mr. Sincerity.

Since she could still hear part of the conversation from the living room even once they reached the kitchen, she didn't kid herself she and Joel had real privacy. Careful to lower her voice, she asked, "Joel, did you hear anything tonight?"

At six foot four, he towered over her. She imagined him doing weight lifting and seriously filling out, and could see why college programs had been eager to sign him. She also wondered if his sheer size had anything to do with Lynne's dislike. Gavin's, too, assuming her instincts were accurate. At five-ten or -eleven, he wouldn't be able to physically challenge Joel. Was this nasty little campaign the alternative?

Joel shook his head in answer to her question, his very dark eyes fixed desperately on her. "I really was asleep. Somebody else did this."

"Who do you think?" she asked, trying to sound nonjudgmental.

"I don't know!" He shot a telling look toward the living room and said more softly, "Lynne and Gavin…you know. But it's not like… I mean, I'll be gone in not that long."

Eve nodded. He was right; a normal kid in Gavin's situation would console himself that Joel might be gone as soon as school let out, if he found a decent job. His eighteenth birthday was in May, ending Rod's responsibility to him as a foster parent. At most, Rod would let him stay until he left for college—and that would be by the first of August if not sooner, given that football players must begin workouts well before the opening day of classes.

On the other hand, she felt really unsettled tonight. The crushed rosebushes—prank. Unpleasant, sure, but still something an unthinking kid would do. The rock through the window—more dangerous, but still a kid might not think about the possibility of it hitting someone in bed. The fire, though, was another story. Given a little more time, it could have consumed the house and killed an elderly man who loved his roses and, yes, was grumpy.

But if someone, say, Gavin, had sociopathic tendencies, he might not *care* if Mr. Rowe died, not if he achieved his ends. He also might not be willing to wait four to six months for Joel to be gone. Or he wanted to ensure Joel was gone for good, instead of being invited back for holiday breaks.

And, God, she might be imagining things. Some kid who lived two blocks away might have it in for Mr. Rowe. Or…had anyone even asked enough questions to be sure he didn't have enemies besides neighborhood kids? A grandson he'd cut off, or something like that?

Suddenly aware of a building headache, she said to Joel, "You're right. None of this makes sense. And it may be chance that Mr. Rowe thinks you're responsible, but we have to consider the possibility that whoever is doing this is trying to set you up. The gas can that came out of the garage, your window screen askew, those could be part of a setup." Seeing his stricken face, she hesitated. "Let me think about what we should do, okay?"

Joel's head bobbed. "You still believe me?"

He was begging. The thought flashed through her head that she *should* hesitate now, before answering. This faith in him was unreasoning. And yet, she'd learned to trust her gut.

"I do." She smiled. "We'll get through this."

He had to wipe wet cheeks. "Okay," he mumbled, choked up. "Thanks."

"I do need to get going. What if I take you out to lunch tomorrow? One o'clock?"

He agreed, and she returned to the living room.

"Ben, you ready to go?" She looked at Pruitt. "You'll keep me informed?"

His jaw tightened. "Yes, Ms. Lawson."

She nodded in a general way at everyone else. "Lynne, Rod."

Just before she turned, she saw that Gavin's eyes had narrowed because she hadn't bothered to acknowledge him. Screw the little creep.

Jumping to conclusions, an inner voice murmured.

Maybe, but something about him made her skin prickle.

She and Ben walked out to his SUV in silence, his hand under her elbow. He gave a boost to help her climb in before walking around to his side.

Still without saying anything, he started the engine, checked over his shoulder and pulled away from the curb. Eve stared straight ahead, weariness weighing heavily on her shoulders. Her head throbbed.

Ben made a U-turn at a cul-de-sac, returning the way they'd come. As they passed the Carters' house again, Eve saw that Officer Pruitt was just leaving, Rod and he talking on the porch with the front door open behind them.

"Did you see the way he looked at him?" she fumed. "He's so sure it's Joel."

"Pruitt?" At her nod, he said slowly, "I did get that impression."

"Tell me you didn't jump to the same one." Her fierce tone earned her a sidelong glance.

"Eve, I don't know enough to form an opinion. I understand you care for the kid, but Pruitt doesn't know him the way you do. The fact he didn't get the window screen reattached..." He shrugged. "You have to admit that's suggestive."

"Or it suggests someone else wants to lay the blame on Joel," she shot back.

"Why would anybody do that?" he asked reasonably.

"Because *that's* the point! Not Mr. Rowe at all."

"You think it's the other boy."

"Yes." She knew she was being too passionate, when she should strive to come off as the measured professional. Especially since even she knew she was being irrational. But right this minute, she didn't care. "Or someone else," she said more weakly. "But not Joel."

Ben nodded.

After a minute, she had to ask. "What are you thinking?"

He let out a long breath. "That I'd like to agree with you to make you happy, but I can't." He held up a hand to stop her when she opened her mouth. "I don't disagree with you, either. I don't know either of them. My inclination is to respect Pruitt's experience."

"But not mine?" she said sharply.

"Damn it, Eve!" There was enough light for her to see his hands tighten on the steering wheel. "You asked my opinion. I don't have one. This isn't a playground where I jump in on your side whether you're right or wrong because we're friends."

No, it wasn't. Shame heated her cheeks. "You're right. I'm sorry. I shouldn't be putting pressure on you because I'm upset." Determined to regain control of her churning emotions, she turned her head to stare blindly out the side window. The pounding beneath her temple was as rhythmic as a metronome.

"Eve?" Ben said after a minute.

She was careful to move really slowly when she looked back at him. "Yes?"

"You're pissed."

"Why would you think that? I said you're right.

I shouldn't have brought you with me in the first place. I was putting you on the spot. So let's just drop it, okay? Truth is, I have a crushing headache."

He didn't say a damn thing, leaving her to wonder whether he didn't believe her or thought the conversation had been inconsequential.

She did know it was one she shouldn't have started. No, he *didn't* know any of the players except Pruitt beyond what she'd told him. While they were there, the only thing she'd heard Gavin say was a defense of Joel. Lynne hadn't said a word after greeting them at the door unless she'd talked while Eve was with Joel in the kitchen. So expecting him to jump in on Joel's side had been childish.

And yet, her belly harbored a small, burning coal of hurt anyway. It was there because he *did* know her, but apparently valued Officer Pruitt's opinion higher than hers nonetheless. Because he was a fellow deputy? Because she was a woman? *That better not be why,* she fumed. Because he thought she was too emotional to think clearly? Who knew?

He parked in a visitor slot at her apartment house, and, still without saying a word, got out and walked her to her door.

There, he waited until she unlocked, then gave her a rueful look. "As endings to an evening go, this one sucks."

"My fault," she admitted, almost sure she'd have invited him in if they hadn't been sidetracked.

"No, you were doing your job, that's all. There'll be times I have to do mine and you may not agree with my decisions."

"But if you'd gotten a call, you wouldn't have taken me with you, would you?"

He made a sound. "Probably not. Eve, sometimes it would be dangerous for you to go with me."

She wrinkled her nose at him. "You win. Good night, Ben."

"Hey, not so fast." Voice suddenly husky, he lifted one hand and slid it around her nape. "I'd really like to kiss you, Eve."

"Oh, fine." She laughed at his expression. "I'd like you to kiss me, too."

No matter what, he stoked a fire in her. He kept the kiss closer to tender than passionate, and still warmth flooded her and her knees grew weak. Eve didn't participate so much as…accept. When he finally pressed soft lips to her forehead and murmured, "Sleep tight," it was all she could do to pry her fingers loose from their grip on his coat.

"You, too," she whispered, and backed inside her apartment. The last thing she saw was him waiting, his blue eyes gleaming, for her to close the door and lock up.

CHAPTER SIX

"BUT YOU SAID we could go sledding again. Mommy says if we don't go tomorrow, the snow might all melt, and then we couldn't go until next winter." Which in Rachel's worldview was forever and ever away. Indignation thrust her lower lip out. "Anyway, I've *seen* those movies."

Crap. Ben hadn't looked forward to seeing either of the two movies currently playing that were aimed at the preschool set, but driving that far only so she could whine that she was *cold*, Daddy, had even less appeal. But Mommy was right; two weeks from tomorrow would be March 28, bumping up to April, and it was possible that the snow would have melted from the more accessible—and gently sloped—sledding hills.

"Let me think about it," he temporized. "Right now, you need to go to bed. We'll talk about it again in the morning."

The lower lip protruded even farther. "But, Daddy…"

He bent a look at her that made her give a theatrical sigh and climb beneath the covers.

"You're mean."

He laughed. "No, I'm not. A *mean* daddy wouldn't offer to take *his* little girl out for pizza or hamburgers and to a movie. Or read her seven— count 'em—seven books before bed."

She giggled. "You'll leave the door open, right?"

"How could I forget?"

The bathroom light would stay on all night, serving as a night-light and making it easy for her if she needed to get up. He hugged her one more time, kissed the top of her head as he flicked off her bedside lamp and retreated to the kitchen.

There his smile died. For once, he'd almost hoped Nic would call with one of her many excuses to "switch" weekends. He'd have really liked to spend time with Eve. Instead, he'd had to say, *nope, I have my daughter for the weekend, so maybe next week.* And, though that conversation had taken place over the phone, he could picture all too well how her glow had dimmed.

Assuming she'd been glowing, he thought, disturbed as he'd been most of the week when he thought about her. Saturday, he'd called to find out if they could do something, but she was with Joel and only said, "I'm afraid not." Sunday, a drunken brawl at a biker bar had escalated into a homicide that fell to him and Seth. Tuesday he and Eve managed dinner—pizza again. They planned for Thursday night, and she had to cancel.

"Tomorrow," she'd begun, when he had had to say, "No, I have Rachel."

Ne'er the twain shall meet.

Where was his head anyway? He had good reasons for keeping his life compartmentalized. Was he second-guessing himself?

Yeah, that's exactly what he was doing. Ben sank his fingers into his hair and yanked hard enough to hurt. If Eve was along, he was betting Rach would have more fun. He wanted to see Eve. Really, what was the harm?

Rachel might develop an attachment to Eve.

Not in the course of one outing, for God's sake. Or even a few. As long as he didn't give her any reason to think Eve was more than a friend, why would she? He wouldn't include Eve *every* weekend, just once in a while.

Jolted, he thought, *I'm assuming Eve wants to be included.*

He kept thinking she'd cooled off some this week. If so, it had begun last Friday night, when he declined to come out fighting on Joel Kekoa's side.

She'd *sounded* genuine when she apologized for trying to drag him into a situation he knew nothing about. He'd have thought no more about it if she hadn't seemed so distracted this week.

And, yeah, there was the fact that Eve hadn't mentioned Joel either Tuesday evening at dinner or during their several phone conversations, which he'd have thought would be natural. He had had to ask if anything more had happened, and her answer was terse.

"No. There's no real evidence to implicate him. Joel volunteered to help rebuild the deck, but Mr. Rowe refused. The week has been quiet."

"You know something else will happen," he'd suggested.

"One more incident, and I'll move Joel to another foster home." She had changed the subject, clearly uninterested in discussing it with him, and he couldn't blame her.

He also couldn't give her what he guessed she wanted, which left them at an impasse.

Having Rachel with them would mean they *couldn't* talk about Joel.

Win-win.

"Fine!" he snapped, startling himself when he realized he'd said it aloud.

He checked to make sure it wasn't too late to call, then grabbed his phone.

Eve answered on the third ring. "Ben?" she said, sounding surprised. "Is everything all right?"

"Sure. Just wanted to hear your voice."

"That's nice. Don't you have Rachel?"

"Yeah, but she's gone to bed."

"I see."

He wanted to believe that was one of the meaningless things people murmured, but knew better.

"Truth is, uh, I was wondering if you're free tomorrow."

"Tomorrow?"

"Rachel wants to go sledding again. I was hoping you'd come with us."

"I would love to go," she said promptly. "Even if I secretly suspect you're asking because you're convinced I'll be able to keep her interested for more than five minutes."

Relief loosened Ben's throat, and he laughed. "Damn, you've got me. What I really think is that you're more fun than I am."

Her snort somehow still sounded feminine. "I can't remember the last time anyone called me 'fun.'"

"I think you are." Hearing the hushed quality of his voice, he thought, *Uh-oh*. Hastily, going for humorous, he said, "I'll bet you'd have cut loose on the dance floor with a date who wasn't too uptight."

Eve laughed. "Maybe. Okay. What time?"

They made arrangements, then talked for a few more minutes, both keeping their voices quiet even though neither said anything important. He felt something that had been lacking the rest of the week. An intimacy, he decided, surprising himself with a word he couldn't remember ever using before.

No, call a spade a spade: she'd forgiven him. That was good enough.

After letting her go, he walked quietly down the hall to stand in the doorway to Rachel's bedroom, just checking on her. He had done that every night, until he no longer lived under the same roof. Needing to know she was safe before he went to sleep himself.

Tonight, she made a small lump beneath the covers. The band of light from the hall fell across her, letting him see the shimmer of blond hair on the pillow. She mumbled and buried her face deeper in the pillow before relaxing into sleep again.

Real anticipation rose in him as he imagined Rachel's excitement when he agreed to take her sledding, then picking up Eve.

Yeah, this would work out fine.

"SO THEN MRS. MESSNER SAID, 'Caleb'—" Rachel's voice deepened dramatically "—'that wasn't nice. How would *you* like to have a favorite shirt ruined by paint?' Only, *he* said he wouldn't care, and he dumped the *whole* pot of red paint on himself. It got in his hair 'n' everything." She sounded awed.

Eve hid her smile. Rachel had chattered almost nonstop for the past half hour, mostly about school and the apparently colorful cast of characters that made up her days. Listening, Eve had angled her body so that she could look over her shoulder often, which of course also had the benefit of letting her watch Ben, mostly in profile.

And, darn it, even his profile was perfect—his forehead high, his nose thin and straight, the jut of cheekbone sharp, a chin proportioned for the rest of his face. She'd been able to watch when he smiled and that line in his cheek deepened along with the crinkles beside his eyes.

Without being too obvious, she could study his throat, the way his mint-gold hair curled just slightly over his collar. His hands, the taut muscles in his thighs outlined by worn denim, strong brown forearms exposed when he'd pushed up his sleeves once the heater kicked in.

And she could smile at his daughter, who was smart, funny, charming and theatrical. However grudgingly, Eve was gaining respect for Ben's ex-wife. Whatever her other flaws, she had to be a good mother, or Rachel wouldn't be so unaffected, so trustingly certain she'd be liked, so observant of the other kids and even her teacher.

Not to say, she reminded herself, that Ben didn't play a big part in building his daughter's confidence. He talked to her directly, listened as if what she said mattered to him, and didn't give away mixed feelings about Nicole when Rachel talked about her mommy.

"Are you learning to read yet?" Eve asked.

"Uh-huh! I'm in the top reading group, 'cuz I can read whole books 'n' most of the kids only know their letters," she declared. "I wish we could use computers more at school. Mommy lets me type on hers, and play games and stuff."

Ben glanced sidelong at Eve and said, sotto voce, "She grumbles every weekend because I don't have any good games on my laptop."

His daughter giggled. "I do not!"

"I make up for it by reading tons of stories to her every night. *Mountains* of stories. Piles of books vast enough to reach the moon."

Rachel thought that was hilarious, too. She did concede that Daddy read lots to her. Mommy did, too, but not so much anymore 'cuz she said Rachel should practice reading stories herself.

"I bet your daddy reads ones to you that you can't read yet, doesn't he?" Eve suggested.

"Uh-huh. Daddy says we might even start a chapter book. It might take us a long time to finish, but that's okay. I could think about the story 'tween visits and imagine what happens."

Eve got a lump in her throat. What she'd have given at Rachel's age to have a daddy who would suggest things like that. Oh, who was she kidding? There'd been a time her dream had only been big enough to imagine having any kind of daddy at all. Now, with adult hindsight, she knew better. Given that her mother had been a drug addict and on-again/off-again prostitute, any man she'd have picked was unlikely to have been quality father material. Eve had come to believe herself fortunate that her biological father's only role had been to supply sperm.

And then she'd been lucky enough to have Kirk Lawson. She felt sure he'd have read to her if she hadn't been too old by then to need him to.

"Ladies, we're here," Ben declared just then, putting on the turn signal. "Looks like we're not alone, but the more the merrier, right?"

Peering ahead as eagerly as Rachel was, Eve saw that he was right. Eight or nine other vehicles were already here, and people in colorful parkas and hats were pulling sleds and plastic discs uphill while others flashed down.

He parked, bumper almost touching a snowbank, and released his seat belt, turning to look over his shoulder. "Time to bundle up, kiddo, so you don't get cold like you did last time."

"You did buy her some new boots, then?" Eve asked.

"And snow pants, too," Rachel boasted. "Only, we couldn't find any pink ones. These are *blue*." Her tone condemned the color.

"Sorry." He'd gotten out and opened her door, helping her unbuckle. The quilted pants he held up were indeed navy blue, probably made for boys, although Eve wouldn't have said that for worlds.

"We went to Goodwill quick this morning," he told her over Rachel's head, as she squirmed into the snow pants. "Even assuming any of the stores at the mall still have winter clothes, I couldn't see wasting a lot of money on boots and pants that won't fit by the time we do this again."

"That's smart. Those do look warm," she told Rachel.

Eventually, they were all appropriately garbed, Rachel all but waddling in her chunky boots— they had found pink boots—quilted pants and heavy parka. Her hands were encased in mittens, her head covered by a cozy hat. Eve lacked the snow pants, but figured she could endure a cold butt for as long as a six-year-old's attention span lasted.

Ben had donned navy blue insulated ski pants and parka and black leather gloves. The knit hat he pulled out of one pocket was—drum roll, please—navy blue. Of course, he looked incredibly sexy no matter what he wore.

He had an actual sled, she was pleased to see, instead of one of those round plastic discs that seemed to spin people around even as they shot down the slope. Having a tendency to vertigo, Eve didn't think that looked like much fun. Who got carsick when they were sledding? She didn't want to be the first.

"It was fun last time," Rachel confided, reaching for Eve's hand. She held her father's on the other side. "'Til I fell off and got all wet and cold."

Ben grimaced over her head. He'd told Eve they had only gone down the hill three times.

Eve laughed and squeezed Rachel's hand. "Falling off is half the fun. Today, you're well padded. All you'll do is bounce."

It was a beautiful day, besides: the sky was crystal clear, a bottomless blue, the snow sparkled in the sunlight, and yet it was cold enough despite the lateness in the season to keep the snow crisp underfoot. Eve's breath puffed out in small clouds.

Once they were at the top of the slope, she waited while Ben went down with his daughter, after which Eve took a turn with her. In no time, Rachel had become fast friends with a couple of kids close to her age. She and another girl spun down the hill in a blue plastic saucer.

"Ugh," Eve muttered. "Makes my stomach spin."

The other girl's mother laughed. "It's even worse when you're actually doing it. You notice I'm doing a lot of standing around and generously letting the rest of the family take my turns."

Eve laughed.

Of course, then Ben wanted to take a turn with her, which involved her settling carefully on the wooden slats of the sled and scrunching up so he could sit behind her and wrap his legs around her, placing his feet on the steering bar. Then his arms came around her, too, as he lifted the rope. He put his mouth close to her ear and murmured, "Now, this I like."

Eve gave a small wriggle that had him laughing.

"Need a push?" a man asked, and a moment later they were sliding.

The hill was just steep enough to make Eve's eyes sting in the cold wind and provide a little bit of a thrill while still being safe for children. As they glided to a stop, Eve wished they could have gone on and on.

Ben rose a lot more gracefully than she did, even with the help of his hand on hers, tugging her up. In the cold, color had risen in his cheeks and his eyes were intensely blue. He kept tugging until she bumped up against him, then dropped a kiss on her mouth with cold lips.

"Fun?" he asked huskily.

"It was." She looked around as an excuse to tear her gaze from his. "How on earth did the two of you ever fall off on this hill?"

Pulling the sled, he started upward. "The packed part of the hill was narrower and there were banks on each side. I think there'd been a late snowfall. There've been a lot of people here since then. Plus," he sounded rueful, "*I* thought it would be fun to tumble into the snow."

"Bet you were sorry."

"You're not kidding."

They caught up to Rachel and her new friend near the top. The two were chattering away. "Look!" she told her father. "I want pants like Livvy's."

Which were, of course, pink.

"Next year," Ben promised. "Yours may be blue, but they're keeping you warm, aren't they?"

Yes, they were. She decided to go down with Livvy again, which gave Eve another chance to snuggle in front of Ben and shoot down the hill. They were almost to the bottom when she felt him leaning sideways, pulling him with her. Just as they slid to a stop, they tipped over. Her head was cushioned by his upper arm, but her hip felt the cold.

"Very funny," she said as they untangled themselves and righted the sled. "And ugh. I think my butt is frozen now."

Laughing at her, he pulled off his glove and laid his hand over her hip. "Huh," he said in surprise. "I think it is." Then he patted her, very gently. "You going to start whining that you want to go home?"

Eve gave a saucy smile. "Nope. I'm a big girl." She twirled and started up without him, adding an extra swing to her hips for a few steps.

Rachel lasted for nearly an hour and a half before getting a little whiny. By then, even Eve was wearing down. Livvy's family had departed, the girls mourning the fact that they didn't go to the same school.

"I wish *I* went to school in Stimson," Rachel declared.

Eve imagined Ben feeling a stab in his heart. But to his credit, he only grinned at his kid.

"But then you wouldn't know Ann. And isn't she your best friend?"

Well, yes, but she liked Livvy, too, and now she'd never see her again.

He'd just stowed the sled in the back when his phone rang. When he answered, Eve guessed the call had to do with work—until she heard him say, "Nic?"

Whatever his ex-wife said after that made his face soften. His gaze caught Eve's, and he turned his back, walking a few steps away for a quiet conversation. Eve tried not to mind. When Ben opened the driver's side door and got in, he said with what struck her as an elaborately casual tone, "Nicole wondered how the sledding had gone." He turned his head to grin at his daughter. "Your mom thought you'd be an icicle by now."

"Did you tell her about my new boots 'n' stuff?"

"I did."

Eve didn't comment. Rachel drooped in the backseat once they were moving and the heat was pouring out of the vents, but revived when Ben stopped at a rustic café twenty minutes down the road for a late lunch.

Eve didn't know if the hamburger was really that good or whether she was just starved, but she devoured it and her fries, and watched in amusement as Rachel gobbled a surprising amount, too, and insisted she still had room for pie.

So did Eve. She decided to skip the a la mode,

but enjoyed watching Rachel and Ben share a slab
of huckleberry pie with a huge heap of ice cream
atop it.

Two minutes after leaving the café, Rachel
tipped until her cheek was pressed to the window glass and fell sound asleep.

Ben smiled, looking in the rearview mirror.
"It's always guaranteed," he said softly.

"Does she still nap?" asked Eve, just as quietly.

"She insists she doesn't, but Nic says she still
does most days. Wear her out a little, and she
conks right out."

"She's a sweetheart. And thank you for inviting me. I had a great time."

"Better than dancing?"

"Well…" She pretended to think, holding back
her smile. "Maybe. Except for the cold."

He chuckled and reached over to take her hand.
Eve dismissed her worry about that phone call.

They mostly stayed quiet during the remainder
of the drive, but she was blissfully happy. Ben
never let go of her hand until they reached the
city limits and traffic became heavier. When he
pulled up to her complex, she shook her head as
he reached for his door handle.

"Don't be silly. There's no need to disturb Rachel."

"Okay." His voice was low, gravelly. "I'm glad
you came." He began the kiss as if fully aware his
daughter could wake up at any minute, but it deep-

ened and grew hotter by increments, until Eve, at least, was wanting a whole lot more.

Ben groaned when he lifted his head. "Damn. I want—"

Me, too. "Talk to you soon." She had to clear her throat. "Enjoy the rest of your weekend."

She'd almost made up the stairs before he drove away. She might have felt a tiny pang, because she would have liked to be included in whatever else he and Rachel did, but she couldn't mind too much because he had invited her to join them for their outing. He'd wanted her and Rachel to get to know each other. Her rational side understood completely why he hadn't at first; it wasn't healthy for kids to spend time with a parade of temporary partners in their parents' lives. In fact, given that they'd only been seeing each other for a couple of weeks, the fact that he'd included her today had to mean something. This happiness felt strange, unfamiliar, but good nonetheless.

It meant he liked her. Really, really liked her.

And, no, she wasn't going to squeal, but she wanted to.

TRUST HIS BIGMOUTHED DAUGHTER. Nicole had barely opened her front door to greet them than Rachel began excitedly telling her about the sledding, and Daddy's friend who said Rachel could call her Eve, and how mostly Daddy rode down on the sled with Eve while Rachel went with her new friend Livvy.

And after he'd been careful during the phone call not to mention Eve.

Nicole listened, her arms crossed, her expression pleasantly interested.

Rachel twirled, telling Nic about how the plastic saucer spun until she and Livvy were dizzy and fell down when they got off.

She beamed. "We had lots of fun. I didn't get cold at all, 'cuz Daddy bought me snow boots 'n' pants." She demonstrated how they made her walk like a penguin before Nicole suggested she take her suitcase to her bedroom before she came back to say goodbye to Daddy.

Ben tensed. If Nic didn't want to talk to him, she'd have Rachel hug him goodbye right away. The "take your stuff to your room" tactic was saved for when she had something to say.

The moment Rachel was out of earshot, Nicole raised her perfectly arched brows. "Did you have to introduce your daughter to whatever woman you're seeing right now?"

He made sure to keep his expression bland. "What's the harm in her meeting my friends?"

"Show some discretion," she said sharply.

His jaw tightened. "Rach tells me all the time about the men Mommy is dating. Pretty sure you've introduced her to them."

She tilted her head, looking almost flirtatious.

"Does that bother you?" she murmured. "Knowing I'm dating?"

Yeah. It had bothered him a hell of a lot, although he'd been careful not to give her the satisfaction of knowing.

Satisfaction? What? He thought she *enjoyed* hurting him?

He blocked out the disturbing thought, which was followed by yet another: that this weekend he hadn't wondered even once what Nicole was doing with her free-as-a-bird Friday and Saturday nights. Because of Eve.

"We're divorced, Nic," he said. "Why would I be bothered?"

Her eyes narrowed and her lips thinned. She hadn't liked that.

Well, good, he thought, anger forming a ball in his gut, because he'd had a suspicion all along that she made sure Rachel met the men she was dating so that she *would* tell Daddy about them. He'd been idiot enough to convince himself it was because Nic was having second thoughts and was trying to get a reaction from him, arouse jealousy so she could be sure he still wanted her.

And here it turned out that what he'd needed to do was threaten *her* certainty that he'd always be waiting in the wings.

He wished he knew if it was all ego for her, or whether she felt any regret or yearning for what used to be.

He smiled past her at his daughter who hurried back to fling her arms around his waist. He lifted her, kissed her forehead and said, "You be good for your mom, okay? *And* Mrs. Messner."

She giggled. "I'm always good."

He laughed and set her down. "Bye, honey."

He'd barely turned away when the door closed, damn near hitting him in the ass. Nope, Nicole was not pleased to find out he had a girlfriend.

Bonus points, he thought with satisfaction, walking to his vehicle.

"SETH'S BEEN TALKING to you." Eve pushed her laptop aside on her dining-room table and reached for her teacup. Bailey had called, apparently in an attempt to persuade Eve to tell all.

Her adoptive sister laughed. "Of course he's been talking to me. We talk almost every night."

Eve felt a pang. What would it be like, to close out every day with the same person? To know everything that happened to you during the day, large or small, was important to him because *you* were?

"What's he doing, grilling Ben on our relationship?"

"Something like that. He says Ben is annoyingly closemouthed."

Since Bailey couldn't see her, Eve didn't have to hide her grin. "So he passed the baton to you, figuring women don't keep secrets from each other?"

"I gather you've been keeping a few from Mom."

Eve's amusement went flat at Bailey's pointed comment. "She complained?"

"No, she just sounded a little hurt."

"I have called her twice this week," she gritted out.

"And what did you talk about?"

Feeling mulish, Eve pressed her lips together, refusing to answer on the grounds it would incriminate her. She'd talked about everything *but* Ben.

"She loves you."

"That's not love," Eve snapped. "It's guilt, heavily applied."

"I don't know, I sort of like having a mom who is nosy because she cares about me."

"So now you're trying to make me feel guilty, too?" Eve shot back. "Because I had Mommy and Daddy longer than you did?"

"Well, you did," Bailey said reasonably, then to Eve's surprise laughed. "Okay, I guess that wasn't so subtle. And no, I don't blame you for wanting to keep your dating or sex life private. She fusses every time I come up because I'm staying with Seth and not with them. 'You know, Hope, there are some people who still disapprove of couples living together before marriage.'"

"They're pretty conservative, in case you haven't figured that out by now."

"I have. I've refrained from reminding her that I haven't been lily-pure for a long time."

Shocked, Eve said, "That's not funny."

This time, it was Bailey who was quiet for a minute. Finally she said, "I wasn't talking about *him*."

He—always mentioned with the same tension—was Les Hamby, the creep who had abducted six-year-old Hope Lawson, sexually molested and physically abused her for years until her body had begun to develop, becoming unappealing to him, and then abandoned her. He'd gone on to abduct other little girls, all pretty, all blonde and blue-eyed, until Seth brought Hope home, then determined to track Hamby down. Working with the FBI, against all odds he had succeeded. Hamby's first of what would be several trials in different states would be here, for kidnapping Hope. It looked as if it might happen as soon as this coming fall. Bailey claimed to be looking forward to testifying, although Eve suspected her real emotions were probably more complex. Eve also suspected she talked about them only to Seth.

"I'm sorry," Eve said.

"It was my teenage behavior I was talking about," Bailey said, sounding more subdued. "I… thought the only thing I had of any worth was my body."

"You never told me that."

"I'm not exactly proud of it." She paused. "I did tell Seth. He says he understands."

"Of course he does. I do, too. I've worked with more than a few girls who took the same road."

"I suppose you have." Bailey sounded thoughtful. "Do you get a lot of kids who've been sexually molested?"

"Unfortunately. No class or economic boundaries there. I have a couple girls in foster care right now whose father likely molested all four daughters before the next-to-youngest finally told. The mother insists they're all lying and is standing staunchly by him. He's an attorney and county council member."

"Really? Still?"

"He resigned from the county council, but is still fighting charges. I can't imagine his law practice is exactly booming."

"No."

Bailey said it so softly, Eve felt a pang of—what else?—guilt.

"I'm sorry," she said again.

"No, don't be. Having been outed to the world, I've discovered that most people are as uncomfortable talking to me about child sexual abuse as they would be about death if I were terminal. It's…awkward. Plus, I'm left listening for whispers behind my back. It's true even for Mom and Dad—" she seemed to be thinking that through "—no, not fair, mostly Mom. You and Seth are the only people who really acknowledge what happened to me."

"Excepting reporters," Eve said drily.

"Ugh. Yes." Bailey took a deep breath or let one out, Eve wasn't sure which. "Which brings us back to our parents."

"And Mom nursing hurt feelings."

"Right. My turn to apologize. I shouldn't have mentioned it. My advice is, don't tell her anything about Ben until you're ready." She paused just long enough to be effective. "Now, *I'm* another story. Dish."

Eve couldn't help laughing. "So you can tell Seth what I said, and he can tell Ben?"

"I wouldn't do that." Bailey sounded totally serious. "Cross my heart. If you ever want to talk…"

"I'll come to you." Astonished, Eve realized she meant it. "Promise."

Hanging up a few minutes later, she wondered how it was that her resentment of the perfect, long-lost and miraculously recovered "sister" had transformed into liking and a growing friendship. In barely six months, she'd begun to accept the possibility that Bailey and she might *be* sisters in a real sense, something she'd have sworn was impossible.

Maybe, she thought, *I still resent Hope. But Bailey isn't exactly Hope, even though she is.*

Clear as mud.

CHAPTER SEVEN

FROM THE FAR side of the parking lot, Ben watched people come and go through the entrance to the sheriff's department. Leaning against the cold metal of the fender of his unmarked county car, he held his cell phone to his ear.

"Six thirty?" he suggested.

"I'm working from home today, so if you can pick me up for dinner, that would be great," Eve said.

Hallelujah. Not just music to Ben's ears, it was a full symphony, and enough to make his body stir. Damn, he wanted her.

"No problem," he said, really fast, before Eve could decide it would actually make more sense for her to meet him at the restaurant.

They didn't talk much longer; he'd just unlocked the car with the plan of heading out to track down several people he wanted to talk to when his phone rang and he saw Eve's number.

He had the passing thought that it might be nice if he could work from home, too. Her home, preferably. Although in that case, he doubted he'd do much work.

She ended the conversation by saying, "I'll expect you when I see you," obviously unperturbed by the possibility he might not arrive on time to the second. He hadn't thought there was a woman alive who not only understood why he had to be late or even cancel engagements fairly often, but did the same herself.

No, not fair—there were women cops, after all. And turned out social workers with crushing caseloads scrambled to find time for a personal life, too.

Life is good, he told himself, calculating whether he might be able to get away early for once. Wasn't as if he'd be shorting the county on hours.

Then don't waste time, he told himself as he settled behind the wheel and fastened the seat belt.

As it happened, he did break away early: a whole fifteen minutes. Which meant if he'd actually located all three people he'd set out to interview, he'd have been late.

And Eve would have been okay with it. Would he ever get over the amazement, after years of bracing himself for reproaches or stony silences?

When she opened the door to him, Eve clapped her hands to her face in mimed astonishment. "Oh, my goodness! Early!" She dropped the silly face and teased, "Eager, are you?"

He'd thought about her all afternoon. The warmth in her chocolate-brown eyes when she smiled, the way she'd wiggled her butt to make a point that day at the sledding hill, the feel of her nestled against his groin on the sled. He wanted in the worst way to see her naked, that wavy dark hair tumbling loose over her shoulders and breasts.

He'd had every intention of kissing her on the cheek and escorting her to dinner, reining in the lust until he brought her home.

The laughter on her face had him aroused with stunning speed.

Was he eager? "God, yes," he said hoarsely, and hauled her up against him fast enough to scare her. He knew he hadn't when she lifted on her toes, flung her arms around his neck and pressed a clumsy kiss to the side of his mouth before he quite had them aligned.

Everything about her hit him at that moment. A subtly spicy scent, hair like the heaviest silk between his fingers, the delicacy of her body, the lushness of dark eyelashes fanned on her cheeks. Ben kissed her voraciously, trying to inhale her. He had his tongue in her mouth, tangled with hers, her taste flooding his senses. A grip on her butt lifted her higher. He squeezed the taut cheek, imagining how it would feel to do the same thing when he was inside her.

Shuddering, he wrenched his mouth away from hers and lowered her until she was back on her feet, although he couldn't make himself release her. He swallowed hard, looking down at her.

Her face stayed tipped up to his. She slowly, uncertainly, opened eyes that were dazed, the brown making him think of melted caramel.

"You're beautiful." His voice might have scraped over gravel on its way out. His entire body ached.

And, yes, he'd never been so aware of how beautiful she was, with that heart-shaped face, big eyes and mass of black curls. Delicate and feminine, she still had a hint of someplace a whole lot more exotic than Stimson, Washington.

"I…" She blinked. "Thank you."

"I want you."

Her gaze skimmed down and her lips curved. "I can tell."

He cleared his throat. "If we're going to dinner, we'd better go."

Her eyes met his again. "I snacked all day. But you're probably starved."

That was one way of putting it.

He cradled her face in his hand, his thumb sliding over her parted lips. "For you," Ben said, low and husky.

Her tongue flicked the pad of his thumb, sending an electrical jolt through his body. He groaned. "Eve?" That was all the question he could ask. His brain didn't seem capable of forming words.

"Please," she whispered, and turned her head to nip his thumb.

He exploded into motion, scooping her up and starting through the apartment.

"Did you close the door?"

"What?" He stopped, staring down at her. It took a minute to absorb the question. "Damn. I don't know." He had to turn around and go back to see that, yes, the door was closed. Whether it was locked, he neither knew nor cared. He resumed his progress to the short hall.

"Second room on the right," she murmured, nibbling at his neck. When her tongue swirled in a circle, he stumbled but managed to shoulder open the door.

Rich color surrounded him despite the beige carpet that was standard rental unit. Wall hangings, throw rug, a painting. He didn't focus on any of them. The bed was his object.

A stunning quilt that made him think of the swirl of gypsy skirts covered the bed. Another time, Ben might have paused to study it. Now, all he did was yank it back and let Eve slide down his body right beside the bed. Then he went after her mouth again. God, he loved kissing her.

For a couple of minutes, he was content to do nothing but, sinking into the pleasure of her taste and textures, her enthusiastic response. His hands skated up and down her body, finding every subtle curve.

Suddenly, that wasn't enough. He backed off

enough to grab the hem of her sweater. "Take it off."

She helped, after which all he could do was stare. "So pretty," he said thickly. He'd never seen a woman more finely made: her skin smooth and golden, her collarbone as delicate as porcelain, her breasts not large but just right. The bra was lace-edged white, somehow both innocent and erotic. He laid his hands over her breasts, lifting and shaping, before flicking open the front catch. Watching his face, Eve ducked her shoulders so that the bra dropped.

She also had the loveliest breasts he'd ever seen. Just enough to fill his hands, her nipples tight and dark. He wanted his mouth where his hands were. But when he grasped her around the waist to lie on the bed, she batted at him.

"No fair." She started unbuttoning his shirt. Ben tried to help, but his fingers felt clumsy and finally he let her do it all, then push his shirt off.

She made a pleased sound that arrowed straight to his groin. "*You're* beautiful," she murmured, flattening her hands on his chest, tugging gently at the hair sprinkled over it, lightly touching his nipples.

Ben tipped his head back and closed his eyes, pleasure spearing him. Those small hands felt so damn good. Now she was kneading, occasionally scraping a fingernail lightly across skin that shivered from her touch. She followed the trail of hair down to his belt buckle.

He groaned. "Don't stop."

The look she gave him was almost shy, but then she laid a hand over the ridge beneath his belt and explored its dimensions, humming her approval when his penis jerked.

"Enough," he had to say, voice guttural. Never looking away from her, he managed to get his belt off and set his holstered weapon and badge on a side table. This time she didn't protest when he scooped her up and sent her sprawling on deep purple flannel sheets before following her down. His mouth captured one breast and he suckled, drawing her nipple hard into his mouth. She moaned.

She wore some kind of stretchy pants. Even through the fabric he felt her heat and knew she was already wet. He applied enough pressure to have her moaning and pushing her hips up to meet it.

Ben moved to the other breast at the same time his fingers delved beneath the waistband and found her springy curls. He slid his finger between her folds and stroked in time with the tug of his mouth.

He needed to see her. All of her. Ben rose to his knees to peel off the pants and bright toe socks. Her feet momentarily distracted him. They were small and, like the rest of her, fine-boned, her toenails painted the same rosy red as her fingernails. He squeezed her feet, running his thumbs up the arched instep and watching her toes curl.

Then impatience had him sliding his hands up legs amazingly long given her short stature, smooth beneath his hands, until he reached the V of her thighs. He bent and rubbed his cheek against that springy black hair.

Eve had lifted herself to watch him, braced on her elbows. Her lips were slightly parted, and he could see the tip of her tongue. Her eyes were the darkest he'd ever seen them.

There was a lot he wanted to do to her, but abruptly he realized he wouldn't be doing it this first time. He wrenched off his shoes and socks and shed his trousers, taking a packet from the pocket before he let them fall. He ripped it open and donned the condom under her fascinated stare. By the time his mouth closed over hers again, his hand was back between her legs, stroking, teasing, pressing. When he slid a finger inside her, her fingers dug into his back, the sharp edge of nails stinging and only driving his hunger into something like madness.

Ben found his way between her legs and, keeping some of his weight on his elbows, pushed inside her, harder, faster than he should have given how small she was. He couldn't make himself stop until he was seated deep, when he raised his head.

"All right?" he managed to ask.

She squirmed, her internal muscles flexing. He almost came. *Not yet*.

"Yes," she whispered. "Oh, yes."

He began to move, finding a rhythm she matched, one that had his brain shutting down. He was all sensation. Usually he closed his eyes, but he wanted to see her face. She made little sounds, some of which he caught with his mouth. Needing her to come, he increased the intensity, went deeper, telling her she was perfect, beautiful, until her back arched in a great spasm and her eyes flew open just as the convulsions gripped him and he lost it. Her expression was one of naked astonishment, and he was afraid his was, too, as he thrust again, once, twice, then went rigid above her as he emptied himself in a climax of stunning power. The best he could do coming down was half roll so his shoulder took some of his weight. Some instinct had him grabbing her thigh and holding it over his hips to keep them connected.

EVE ENDED UP lying half atop him, her mind... blank. She only felt. The hard, punishingly fast beat of his heart beneath her ear, the tickle of the gold hair on his chest, the hard, hot wall of muscles. With her hair tumbling over her and him both, she couldn't see more than a couple inches beyond her nose, but who needed to see? She wasn't sure she could so much as lift her head and didn't try.

Eventually her brain started to reboot, and she was almost sorry, because, didn't it figure, doubt hit her first. She'd never felt anything like that before. What if it had been routine for Ben? She couldn't bear that.

Don't be the first to say, *Oh, my God.*

After which her mouth opened, and she mumbled, "Oh, my God," sounding every bit as dazed and stunned as she felt.

The muscles beneath her cheek tightened and flexed. "You under there?" he asked huskily. He gathered handfuls of her hair and lifted, then smoothed it away from her face.

Having him able to see her made Eve feel even more vulnerable. She kept her head where it was, so his view of her stayed oblique.

"I think so." Wow, that voice didn't sound like hers. It was tremulous, uncertain. *Because I am.*

"Good." His hand kept moving, tracing her jaw, her cheekbone, gently stroking her temple, smoothing back her hair again.

Eve let her own fingers spread on his chest and continued her earlier exploration. "You must work out." *Yep. Let's make conversation.*

"Yeah." He cleared his throat. "Run and lift weights."

He'd said something about running once. "Me, too. Running, I mean. No weights."

"In a gym?"

"Winter only. Then I mostly do elliptical. Save my knees for pounding the pavement all summer."

His chest shook with a chuckle. "I know what you mean."

They both fell silent. He hadn't responded to her "Oh, my God," it occurred to her. Now what? Say, *gee, that was fun, and when are you going home?*

Ben gusted a sigh. "I need to take this damn condom off."

Her eyes widened. He'd stayed inside her longer than he should have. *Oh, my God.* No. Wrong time of month. Wow. She should have thought. Note to self: go back on the pill or patches.

"Yes, you should." One, two, three, *move*. She rolled off him and lay on her back, staring up at the ceiling.

Ben heaved himself up with apparent reluctance, and went into her bathroom. She turned her head to watch him go, discovering the back view was very nice. He might be lean, but he possessed impressive muscle definition in his back and butt. She heard the toilet and waited for his reappearance. He looked really, really good from the front, too. She propped her head on her hand and watched him approach.

His mouth tilted in amusement. "I hope that's appreciation."

"It is." That came out so sultry, she surprised herself.

He either liked sultry or the expression on her

face. Instead of going back around to the other side of the bed, he stopped with his knees bumping the mattress on her side.

Eve scooted closer. Close enough to stroke his thigh, as rock-hard as the muscles in his back had been. Head bent, he watched her, his eyes a heated blue that could have incinerated her. Her hand moved upward, cupped him, then rose so that she could wrap her fingers around him and squeeze and stroke.

"We could still go out to dinner," she suggested.

His laugh broke. "You're taking the wrong tactic if that's what you want."

She smiled at him. "Just offering options."

"I like this one."

Yes, he did. The evidence was overwhelming. Eve half crawled to where she could rub her cheek on him, then lick upward. She'd never done anything like that before. Never wanted to. The musky scent and taste surprised and aroused her. She took him into her mouth, grazing him lightly with her teeth, and sucked.

His body shook and an indescribable sound broke from him. His fingers sank into her hair and cradled her skull. "Eve."

When she circled him with her tongue, he shuddered, said her name again, and took control. Before she knew it, his head was between her legs, and she was the one shaking. There was a momentary crisis when he had to search for his wallet and

find a second condom, but all the delay did was
whet her appetite. This time, she shattered three
strokes in, and Ben wasn't far behind.

THE AFTERMATH WAS never good. This time, Ben
was disconcerted to discover he didn't want to
leave her. Three times was not enough, and he
couldn't remember the last time he'd thought that.

In between times two and three, they made it to
the kitchen, Eve bundled in a robe, him wearing
only his pants. They talked while a frozen pizza
heated in the oven, and kept talking while they ate.
He never seemed to run out of things to say to her,
and he liked hearing everything she had to say.

Which was his second sobering thought in a
very short period of time.

It might have been smart to get dressed and
leave after they'd eaten, but by then he'd been eye-
ing her mouth as she sipped her soda and laughed
and pursed her lips, which of course made him
remember how that mouth felt on *him*. Plus, the
sash of her robe had loosened and he was catch-
ing glimpses of that supple body and the curves of
her small, high breasts. He had to have her again.

After that, he groaned, stretched and said, "Shit.
I should go. I have an early morning tomorrow."

"Me, too." Swinging her legs over the side of
the bed and glancing over her shoulder at him, she
didn't sound like a woman who yearned for the
man in her bed to stay the night. "I can't be late

for my first home visit. The mom has a new job, so I promised to be there by seven-thirty."

Inexplicably irritated, he began getting dressed. By the time he buttoned his shirt, leaving the tails out, she'd put on flannel pajama bottoms, a thin tank top and the robe as well as sheepskin slippers.

She glanced around. "Got everything?"

God forbid he left any trace of his presence. "Yeah."

His tone must have been forbidding, because Eve didn't say anything on the way to the door.

There, he pulled her to him for a hard kiss, lifting his head to see her blinking a couple of times, as if he'd befuddled her. "I wish I didn't have to go," he grumbled, even though he hadn't meant to say that.

"I wish you didn't, too," she said softly, erasing his irritation and what had felt uncomfortably like fear.

Fear? Of course he wasn't afraid. What a stupid damn thought. He'd felt some uncertainty, that's all. But this was good. They'd had amazing sex, and she didn't want him to go, which meant she'd want him back in her bed. The fact that she was fine with him going home...that was good, too. It meant she wasn't getting overly sentimental, imagining love and forever.

Perfect, he told himself, shrugging on his coat

and hunching against the cold rain that trickled down his neck as he hurried out to his SUV.

If he noticed how *un*colorful his apartment was when he walked in, how *un*homey, how quiet, how empty, well, none of that was exactly news, was it?

"Do you just have a booth, or have you entered any quilts?" Eve asked, phone held to her ear while she manipulated the computer mouse with her other hand.

Her mother did machine quilting for people who liked to piece quilt tops but weren't into hand-quilting and didn't have a sewing machine capable of handling the multiple layers and wide surface of even a twin-size bedcover. Karen's machine quilting was superior, too: intricate and original, always perfect for the design.

But she also pieced and quilted her own work, which qualified as art in Eve's opinion. Not just Eve's opinion—Karen Lawson quilts frequently won contests at quilt shows and the county and state fairs. They'd been featured in magazines and sold for hefty prices.

She'd been a kindergarten teacher until her own six-year-old child was abducted. Then, she always said, she couldn't work with children, especially ones so close in age to Hope before her disappearance. So she'd quit and sought a way to bring in a second income and yet allow herself the time she was compelled to devote to the never-ending search for Hope. Quilting had been a hobby. She decided to make it a business. Eve suspected she earned more now than she would have as a teacher.

Plus, she'd given Eve a couple of glorious quilts, including the one on her bed, and, more recently, had given Bailey one that Eve happened to know was on Seth's bed. Bailey had said she'd buy a bigger bed so she could use Mom's, but decided not to bother since she'd be moving in with Seth as soon as she graduated from the University of Southern California in May. Which was…less than two months away, Eve realized in surprise.

She tuned into what Mom was saying, and was able to replay enough to know she had entered a couple of quilts in the show as well as having a booth, but she'd be home by late afternoon Sunday and wanted Eve to come to dinner.

"You can help me celebrate."

"Such confidence," Eve teased, and her mother laughed. "Of course I'll come to dinner. I can even get there early and cook, if you'd like. With you having such a busy weekend…"

"You know I love to cook. I'll spend the whole weekend sitting, manning the booth. Doing something else will be a relief."

Arguing never did any good, so Eve didn't bother.

"Why don't you invite Ben?" her mother suggested, her tone warm, cordial and elaborately casual. "We'd love to get to know him better."

Alarm zinged through Eve like static electricity. "Mom, it's too soon." But, oh, she wished it wasn't. Yearning filled her. Bringing Ben home to her parents felt so right.

"Why?" Karen asked reasonably. "It's not as if we haven't already met him. I used to see him when I stopped by the station to find out if Seth had any news. With Ben and Seth such good friends, we're bound to see more of him. It would be lovely if his daughter could come, too. I bet she'd like to see my quilts."

Eve bet she would, too. Some of Mom's best sellers were crib quilts, the kind kids would treasure and save for their own children and grandchildren.

"This isn't his weekend to have Rachel," she said.

Her mother clucked her tongue. "Oh, what a shame. Another time, then."

"Mom…"

"What's the harm in asking? Unless this, well, isn't that kind of relationship?" her mother asked delicately.

I want it to be. The surge of longing took her aback. It was way too soon to let herself dream. The fact that she already was…well, that took her aback, too. It wasn't like her.

No, but he had invited her to spend the day with

him and Rachel, and that meant something, didn't it? And…even though he hadn't talked about how he felt, surely he couldn't have made love to her with such heart-stopping passion and tenderness if this was just sex for him.

And I am being an idiot, she thought. Such an idiot that she heard herself tell her mother she'd ask him.

"But he may not want to come," she warned, "or he might be tied up. If he gets called in to work. You know."

Mom knew. She had become something of an expert on the topic of child abduction and abuse during her long campaign to not only find Hope, but to raise public and legislative awareness and increase tax dollars spent on weaving the kind of connections between agencies that brought children home.

"Of course I understand," she said.

Eve promised to let her know, then heard about how Dad's back was bothering him, but he was so stubborn, refusing to go to the doctor. *Stubborn* was hardly an adequate description of Dad. He was like a stone letting water drip down on him, knowing how slow any impact would be. Dad would listen, nod without comment, then do whatever he wanted anyway. Mom surely knew her nagging was wasted.

Eve hung up the phone and did some deep

breathing to combat a brief panic attack. Ask him, or not? *I said I would.*

Doesn't mean I have to follow through.

Go with the moment, she finally decided.

ALTHOUGH THEY'D TALKED briefly on the phone a couple of times, Ben didn't plan to see Eve again until Friday night. That was a deliberate choice. Sooner made him look too involved. Too…eager.

God, yes, he heard himself saying.

He frowned as he strode out of the courtroom where he'd just finished testifying. The defense attorney, one of his least favorite, was the kind of slime whose go-to strategy was to blacken any victim's reputation. Make a woman look like a slut, the jury would buy the defendant's insistence that the sex had been consensual, that she liked it rough and that's why she had all those bruises afterward. Unable to shake Ben, he'd kept his cross-examination short. Ben was still pissed.

As he stepped off the elevator, he saw a woman wearing a snug black suit and three-inch heels hurrying across the lobby toward him.

He stopped dead. "Eve?"

Damn, she looked good. She always did, but in heels her legs appeared even more sensational. Whatever she had on beneath the jacket was fire-engine red, and small gold hoops swung from her earlobes.

"Ben." She smiled. "Testifying?"

"Unfortunately."

She laughed. "Best part of your job, huh?"

"Safe to say." He shook his head to rattle his brains back into place. "What are you doing here?"

"On my way to a hearing in juvenile court. I'm probably here as often as you are."

"I've never noticed you before." And he couldn't believe he hadn't, especially if she usually looked as she did today. Except he liked her hair better loose, not woven into some kind of complicated braid and bundled at her nape.

"Just chance." She glanced at her watch. "I need to run. See you Friday."

"Yeah." His feet didn't move, and neither did hers.

"Sunday I'm having dinner at Mom and Dad's. Mom was hoping you might like to come."

Dinner with her parents? Dread filled him.

This smile looked forced. "Mom wanted you to bring Rachel. I think you're incidental to her main goal. No grandkids, you know. Plus—" a shadow crossed her face "—Rachel looks a lot like Hope did. You know. Before."

God. He hadn't thought of that.

"I told her you wouldn't have Rachel this weekend, though," she said hurriedly, "so don't worry about it, Ben. Listen, I'm going to be late. Friday, right?"

Shit. Annoyed to have been put on the spot, Ben had felt his resistance crack when she said that about Rachel. It hadn't occurred to him, but she was right; Seth had had the last school picture taken of six-year-old Hope Lawson posted everywhere when he mounted his search. And, damn it, there was a resemblance that went beyond the superficialities of age, hair and eye color. If you studied them feature by feature, it wouldn't be there, but at first glance...yeah.

And now he felt guilty for something that wasn't his fault. Even so, it was enough for him to say to her back, "Eve?"

She paused and turned, her expression pleasantly inquiring. It was her professional face, the one that revealed nothing of what she was really thinking.

"I can come Sunday."

She studied him for a long, thoughtful moment. Then she said, "That...would make my mother happy. Thank you."

Would it make her happy? He was afraid so, and was concerned now that she'd read something into his acceptance that wasn't meant.

He nodded curtly and walked away, not liking his agitation. What had she been thinking, pushing like this? Using the sadness that always clung to her to manipulate him?

He stalked across the parking lot, hardly aware of his surroundings. When he reached his car, his head cleared enough for him to look around and feel a jolt. He was a cop. Cops didn't walk around with their damn heads fogged.

The agitation had finished its job, leaving his emotions balled in his belly. What he mostly knew was, he didn't want to go with Eve Sunday and have her beaming parents evaluate him as her guy. But he couldn't hurt her by canceling, either.

He'd have to hide his irritation—but he'd also have to find a way to let her know anything else like this was off the table. Dinner with the parents suggested something that wasn't happening, and she needed to know that.

CHAPTER EIGHT

"WHEN IS RACHEL'S BIRTHDAY?" Karen Lawson asked brightly. "Eve said she's six?"

"That's right. She turns seven in April." Ben didn't look at Eve. He was not enjoying himself. He couldn't call what her mother was doing an interrogation, but it was damn close. Maybe this was normal; he wouldn't know, since neither he nor Nicole had mothers. No matter what, he resented being set up for this.

"What a doll." Karen beamed at him. "And so poised for her age."

"She is."

"Why, she reminds me of—"

Her husband gave his head a shake so abbreviated, you had to be looking to notice it.

She didn't finish, although the resultant silence was awkward.

Damn, Ben thought, Eve had been right. Her mother was drawn to his daughter because she looked like her own child before she'd been snatched.

He risked a glance at Eve to see that her head

was bent. She was using her fork to make swirls in her mashed potatoes.

Karen's smile might have been a little forced. "I hope everyone has room for dessert. I made my Kahlúa-almond cheesecake."

The temptation was too much, even if Ben had planned to plead a need for an early night. "That sounds really good," he admitted. "Count me in."

Eve popped to her feet. "Let me clear the table, Mom." She'd done little but push her food around on her plate, which explained why she was whisking it out of sight so fast. She grabbed her father's empty plate, too, and carried both to the kitchen without so much as glancing at Ben. Karen took his and her plates and followed her daughter.

"That was some fine work you and Seth did, arresting the two who robbed the jewelry store," Kirk remarked with the air of a man who felt he had to fill the silence.

"Thank you, Mr. Lawson."

"Kirk, please."

Ben nodded. "The owner was injured badly enough he'll be left with some disabilities. Solving that one was a real priority for us."

Ben hadn't heard Karen returning until she said, "It was so awful, and to think both men were local residents." She clucked.

Why that made it worse, he wasn't sure. Pretty well every zip code counted some scum among the residents, he felt sure.

"Coffee?" she asked.

"Please."

Eve returned and, without saying a word, removed serving dishes from the table. Her father's worried gaze followed her as she retreated to the kitchen again.

He asked a few questions about the investigation, which Ben answered. From their brief acquaintance, he liked Kirk Lawson.

"Have you ever had a break-in or suffered a significant theft at your shop?" he asked, suddenly curious.

Kirk shook his head, smiling crookedly. "Don't keep much money on the premises, and I'm careful about who I hire. One of my guys has been with me fifteen years or more." He seemed to ponder. "One about ten, I guess. I've added a couple of young guys this past year or two, but so far they're working out fine."

Ben studied the craggy face of Eve's father. He'd seen how Kirk listened to conversations, hearing what wasn't said as well as what was. "You have good judgment."

His blue eyes met Ben's. "I'd like to think so."

Ben tensed. What did that mean? *Take it at face value*, he told himself. Didn't matter if Kirk liked him or not anyway; contrary to what Karen seemed to believe, Ben was not here to gain the approval of Eve's parents.

He was here because he hadn't been able to say no.

Eve set a cup of coffee in front of him, her smile pleasant but not in any way intimate. She'd been reading the vibes, he had already realized. He hoped her parents hadn't. They were nice folks; he didn't want to offend them.

The coffee and cheesecake were both extraordinary. Karen was a fine cook. Ben told her he couldn't remember a better meal, and her cheeks turned pink with pleasure.

"Eve's just as good a cook as I am," she claimed, smiling at her daughter.

"Gee, Mom, do you want me to show him my teeth, too?" Eve said tartly.

"What?"

"You don't have to try to sell Ben on my fine qualities." She softened her acerbic statement with a smile that held genuine affection. "Either he's smart enough to notice them, or he isn't."

Ben gave a huff of laughter. "Now, what am I supposed to say to that?"

Her gaze met his coolly. "Absolutely nothing."

His momentary humor evaporated. She looked angry. Had he really been such a jackass tonight?

He couldn't tell if her mother was oblivious or trying to intervene when she said, "We'd love for Eve to go with us to Hope's graduation in May. We're so excited!"

"I understand why you're proud of her. It's pretty amazing Bailey—ah, Hope—managed to put herself through college."

Karen was pleased. She talked at length about everything Hope had accomplished, while Eve listened with a smile that never wavered. Ben asked where Eve had gotten her BA.

Her gaze touched his. "Whitman College."

He knew Whitman to be a nationally ranked private liberal arts college and was impressed. It had to be tough to get into.

"Were you happy there?" he asked.

"Yes. Very."

He tilted up his cup to take the last swallow of coffee, and hadn't even set it down when Eve said, "Mom, I hope you'll forgive me for leaving you with the mess, but I have an early morning tomorrow."

"Oh!" Her mother looked startled, but said, "You've already loaded the dishwasher, for goodness' sake. There's not much else to do. I'm just sorry you have to run off."

Weirdly, Ben felt some disgruntlement. He'd been wondering if he might not be offered a second slice of that cheesecake, for one thing. For another...damn it, *he* was the one who should be trying to cut the evening short, not Eve.

But before he knew it, he was helping her with her coat, shrugging into his own and thanking

Karen for dinner. He shook hands with Kirk and walked with Eve in silence down the driveway to his SUV.

Once they were both buckled in and he had the engine running, Ben cleared his throat. "Your mother really is a good cook."

"I'm glad the evening had an upside for you."

Uneasiness stirred. "What's that supposed to mean?"

"Really?" She slanted a look at him he was just as glad he couldn't see well out here in the dark.

Driven to it, he asked, "You don't think this was a little too soon for a 'meet the parents' deal?"

"That's not what it was!" Eve fired back.

"Uh-huh."

"You've met them before."

He unclenched his jaw. "That's not why I was there tonight, and you know it. I was given the third degree because I'm dating their precious daughter."

There was an odd moment, then he heard her breath hitch.

"If I really am, I'll count myself blessed. And that wasn't the third degree. It was pleasant conversation."

"Sure it was."

She shook her head. "Why didn't you say no?"

"Because—" Shit. He knew better than to say this. Midstream, he switched gears. "I didn't think much about it until I saw the way your mother was looking at me."

"Try again," Eve suggested, as steely as him at his best.

Ben gave up. "What you said about Rachel looking like Hope. It made me feel…" He hesitated.

"Sorry for me." She gave a small laugh. "How heartwarming."

"Not sorry for you. Bad for you. That's different."

She shook her head.

He was frustrated to realize he was turning into her apartment complex. "Eve…"

"I suppose I should thank you for coming." She freed herself from her seat belt before he even braked to a stop in the visitor slot. Once he had, she opened her door.

"Eve, let's not end the evening like this."

"No? You had in mind a quickie before you went home?"

"You know that's not what I meant!"

"Do I?" She slid to the ground. "No, please don't walk me up. It's not necessary."

He hated and resented the fear that had a grip on him, but it was real and told him he was losing her.

Had lost her.

"Eve," Ben said hoarsely. "Stop."

She paused just before slamming the passenger door, her eyes dark and turbulent in the harsh lighting.

"I was a jerk."

"Yes, you were," she said after a moment. "Why?"

Good question. Like it or not, he'd agreed to having dinner at her parents' house. He hoped they hadn't noticed his reluctance, but he'd known Eve saw through his thin veneer of civility to the resentment beneath.

Had he been trying to make sure she understood that theirs wasn't that kind of relationship, and he was irritated at what he saw as her pushing?

Ben didn't think it had been that conscious, not initially, at least.

This was where he should say, *Eve, I like you, I enjoy your company, but I'm not looking to get married again. You need to know that.*

But if he said it, she was gone. No doubt whatsoever. And just thinking that was enough to tighten the band of fear until it made it hard to draw a breath.

If this was as casual as he wanted it to be, he should be feeling philosophical. There were other fish in the sea. He knew women noticed him. They flirted with him. If sex was all he wanted, he could have someone new in his bed by next weekend.

Slammed by shock, he felt as if he'd walked into a sliding glass door. *Wham.*

He was staggering back when Eve shook her head, closed the door and started for the lobby.

Ben leaped out and followed her. "Eve, just give me a minute."

She had a tight grip on her bag as she turned very slowly. "It's cold out here."

"Let me say this." He needed time to think, but she wasn't giving him that. Residual resentment, fear, guilt, all churned in his belly. "I've only been divorced for a year. I never expected my marriage to fail. My parents—" He shook his head. Didn't matter. "I felt like I'd screwed up. For a long time, I thought maybe I could fix it. I've taken women out a few times, but, uh, you mean something. They didn't. It's…taking some adjustment. If you can't deal with that…" His throat seemed to have thickened. "I understand. I should have said this sooner, told you why I didn't want to go to dinner with your parents yet."

Yet? Do I mean that?

More shock came in the wake of realizing he did. He didn't know what he felt for Eve, but he thought about her all the time, wondered how her days went, hated the idea of her heading out at night alone as she'd been prepared to do after the fire her kid Joel had been accused of setting.

The passion between them was explosive.

And, shit, the sight of tears swimming in her eyes just about killed him.

He took a step forward, then made himself stop. "I'm sorry."

"No." She wiped under each eye. "I'm the one who should be sorry. I knew I shouldn't have even asked you. I was really annoyed when Mom suggested I bring you. I should have just said no. You and I've only been seeing each other for, what, a month?"

Five weeks, he thought, annoyed that she didn't know.

"I just thought…" She hunched her shoulders. "I don't know what I thought."

"It's all right, Eve." He crossed the distance separating them in a couple of strides and gathered her into his arms. "I was a jerk. Your parents are nice people. I've known your mother, especially, for a while. There wasn't any reason we shouldn't have dinner with them."

"Yes, there is." She rubbed her cheek against his jacket. "No pressure. I promise. It's way too soon for either of us to know where our relationship is going."

He had a sudden need to pin her down, not let this parting be open-ended. "Can we have dinner tomorrow? I'd really like a chance to make up for tonight."

"Yes." Her smile glowed, but it was tremulous,

too. "You don't have anything to make up for, but I'd like to see you."

"God." He bent his head and kissed her, hard, deep, desperate, and needed the response she gave so freely.

Even so, she didn't invite him in. He'd left his truck running, so she backed away, gave him a last smile that quivered on her lips and let herself into her building, leaving him outside.

PLEASED WITH HERSELF because she was actually a couple of minutes early for once, Eve was almost at the Mexican restaurant to meet Ben when her phone rang. After-hours calls were rarely good. A glance at the name ratcheted up her apprehension. She touched her earpiece.

"Joel?"

"Ms. Lawson?" He sounded young and scared. "Something bad has happened."

"Tell me." Turn signal on, she pulled over to the curb.

"Um, Mr. Rowe feeds some stray cats."

Her sinking sensation came from two causes. She was going to hear something she didn't want to hear—and she'd just learned something about the grumpy old man that made her like him.

"One of them is dead. It was right outside his kitchen window, hung with twine from the eaves."

Her stomach lurched. "Oh, no."

"It was this really friendly cat, you know, one of those orange and black and white ones?"

"A calico."

"I used to pet it whenever I saw it." He sounded miserable.

"Not it. She."

"What?"

"Calicos are almost always females," she heard herself say. "It's a genetic thing."

He apparently couldn't think of a single response to this fascinating fact, shared at a completely inappropriate time.

She closed her eyes. "I suppose he accused you."

"Yes. But I'd never hurt an animal!"

This was the moment when she needed to seriously consider the possibility that Joel Kekoa was playing her, that in fact he had a hidden vicious side.

Why would it suddenly appear now?

Because in the past Joel's targets had been more random, maybe not so close to home? Because nobody had ever accused him before?

Both possible, she had to admit.

And didn't believe any of it. She would stake almost anything on her certainty that the shock, bewilderment and hurt she'd seen on his face were genuine. And then there was her gut level unease about Gavin.

"Ms. Lawson?" It was almost a whisper.

"I had to think for a minute," she said, assuming a calm mantle. "I said last time that we'd have to move you if anything more happened. I still think that's best."

"But…where will I go?"

"That's what I'm trying to figure out." If she couldn't come up with another solution, she'd ask her parents to let him spend the night. He couldn't stay where he was. "Joel, I'm going to make some calls. I'll find someplace. Right now, I want you to go pack your stuff, at least everything you'll need in the immediate future. We can grab the rest later. I'll aim to be there within an hour. Okay?"

She could hear him breathing. Panting. He had to be scared.

"Joel?" she said gently.

"Yeah, I just— Rod and me, we were good. You know? And now I can see him looking at me and thinking I did this shit, but how *can* he?"

Eve's answer was honest. "I don't know. Right now, let's focus on making sure you aren't next door to Mr. Rowe even for another night. Then we can talk about everything else."

"Okay," he said, sounding subdued. "Should I tell them?"

"Is Rod home?"

"No— Yes. I think he just came in the door."

"All right. Don't get drawn into a shouting match. Just say, I didn't do it, but Ms. Lawson thinks it's better if I don't live here anymore, so she's coming to get me. Then go to your room."

"I don't have a suitcase."

She bumped her head a couple of times on the steering wheel. "Grab some garbage bags. I was going to give you luggage for a high school graduation present, but I'll buy some tomorrow."

"Really?" Now he sounded as if he was going to cry.

"Really. It'll be okay, Joel. I promise."

He said another, shaky, "Okay" and was gone.

Her next call was to Ben.

"Eve? What's up?"

"I'm sorry," she said. "I hate to bail on you last minute, but one of my kids has had a crisis and I need to deal with it."

"Is it anything I can help with?" His voice had become a little huskier, as if he was worried about her.

Did he mean it? She ached to say, *Yes, please,* but knew better. This was her job, not his. Blurring those lines last time hadn't gone well. Chances were the police had been called, but the responder would be a uniformed officer—probably Pruitt again—not a detective. This wasn't the first time she'd dealt with a kid in crisis, and it wouldn't be the last. Her kids had good reasons for being angry, and they did sometimes commit crimes. Joel was unusual in that she'd swear he *wasn't* angry—and that he had nothing to do with this series of nasty crimes.

"Thank you," she said quietly. "But, no. I can deal with this. I just need to find a placement and move a kid."

"All right," he said. "We can aim for another night."

Her gaze settled on the dashboard clock. "You're probably already at the restaurant," she realized.

"Yeah, I'll get an order to go. It'll beat whatever I have in my freezer."

What if she asked him to come over later? But…she knew it wasn't a good idea. He'd want to hear about what happened, and she'd get annoyed if he even hinted that Joel was responsible for everything that had happened. Even though… well, she couldn't exactly blame him. Even she'd had to consider the possibility, and Ben didn't know Joel.

Anyway, she could get through a night without seeing Ben.

They said goodbye, both quietly, as if… Eve didn't know, and didn't let herself think about it.

Her next call was to a favorite receiving home. Both husband and wife had a gift for handling troubled teenagers. When Tony Santos answered, she said, "I need a great big favor."

"Not the first time you've asked for one," he

said with amusement. "And let me guess. You need a bed for a kid tonight."

Eve laughed. "You know me too well."

"Hah," he said, the smile still in his voice. "I think it's more the other way around." He became abruptly serious. "You're in luck. A kid was moved just a couple of days ago. We can take your boy, whoever he is."

"Bless you." Some of the tension left her. "Let me tell you what's going on."

LATE AFTERNOON THE next day, Ben happened to see Ed Pruitt in the parking lot. Ed detoured to meet Ben.

"Your friend tell you the latest about the Kekoa kid?"

Well, damn. Whatever it was, Ben understood why she *hadn't* told him.

"No. She insists he's a great kid."

"The neighbor says otherwise. And this was ugly." He described the gruesome scene and the elderly man's horror. "I don't like the combination," Ed said more slowly. "Arson and animal torture. You know where that's going."

Ben knew. He felt a chill. Ed was right—pyromania, bed-wetting and animal torture comprised the classic triad, infamous for being in the background of too many serial killers. The bed-wetting was an unknown, but killing the cat could be seen as practice for what this perpetrator really wanted to do—kill a human being. And since every one of these incidents had been directed at Rowe…

Jesus, he thought. "Have you suggested to the old guy that he needs to be extra careful?"

"I did," Ed said grimly. "I didn't want to go too far in stirring him up, though. Rowe is a little wacko already. He has a handgun. I could see him being the kind to go after the kid."

"Eve was going to move the boy, you know."

"I didn't." He seemed to think it over. "That's smart. Let them both cool off."

"Which is fine if Joel's the one who really did all this crap."

Pruitt shook his head, his expression making plain his opinion. He said only, "Let's hope for the best," and went on his way.

Still on his way in, Ben called Eve and only got her voice mail. He'd hoped they might get together tonight. The fact he hadn't heard from her made him uneasy.

Maybe a break was good, though. He'd cracked under pressure the other night and said things he hadn't thought through. His own turnaround left him dizzy. Could he really be getting serious about Eve?

Yeah. He could. Without having seen it coming, he already was. And, damn, that had him rattled.

A little space to come to terms with how he felt about her *and* how he felt about Nicole might be smart. Funny how telling himself that didn't help, though. He wanted to see Eve, be sure she hadn't actually written him off after his jerk behavior. It was reassuring, in a way, to know last night's crisis hadn't been fictitious.

But, damn it, why hadn't she called him or taken one of his calls?

Brooding, he nodded at the desk sergeant and keyed in the code to let himself through the heavy glass door that gave access to most of the sheriff's department. Along with a couple of conference rooms, patrol and IT were ground floor, specialty units upstairs. Records and the lab had been consigned to the basement.

He took the stairs two at a time, strode down the hall and entered the detective bull pen, only to see the instantly recognizable back of a woman talking to Seth. Unfortunately, it was not Eve who had stopped by. It was her mother. He would have retreated, but it was too late.

Having seen him, Seth had a smirk on his face. Karen looked over her shoulder, her expression brightening.

"Ben! How nice. I was hoping you'd be here. I brought cookies."

"That's great," he said, smiling. "Seth always shares."

Originally, she'd brought the cookies weekly as one of her ways to put pressure on Seth to make sure he kept up the search to find her long-lost daughter. Seth had begun to quietly groan when the desk sergeant called up to let him know Karen Lawson was here to see him.

Since Hope's appearance, Karen had kept the cookies coming out of gratitude.

Ben hadn't minded at all. Her cookies were the best.

Now she beamed at him. "I brought some for you, too, this time."

Seth's smirk hadn't let up at all.

Ben accepted the lidded plastic container from her and kissed her cheek. "Peanut butter. My favorite. Along with those ginger-molasses ones."

"I'll make those next time," she said, obviously pleased.

There was silence in the bull pen until she was gone, after which some good-natured mockery came their way from other detectives.

Seth told them they were just jealous, then peeled off the lid of his container and placed it by the coffee urn.

"I can't tell her I hate peanut butter cookies," he mumbled for Ben's ears only.

"I kind of noticed, since you've been giving them to me." He sank down into his desk chair, watching as every coworker in the room suddenly decided he needed a cup of coffee, and, gee, why not a couple of cookies.

"It was so *nice* you could have dinner with them," Seth told him in as near a falsetto as he could get, dropping it as he continued, "She's thrilled that Eve is dating you. She didn't quite go so far as to say how wonderful it would be if she gained both of us as sons-in-law, but the implication was there."

Ben winced.

Seth wasn't smiling anymore. "You'd better watch yourself there."

Ben clasped his hands behind his head, his chair squeaking as he leaned back. "Is that a threat?"

"Should it be?"

Ben let out an incredulous laugh. "You're asking me my intentions?"

Seth's face underwent some gyrations. "Yeah," he said finally, sounding uncertain. "I guess I am. Kind of."

"Keep it that way."

The other detective frowned. "What way?"

"'Kind of.'" Just like that, he leaned forward, crossing his forearms atop his desk blotter. He had a bad feeling he was baring his teeth. "What's between Eve and me is none of your goddamn business."

One side of Seth's mouth lifted. "Hit a hot button, did I?"

Ben felt his jaw set and didn't say anything.

Thank God his phone rang just then. His relief vied with nerves when he saw that Eve was the caller.

He rose to his feet and was already walking away from his desk and his buddy Seth as he answered. "Eve." By the time he reached the hall, he was smiling. "Yeah, tonight's good for me. I don't mind doing Mexican again. Had burritos last night, I'll make it fajitas tonight. Six? Sure."

When the call was over, he headed for the men's room instead of returning immediately to his desk. He was glad to find he was alone in here, needing a minute to deal with this swing of emotions. He went to the sink and splashed cold water on his face, then dried it, meeting his own eyes in the mirror.

One thing he knew about himself: he hated uncertainty. Keeping his head spinning had been one of Nicole's specialties. Still was, apparently, unless she really was having second thoughts. This thing with Eve, though, he couldn't blame her; *he* was the one who kept screwing up, making their relationship a roller coaster, and not in a fun way.

With a last, disgusted look at himself, he tossed the paper towel in the trash and headed for the door.

CHAPTER NINE

CUDDLED UP TO BEN, Eve sighed. "I hate prom season. Have I said that before?"

He chuckled. "Don't think so. What brought that on?"

"Oh, the girls are already starting to fuss about it. Will some guy ask them. Will the *right* guy ask. And then there's the dress, the shoes."

"It's as bad for guys, you know. Do you know how humiliating it is to have a girl turn you down?"

Shocked, she straightened and swiveled to face him, tucking one leg under her. They'd been lounging on her sofa, his feet stacked on her coffee table.

"Did that happen to you?"

He grimaced. "Yeah. Nicole was peeved at me, can't remember why, but she made her point by going to prom with another guy. I hated him. Took another girl to pay her back and seethed the whole evening."

Eve found herself laughing, even though she could guess how painful that had been for everyone concerned. Maybe especially Ben's date and

Nicole's date, who must have figured out pretty quick that they were mere pawns.

"That was petty," she said incautiously, before remembering her resolve not to criticize his ex. "Although, of course, that depends on what *you* did."

"Nothing very bad." He appeared momentarily pensive. "Didn't return a call quick enough, didn't blow off something I'd planned with a friend when she asked, spent too long talking to some other girl."

"That sounds...difficult."

He blinked a couple of times and focused on her. "Nic was pretty insecure. With reason. I think I told you she lived in foster homes. Three or four during the time I knew her. Thing was, her mom would start counseling, something like that, and the judge would let her have Nicole and her younger brother again. Couple months later, Mom would go off the rails again, they're back in foster care." He shook his head. "It sucked."

"I've seen that happen more than I like," Eve admitted. "Most of the judges I work with can see the dangers of treating kids like yo-yos. But there's one, who shall remain nameless, who has a huge bias in favor of biological parents." She paused. "You understand, they are all, to some degree, directed to give priority to keeping families together."

He nodded.

"Most balance that expectation with enough realism to see how quickly kids can be damaged when they can't count on anybody."

"That was Nicole." His mouth twisted. "She used to talk about how she never wanted to put her own children through anything like that. Marriage was permanent."

"But it's a hard goal to achieve for someone with her history," Eve said gently.

Ben took her hand, his thumb sliding in circles on her palm as he studied her.

"We got sidetracked." Apparently he'd said all he intended to about his ex-wife. "What had you thinking about prom?"

"Just that the teenagers are all fussing about it."

"I remember you saying the girls can't afford the dresses." He frowned. "Prom night costs even more for the boys. They not only have to rent a tux, they have to pay for flowers and dinner. And, geez, these days the girls probably expect them to rent a limo."

"I think a lot of the boys in foster care just don't go. The girls, at least, can take advantage of the dress exchange." His inquiring look had her explaining about the annual event, when girls donated the dresses they'd never wear again, or in some cases traded in last year's for a different dress. "We've talked some stores into giving dresses and shoes, too, and some salons into doing girls' hair gratis. Ditto with tuxedo shops, but, like you say, the dinner is another story."

"The Kekoa boy planning to go?"

The question sounded casual, but his gaze was sharp enough to make Eve wary.

"He hasn't said anything. He has bigger things on his mind."

Ben nodded. She wondered if he knew he was giving her a hand massage: squeezing, gently tugging on her fingers, pressing on the pads. It worked nicely as foreplay, making it hard to concentrate on the conversation.

"You said something once. Implying you had ideas for filling in the gaps for foster kids."

Surprised that he remembered, Eve nodded. "There's this amazing nonprofit in King County called Treehouse. Their mission is to give foster kids a childhood and a future. That's a quote." Seeing his interest, she continued. "They have multiple programs. Probably the most important is coaching and support designed to improve success at school. But they operate a free store where foster kids can get new and like-new clothes, books, toys. You know. Oh, and Christmas gifts. They also help pay for expenses for sports, music, dance. Those extras are often beyond the means of foster parents who'd be otherwise willing."

"Sounds expensive," he commented.

She wrinkled her nose. "That's the catch, of course. I've been studying what they do, talking to some of the people involved. They raised almost ten million dollars in the year I saw figures for."

"Ambitious."

"But there are a whole lot more kids to serve in King County than we have up here." Eve heard her enthusiasm, and didn't try to squelch it. This was a dream of hers, and she really thought it was an achievable one. "We could launch it on a smaller scale."

"You said if you ever started a family, you couldn't keep doing your job. Is this what you were thinking about?"

"Hmm? Oh, I could probably go half-time with DSHS."

His eyebrows rose. "Or does that mean full-time instead of time-and-a-half."

She made a face at him. "Something like that."

He laughed and lifted his arm. "Come here."

She shifted again so she could snuggle against him. He nuzzled her hair. He must have decided they'd talked long enough. He never actually spent the night, which gave them a limited window in which to make love before he needed to go home.

So it came as a surprise when he remarked thoughtfully, "You said 'we.'"

Distracted by his nearness, it took her a minute to parse what he was asking.

"A couple of friends and I've talked about it. One is another caseworker, the other a foster parent. I think I could find a core of volunteers pretty quickly, too. Starting with family. Bailey sounded interested, as much as her studies allow." Bailey had been accepted into the graduate program in psychology at the University of Washington, starting this fall. She and Seth planned to stay in Stimson unless the commute proved too difficult.

More slowly, not sure whether introducing the subject of either of her parents was a good idea, Eve said, "Mom, too. She's been teaching a quilting class at a teen shelter. It's really made a difference for some kids. It gives an outlet for creativity, teaches patience along with basic sewing skills and provides a relaxed group session where girls feel comfortable opening up."

"Girls only, huh?" He sounded amused.

"At the moment. Quilting is traditionally a woman's art, you know."

"So she has these street kids taking part in quilting bees, huh?"

"Yep. First they take sewing lessons, cut out and piece their quilts, but then they hand-quilt them."

He didn't move or say anything for a minute. Eve waited him out.

"There's more to your mother than meets the eye," he said finally.

She scooted back a little again, wanting to see his face. "That's true of most people, don't you think?"

"Maybe." Creases lined his forehead. "She

comes off as so…sweet." His glance at Eve appeared wary. "Clueless. Ah, no insult intended."

Eve still wasn't sure talking about her mother was a good idea, but she didn't take offense, because she knew what he meant.

"Mom is sometimes a little oblivious," she admitted. "But I think some of her supersweet, homemaker persona is facade, too. You've seen her quilts, so you know she's an artist."

"Only the one on your bed. But, yeah, it's nothing like what I think when I hear the word *quilt*. It's…" he frowned. "I don't know. All about movement and color."

"Right," she said, pleased. "There's balance and flow and a clash of colors exactly where they're needed."

"Okay."

"My point is, if you hadn't seen one of her quilts, would you ever have guessed she was capable of that kind of vision?"

"No. I'm always surprised she isn't wearing a sweatshirt with puppies and flowers on the front."

Eve laughed. "Exactly. Someone just meeting her would never guess she had what it took to put pressure on police agencies to find her missing daughter, either, or support and advise other parents in the same position. Mom is a lot tougher than meets the eye."

His mouth quirked. "*Relentless* is the word I'd

use. But instead of placards or endless phone calls, she wages war with cookies."

"And photos." Her own smile was probably awry. "Don't forget the pictures."

"No. They drove Seth nuts."

"I know. She might have read that it was the thing to do, but I also suspect it might be instinct. Make the cops *see* your child. Grip their hearts, and they'll do more."

He made a sound in his throat. "Just don't say that publicly. We couldn't do our jobs if every investigation became gut-wrenching."

"No, I hadn't thought about it, but I can see you have to protect yourself to some extent, don't you?"

"Yeah," he said roughly. "We do. There might be times you'll think I'm a cold bastard, Eve, but sometimes I have to be."

"I do see that." She lifted her hand to his face, loving the texture of his evening beard beneath her fingertips, the softness of his lips when he turned his head enough to kiss her palm. "I've never seen you as cold."

The furthest thing from cold, she thought. Ben was still an enigma to her. He'd begun to open up—talking about his ex-wife tonight, for example. In fact, this past week had been really good. After dining out Tuesday evening, she'd offered to cook for him tonight. Tomorrow afternoon, he'd be picking Rachel up for the weekend, and had already asked Eve to go with them to see a play aimed at children put on by a community theater.

But there was still a part of him he guarded. She knew nothing about his parents or why he'd become a cop. She didn't understand what caused the shadows in his eyes.

What she had finally accepted was the need for patience. In his own time, he'd tell her. She could be endlessly patient with her kids. But maybe, she reflected now, it was something like what he'd described. She, too, had to maintain some distance. She could believe in her kids, care deeply, but never let herself truly love them. If she did, the job would be too painful to do.

With Ben, it was different. She was falling in love with him, if not all the way there. The natural awareness of her vulnerability was increased by the imbalance between them. He knew so much about her history, her wounds, her bitterness and even pettiness. She still had trouble sometimes understanding what drew him to her, but she'd begun to believe he was falling in love with her, too.

She needed to believe that.

"You can stay for a while, can't you?" she said with sudden urgency.

"You kidding?" The grit was there in his voice. "I definitely don't feel cold right now."

Cold? It took her an instant to remember the last thing he'd said, about how he could be a cold bastard. There was nothing cold about his eyes right now, as blue as the heart of a fire.

"I can tell," she whispered, rising to her knees, letting him pull her forward until she swung one leg over him to straddle his thighs. It was one of her favorite positions.

They never made it to the bedroom. Although she'd added a box of condoms to the drawer in her bedside table, Ben had apparently replenished the supply in his wallet. She'd started on the pill again, but hadn't said anything. She'd never made love with a man without insisting he also use a condom. Because it was safer, she'd always told herself, but suspected the reason had to do with keeping some distance, however small.

The bad thing about making love on the sofa was that Ben didn't stay as long afterward. She had to climb off him, and then he had to go dispose of the condom, which made it logical for him to pick up clothes and start putting them on as he returned. And since she didn't like to sit there naked when he was dressed, she would do the same, and before she knew it, she'd be kissing him goodbye at the door.

This was a weeknight, she consoled herself, and she ought to try to get some sleep. She had another court appearance tomorrow afternoon, and a lot to try to squeeze into the morning.

But after she'd finished cleaning up the kitchen

and had gone to bed with a book, she wished she
had him with her instead.

THE WEEK HAD been really good, the only down-
side that he and Eve were lucky to be able to exchange a couple of chaste kisses over the weekend.

A little ruefully, Ben remembered telling himself a very short while ago that he'd include Eve
in activities with Rachel only occasionally. That
plan would have had him not seeing her at all
this weekend, which he'd found unacceptable. So,
lunch and the play, he'd decided, only they all
had so much fun, she stayed for dinner, then together they watched a DVD she'd offered to loan
to Rach, an old TV movie, *Sarah, Plain and Tall*,
about a mail-order marriage. His daughter loved
it. Afterward, while Rachel brushed her teeth, Ben
walked Eve to her car.

That kiss couldn't be called chaste. It left him
aroused enough to keep him from sleep for several hours.

When he dropped off Rachel, she just had to
babble about Eve along with everything they'd
done this weekend. He almost wished Nicole
would get bitchy, but instead she seemed sad.
That bothered him more than he should let it. All
evening, he found himself wondering what was
going on with her.

Tuesday, he cooked for Eve. Worth it, to ensure
a bed was nearby.

That wasn't all he looked forward to, though. Eve never bored him. They could spend an hour dissecting a movie, or he could tell her about something bothering him on the job or a troubling investigation and she'd listen, offer advice if he asked for it, challenge him if he needed that, or go straight to sympathy. He did the same for her.

He was waiting for her to open up about her childhood, although he was aware if she did, he'd be expected to reciprocate. Increasingly, he thought he could do that. The serious talk he'd meant to have with himself about the future somehow never happened.

Wednesday was the first of April. April Fools' Day. On the way into work, Ben braced himself for the usual childish pranks. None had yet materialized when his phone rang midmorning.

Dead body, presumed to be the homeowner, apparent homicide.

"On my way," he said, starting for the door before the address registered.

He swore under his breath. Clement Rowe's house. For Eve's sake, he hoped Joel Kekoa had one hell of an alibi.

Two uniformed officers waited in front of the house. Ben knew the older guy, Barry Gunter, but not the younger, who had to be a rookie. His face was pea green, and when Ben got close he smelled puke.

He acknowledged Barry and nodded at the second man. "And you are?"

"Landon Engell."

Ben switched his attention back to Barry. "What do we have?"

"Postal worker asked us to check on the old guy. His mail from Monday on is still sitting in his box, and his newspapers are piling up." He nodded to the plastic box attached to the post that held the mailbox.

Ben held up his finger and walked over to look into the box. No Sunday paper, he saw at a glance—with all the advertisements inside, it would have been obvious, but three regular dailies were crammed in. Which meant Rowe had died sometime after he'd taken in the Sunday paper, but before his usual time to come out to pick up the Monday one, which had a morning delivery.

He returned to the two officers and nodded at Barry to continue.

They had rung the doorbell and knocked, with no response, then circled the side of the house to look in the garage window. The one vehicle registered to Clement Rowe was there, so they'd continued to the partially burned back deck and peered in the sliding door. They had seen a set of feet sticking out from behind the kitchen island.

"I was going to break in," he said, "but the slider was unlocked."

"Did you put on gloves before you touched the door?"

"I did."

"Okay."

"Looks like he was battered to death. A lot of splattered blood, dry now. It's an ugly scene."

Yes, they'd done a quick search; the house was otherwise empty.

"All right," he said. "Thanks. I've already called for the coroner and the crime scene folks. I'm going to do a walk-through myself right now." He asked them to stay for now, if possible, and make sure neither curious neighbors nor reporters approached the house.

He, too, started on the front porch, noting that drapes were drawn tightly, and that the front door had a peephole. Would he have opened the door to Joel? That seemed unlikely, which had Ben making a mental note. Who would Rowe have opened the door for? Had the guy paid any attention to Pruitt's suggestion he be especially cautious?

Ben completely circled the house, studying the ground and deck carefully. Unfortunately, a fairly heavy rainfall Monday had probably washed away any blood out here. Finally, he snapped on latex gloves and let himself in through the sliding door, sidestepping to avoid the splotches of blood on the vinyl floor. He didn't go close to the body, only stood to one side of the island so that he could see the mess that had been Rowe's head.

Overkill, he thought, maintaining his detachment. Chances were, the first blow had done the job. Either there'd been a lot of rage, the killer had been high and just swinging away or he'd been having fun.

He saw no weapon, unless it was beneath the body, which seemed unlikely.

The two bathrooms and the kitchen sink appeared pristine. The killer might have cleaned himself up, then washed the sink, bathtub or shower, but Ben didn't believe that. No scent of cleanser lingered in the air, and the behavior seemed too controlled compared to the murder act itself. Even so, he'd ask the crime scene investigators to look for blood, which wasn't as easy to wash away as most people believed. Especially teenagers—he had to believe they held on to some naivete.

Even in the middle of the night, would Joel have walked a mile or more across town as bloody as he would have been?

The only bed in the house was carefully made. Rowe had been dressed, down to what looked like orthotic shoes. No slouching around the house in slippers for him, apparently.

Ben returned to the kitchen to see a couple of people on the deck, peering in the glass. He let them in.

Unfortunately, the county was small enough

not to have a dedicated coroner. Bob Deeter was a prosecuting attorney, as well.

Ben didn't need to be told that Rowe had been dead for two to three days. He hoped the pathologist would be able to be more precise, but felt sure they'd find the crime had happened sometime Sunday night.

Letting the techs do their thing, he started canvassing and found only one woman home, hardly a surprise in the middle of a weekday. She lived across the street, though, and proved to have been observant. Mr. Rowe was an early riser who went out for his paper at about 7:00 a.m. every day, she said, then fetched his mail within minutes of the postal truck passing.

"He must watch for it, although…" She hesitated, appearing embarrassed. "I feel bad saying this."

"He'll never know," Ben pointed out.

"No, but— Oh, I just had the thought that I couldn't imagine who would be writing him. He was so unfriendly. I guess he mostly got bills. I doubt he'd changed with the times enough to do his bill paying online."

"So I've gathered."

"You've heard about all the trouble he's had recently."

"I do. Do you know the neighbor boy he accused?"

Now her middle-aged face crumpled in distress.

"Joel is such a nice boy, I just don't believe it. He's mowed my yard the past couple of years, and does extras without asking for a penny more. He just doesn't seem the type..." She gave an almost laugh. "You must hear that all the time, don't you? I read it all the time in the newspaper. The neighbors are always the last to notice anything wrong."

Ben gave her a sympathetic smile. "That is sometimes the case. With Mr. Rowe, though, I'm sure you were all aware of his idiosyncrasies."

She made a face. "Unfortunately."

"And a postal worker cared enough to call the police to check up on him, which doesn't always happen."

"I'm just sorry I didn't notice he wasn't following his usual routine," she said unhappily.

He worked her back to Sunday night, but she'd neither heard nor seen anything out of the ordinary. Eve on his mind, he asked if she knew Gavin. Not as well, she said, but told him what a handsome boy he was and what a nice smile he had.

He thanked her, left a card and walked back to the Rowe house.

He wanted to call Eve and let her know what had happened, but knew he couldn't. Her passionate defense of a kid she cared about was one of the many things about her he liked. But he couldn't have her jumping to intervene before there was any reason.

God, he hoped Joel wasn't the killer.

"JOEL HAS BEEN ARRESTED," Eve repeated numbly.

An officer of the court had called to inform her that Joel was in custody at the juvenile detention facility, and had been asking for her.

"Tell him I'm on my way," she said, still battling a feeling of unreality.

She told her supervisor what little she knew, then flew out to her car. She started it, then decided to call Ben before she went anywhere. He could find out what had really happened for her, so she didn't go in ignorant.

Thank God Joel is a juvenile, she thought, listening to the rings. A few months older, and he'd be housed in the county jail.

"Eve."

"Ben?" she said. "I'm hoping you can help me. I hear Mr. Rowe has been murdered, and Joel is under arrest."

"That's true." His tone had an odd note. Resignation? "I'm the arresting officer, Eve."

Her "what?" was almost soundless.

He must have heard it anyway, because he said, "You know I had to investigate without bias. I'd have liked to call you, but I couldn't."

She grappled with the news. *Ben* had arrested Joel. Probably handcuffed him, read him his rights.

The Ben who had made such tender love to her last night.

"Did you arrest him at school?" she demanded.

"I did."

"Why couldn't you wait?" she asked.

"We found a bloody baseball bat in his locker at the high school. If you were the parent of any other student at that school, would you have wanted us to let him finish his classes for the day?"

No, but— "He didn't do this."

"Eve, I don't have time to argue this with you right now. The court will appoint an attorney for him—"

"If I have to pay the bill myself, I'll find him someone better than that."

He couldn't have missed how grim she sounded. Angry? She examined her dark storm cloud of emotions, and wasn't sure. No, not true—she just didn't know yet if that anger was aimed at Ben specifically.

"I'll talk to you later," she said, and ended the call with a stab of her thumb.

A redbrick wing extending behind the courthouse housed the juvenile detention facility. She parked and hurried in.

Apparently she'd already been cleared to see Joel, because the clerk only murmured, "Ooh, that's a bad one," and thrust the clipboard over the counter for her to sign.

A minute later, she was left in a room that held only a small table with a chair on each side. An expansive window, webbed with wire, would allow the guard to watch conferences without hearing anything that was said.

The door swung open and a uniformed male guard pushed Joel in.

Eve half rose to her feet, forcing herself to sit back down. Physical contact between them wouldn't be permitted.

He stumbled and came close to falling. Eve was furious to realize that his hands were cuffed behind him.

"Please remove the cuffs," she said icily.

The guard gave her a dark look, but said, "Yes, ma'am," and complied, backing out to take up a stance where he could see them.

"Oh, Joel. I'm so sorry."

"They think I *murdered* Mr. Rowe." His eyes held horror. "And…whoever did it used my baseball bat."

She drew a breath and willed herself to be calm. "Tell me what you know."

"They got a warrant. I don't know if they've searched at the Santoses' yet. I was called out of class to be interviewed, but first the vice-principal opened my locker for the detective." His gaze became accusatory. "He's that friend of yours."

"I know."

"Anyway, the bat was there. It was wrapped in a garbage bag. Detective Kemper said it was covered with blood. And now they say it has my fingerprints on it." His voice shook. "They pulled it out enough to show me the hand—you know, the part that didn't really have blood—and I said it was mine. I mean, it had my initials burned on it."

"It's wood?"

"Uh-huh. But, Eve, I didn't have it with me. I mean, you know I didn't, 'cuz you picked me up and took me to the Santoses'."

"I know you didn't," she agreed, but was aware that her saying so to Ben wouldn't exactly be a compelling indictment of the case. After all, it had been a week since she'd driven Joel to the receiving home. He could have had a friend give him a ride over there since, or even walked the mile and a half or so.

"Where was the bat the last time you saw it?" she asked.

"All my sports stuff was out in the garage at the house. You said we could get everything later."

"What else did you have there?"

He frowned, thinking about it. Basketball, football, baseball, mitt, skateboard was what he came up with. "And my bike," he added. "I was going to call you and see if I could go get it, because I could ride it to school."

"Joel, do you still have a key to Rod's house?"

He looked puzzled. "I guess. I mean, sure." His voice slowed as his understanding of what this admission meant dawned on his face. "I didn't even think about it."

"I didn't, either." She'd give a lot to have taken

the blasted key from him last Monday and handed it over to Rod.

Right, as if that would have made a difference. Any self-respecting prosecuting attorney would argue that, in the three years he'd lived in the home, Joel could easily have had copies of the key made.

"I don't even know for sure the bat was still there," he said in a low, panicked voice. "I haven't done any sports since football season ended. I've been busy with school and college applications and, you know, thinking about other things."

"Okay, Joel. One more question."

He waited.

"Who would have had the combination to your locker?"

"Nobody! I mean, I don't know. I didn't give it to anyone."

"But kids with lockers near yours might have seen you dialing it."

His shoulders slumped. "Yeah, I guess so."

Not to mention friends of his who hung around while he grabbed something out of his locker— or any enemy who had loitered nearby in the hall for no other reason than to memorize his combination. Why would he have bothered to be especially surreptitious?

From somewhere, she summoned a real smile. "I'll find out what, if any, other evidence they think they have against you, and I'll hire an attorney."

"They said the court would pay for one."

"I'd rather get someone I have more faith in."

"You believe me?" He was about to cry. "You know I didn't do it?"

"I know you wouldn't do anything like that, Joel. I didn't believe it for a second." She hardened her voice. "I'm on your side. Whatever it takes. Do you understand?"

He gulped, sniffed and wiped his face with his sleeve.

Eve made eye contact with the guard and then rose to her feet. "I need to go now, Joel. You just hang in there. They had to arrest you after finding the bat in your locker. That doesn't mean the investigation is complete. You know that, right?"

He nodded. The guard stepped up behind him, cuffs in his hand.

"Are those really necessary?"

"Yes, ma'am, given the severity of the crime," he drawled, his tone just a shade short of offensive.

She clenched her teeth together and watched Joel be cuffed, gave him one last reassuring smile and waited until he was gone before retracing her own steps out of the building.

CHAPTER TEN

BEN SAW EVE'S car when he was still a block away from the Santoses' house and cursed.

Seth, who was in the passenger seat, said, "You didn't expect her?"

"How'd she know we were going to serve the warrant now?"

Intelligent guesswork, that's how. She'd undoubtedly spoken to the couple who ran the receiving home, and learned no search had yet taken place.

It wasn't that he was avoiding her. He had intended to call her or even go hammer on her apartment door later. But this wasn't ideal for a first chat about Joel.

He'd damn well better not find her just putting a load of Joel's clothes in the dryer, he thought.

Nah, she wouldn't do that.

You so sure?

He said another obscenity, just because, and pulled up to the curb.

When he rang, the door was opened by a short, stocky Hispanic man, younger than Ben had expected. The guy's gaze dropped to Ben's waist where his badge showed.

"I'm Detective Kemper, and this is Detective Chandler. We have a warrant to search your home."

"May I see it?"

Ben handed it over.

The guy perused it, finally handing it back. "You know I'll be watching to be sure you don't search any of the other boys' possessions."

"We are interested only in specific areas of your home." Ben stepped into a shabby living room, where a plump, brown-haired woman and Eve stood with crossed arms and matching glares.

"I assume you're the Santoses?" Ben said.

"Yes. I'm Tony, and this is my wife, Laura."

Ben nodded. "Eve." Seth's echoing greeting came from behind him.

"Detectives."

Her voice singed his skin. Ben didn't look to see how Seth had taken it.

He asked to be taken to Joel's bedroom. Seth went for the laundry room, which turned out to be a glassed-in back porch.

Glancing into other bedrooms upstairs, he saw that each held a pair of twin beds. No kid would have his own room in this kind of setup. Tony stood in the doorway, never taking his eyes off Ben as he crouched to look under the bed, then went through the closet and the dresser drawers on Joel's side. He closely examined the pair of high-tops and some slightly dressier leather shoes that sat side by side on the closet floor. Size thirteen. Neither pair looked as if they'd even been worn recently, much less cleaned.

Finding nothing but the expected clothes and school books, Ben looked at Santos. "Where are the dirty clothes that haven't made it to the utility room?"

"Hamper in the bathroom." He led Ben there.

Red plastic, the kind parents bought for their kid to have in a college dorm room, it was getting pretty full. Ben dumped it out. Santos narrowed his eyes at a sweatshirt that reeked of beer, but said nothing. Ben wouldn't have expected a kid to put clothes saturated with blood in the hamper, but had had to look. He replaced all the clothes.

"Do you look through the boys' drawers or closets on a regular basis?"

Santos's eyes flickered. "Yes. I warn them I will be. Not because I distrust them all, but because one who is into drugs could stash his supply in another boy's sock drawer."

"Would you do that right now, with me observing?"

"But you're not looking for anything small."

"No, his bloody clothes would almost have to be in a plastic bag." He'd expect the shoes, too, to have gotten spattered, at the very least, but he didn't say that.

"That, I will look for."

Ben followed as the guy opened every closet and drawer and looked under beds. Nothing.

Back downstairs, he thanked Santos. "That was above and beyond." Already pricklingly aware of Eve's presence, he saw her surprised glance at Santos.

"Murder isn't a petty crime," the man said.

"No, it isn't." Led by Mrs. Santos, Seth appeared from the kitchen, shaking his head.

"Nothing in the laundry room or garbage can."

"Our garbage pickup day is Friday. And, with rare exceptions, we do laundry only on weekends," Mrs. Santos explained.

"Would you have noticed if one of the boys had run the washer sometime during the week?"

"Yes," she said flatly. "If nothing else, I'd have issued a warning that he had to plan better the next week. Because we have kids coming and going, we maintain a routine they all understand from the beginning, and have fairly strict rules. We keep a close eye on them. We are rarely both gone at the same time, even during the day, and never in the evening. Our bedroom is at the head of the stairs. We sleep lightly. Hard to imagine one of the boys sneaking out successfully."

Which didn't mean it hadn't happened.

Ben and Seth had no choice but to leave empty-handed.

Eve made no attempt to speak to them or to follow them out.

Neither said anything until they were in the car.

"He could have thrown the bloody clothes in a Dumpster or anyone else's garbage can," Seth said after a minute.

"And walked home naked? There's no way he wasn't covered with blood."

"What if he came prepared? Clean clothes in his backpack. He could even have worn a raincoat, something like that."

Ben only shook his head. Their inability to find the bloody clothes and shoes had introduced a note of doubt for him that would bug him until he had an answer.

Seth refrained from commenting on how pissed Eve had looked, which Ben appreciated.

They talked a little more on the way back to headquarters, but achieved no insight. Ben was primary on this investigation, Seth backing him up only when necessary. They never served a warrant alone.

Back at their desks, the last thing Seth said was, "The kid may have the innocent act down, but he still looks good for this. Given that the victim accused him. Sort of a voice from the grave."

Ben grunted. Unfortunately, Seth was right. That still didn't mean Ben wouldn't be checking up on other neighborhood teenagers who may have held a grudge against the man no one liked, as well as talking to any family he could track down. Damn it, they might even find Rowe actually did belong to something like the Eagles Club or Veterans of Foreign Wars and therefore had, if not friends, at least friendly acquaintances. People who knew more about him and his history.

And no, Ben told himself, he wasn't considering other possibilities besides Joel Kekoa to placate Eve.

EVE WASN'T ENTIRELY surprised when she heard the intercom buzz that evening, or that it was Ben who wanted to be let in.

She pushed the button to release the front door lock, then waited for his knock.

"Hope this isn't too late," he said when she opened her door.

It was eight-thirty, long past dinnertime, but she hadn't been thinking about getting ready for bed yet.

"No, this is fine." She backed away, feeling too tense for a kiss, assuming that's what he intended. "Would you like a cup of coffee?"

"Thanks." He followed her to her small kitchen, leaning a hip against the counter and watching as she operated the coffeemaker and took down two mugs. When she didn't say anything, he did. "I spent the evening canvassing Clement Rowe's neighbors."

"Are you going to tell me what you learned?" she asked, trying for polite.

"Nothing that's any help to Joel." When she

whirled around to face him, he shook his head. "Nothing bad about him, either."

"In other words, a big, fat nothing."

"No, I tracked down other teenagers who live nearby, but none sent up a flare for me. The neighbor who lives directly behind Rowe's house had a squabble with him last month over a fence. Sounds like they almost went to court over it, but the neighbor decided the headache of digging in to claim the extra six inches of ground he thinks is his wasn't worth hiring a lawyer, so he swore a lot, moved his fence posts and made sure the slats blocked all view of his backyard from Rowe's side."

"That was mature." When defending territory, people rarely were, from what she'd heard. Think how many wars had been fought over not much more than that six inches of ground.

"Mostly, people shrugged and sounded tolerant. The guy was cranky and considered a little loony. Parents warned their kids to stay away from his yard."

The coffeemaker burbled, but she ignored it. "What about Rod Carter and his family? Did you talk to them?"

"Of course I did." Ben's face was unreadable. "They're shocked. Carter showed me where the sports equipment is stored in the garage. Snowboards and skis on an overhead rack, plus an inflatable yellow raft for the river."

She nodded. Joel had told her about some good times he and Rod had had, floating down the river when it was low midsummer.

"He'd built a crude bin that held everything from an ancient lacrosse racket—no," he corrected himself, "Carter called it a stick and said he played in college—to balls, bats, tennis rackets, mitts." Ben shrugged, his eyes watchful. "Front door key works on the side door into the garage, too."

"And you know I didn't have Joel give back the key the night I removed him from the home, even though I should have."

"I do know that, but it really doesn't make any difference, Eve. The kid might very well have several. You can't tell me in three years he hasn't lost a key, then found it later after Rod had already made him a replacement."

She couldn't argue, since she'd thought the same thing. At least Ben hadn't said that Joel had made copies specifically so he could get back in the house when he no longer lived there.

"Gavin was really cooperative. He was out with friends Sunday evening. And, yes, I confirmed that. Once he was home, nobody in the house heard anything unusual overnight. Which isn't surprising, since their garage is on that side of the house."

"Joel's is the only bedroom that has a window looking out at Mr. Rowe's house."

"Right. It's a good possibility there wasn't any

noise to be heard if the killer got in the first swing before Rowe could get out a shout."

She crossed her arms. "So you're confident Joel did it."

"I'm still investigating, Eve."

"But?"

"Events have been building toward this. Every step of the way, Rowe accused Joel and only Joel." His voice was hard, his logic relentless. "You tell me, Eve. If the other boy was pulling all that crap, why didn't Rowe suspect him? What possible motive would Gavin have to go after the neighbor, given that they hadn't had any major conflict?"

To give herself a moment, she turned to pour the coffee. She was disturbed to see that her hand trembled.

Finally, she drew a deep breath and faced Ben again, struggling for calm. "There are any number of reasons he could have had it in for Joel that weren't based on anything Joel did. You know that. Mr. Rowe might have been prejudiced."

"Joel is Hawaiian, not black."

"You think that is a meaningful difference to the kind of person who judges on the color of your skin?"

"You mean, there are people who don't like Hispanics, either."

"News flash. There are plenty of people who don't, Ben." She didn't dare pick up a mug and offer it to him. "You're surely not that naive."

"No," he said slowly. "I'm not."

"It's also possible somebody made sure Mr. Rowe believed it was Joel who did all those things."

"You don't mean 'somebody.' You mean Gavin."

Eve lifted her chin. "Yes. Why won't you listen to me? Behind that charm, Gavin is sly at the very least."

"Do you have some evidence to back up that assertion? Or did you catch some fleeting expression on the kid's face?"

The fact that the answer would have been option number two didn't negate her certainty.

"I have two degrees that are focused on working with troubled children. On top of those, I've held my current job for almost five years. I know teenagers. Give me some credit here."

He gusted out a breath, bent his head and kneaded the back of his neck. When he straightened, his expression held weariness but also resolve.

"Eve, I have to ask myself if your own history isn't influencing you."

She froze.

"Don't take this the wrong way, but I can't help seeing echoes of your family. In a big way, Joel became the outsider once his foster father remarried. Gavin is the biological child." If she'd thought him relentless before, that had been nothing. He held her gaze, his very blue eyes implacable. "Joel is darker-skinned than everyone else in the family. Anyone looking at them would know he's adopted or a foster kid. In contrast, Gavin is blond, handsome, favored by his mother." He paused. "Are you sure you're not identifying unconsciously with Joel and seeing Hope in Gavin?"

Everything she'd felt for this man crashed and burned in that instant. He had been judging all along, seen her as the misfit who resented the beautiful blonde daughter who *belonged*. She'd been fooling herself to so much as dream that he could feel anything lasting for her. She was such a jarring contrast to his beautiful blonde, blue-eyed daughter and his own gilded looks.

Something changed in his face when he saw her shrink back, but she didn't know or care what he thought. "Eve…"

She might have remained speechless if rage hadn't risen to overcome the pain. It enabled her to straighten her shoulders, to stare him down. "You really believe I could be so shallow, so vengeful, I'd want an innocent boy to be accused of a brutal murder because he's *blond*?" Except for the bite at the end, every word had been icy cold.

Lines deepened on his face. "We're all unconsciously influenced by things that have happened to us. Damn it, I had to ask!"

"No, you really didn't. Now I'm asking you to leave, Detective."

"Eve, don't do this."

She didn't let her gaze waver. "You've worn out your welcome."

"You're misunderstanding me. This wasn't about us."

"Oh, yes, it really was."

"I hurt your feelings, and I didn't mean to."

Eve actually laughed. The sound wasn't pretty.

He flinched. "All right. I'm going, but we'll talk again once you've cooled off."

He backed out of the kitchen doorway and she stalked past him, going straight to the door, which she opened. Ben grabbed his jacket off the back of the sofa, hesitated, then left without another word.

She closed the door, locked the dead bolt and put on the chain. Back in the kitchen, she dumped out the coffee, unplugged the machine and turned out lights as she went to her bedroom.

Not until she took out her toothbrush and made the mistake of looking at herself in the mirror did she break down.

WHAT DID I DO?

The lights in her window went out. Stunned, Ben sat in his SUV outside Eve's apartment building and tried to understand how he could have been such an idiot.

Of course Eve wouldn't identify with a boy like Joel to the extent of blinding herself to his viciousness. Of course she wouldn't hate another boy—a sixteen-year-old kid—only because he was fair-skinned and blond like her sister.

He closed his eyes, remembering how gentle and funny and natural she was with his own daughter, who bore more than a passing resemblance to Hope when she was snatched. He'd seen Eve hug Bailey, the way they'd teased each other, the warmth he hadn't expected between them.

He'd heard the way she talked about her "kids," with affection, patience underlying even exasperation. She'd expressed worry about one girl she saw as a train wreck waiting to happen, frankly admitted that one boy had committed arson even though she kept fighting in his corner. She was too smart to delude herself about Joel if she had seen anything to give her so much as a qualm.

She'd asked him once why he believed Officer Pruitt's gut feeling instead of hers. Ben had no idea what he'd answered, but now he thought, *I know Eve, and I don't really know Ed Pruitt.* They both wore a badge; he hadn't heard anything bad about the guy, but he'd automatically taken his side instead of hearing what Eve was trying to tell him.

This wasn't the first time he'd sabotaged his relationship with her, but the agony in his chest told him there'd be no comeback this time. He couldn't blame her. He'd just accused her of indefensible behavior. Why would she forgive him?

A car pulled into the parking lot, the headlights

sweeping over Ben's SUV. Staring straight ahead, he was barely conscious of it passing him and turning into a slot not far from Eve's car.

Being this honest with himself felt like stripping off a few layers of skin. He did it anyway.

Was he conflicted enough about where things were going with Eve that on a subconscious level, he'd actually been trying to sabotage the relationship?

He groaned. Why would he do something that stupid? Because he really thought, with Nicole sending different signals lately, that he could get her back?

Or he was afraid to fall in love again? Afraid to trust anyone not to hurt him, the way Nic had?

Had believing he still loved Nicole felt safe to him, in some twisted way?

He shook his head at that, even as he accepted the possibility. Maybe he'd liked to think of himself as steadfast. Or—shit—if he ever really made himself examine his marriage, he might start to wonder whether she'd ever loved him at all. Or had he just fulfilled her need for someone to give her what she craved—utter devotion?

A sound broke from his throat. He sounded like a big-eyed puppy, endlessly loyal despite the occasional kick.

Truth was, he'd accused Eve of being unconsciously influenced by her history, when he might be the one who really had been.

Nice thought.

He leaned his head back and closed his eyes for a minute. Where did he go from here?

To his empty apartment, now filled with memories of making love to Eve on that sofa, her cooking with him in the kitchen, showering in his bathroom.

Slowly, his mind cleared despite the pain in his chest, the knot in his belly.

All right, if he believed in Eve, that meant he had to take what she'd said seriously. He needed to flip everything he thought he knew about Joel Kekoa, Clement Rowe and Gavin Shaffer upside down. Consider other possible motives. Other scenarios. For example, how did the bat get into Joel's locker? Kids carried backpacks to school, not long, mysterious objects wrapped in black plastic. Could either he or someone else have put it there completely unseen?

Not likely. So why hadn't he been asking questions at the high school?

Because, whatever I told myself and Eve about the investigation being ongoing, I did believe I'd already arrested the killer.

Incredulity and disgust felt.like a hard slap in the face. Damn, that's what he'd been doing tonight: if he could undermine Eve as a credible character witness, his own opinion would be justified. And, hey, he'd be saved a lot of hassle pursuing this investigation.

Ben refused to believe he was that man, but he had to prove it, to himself if not Eve.

A LOCAL AND very successful criminal attorney, Vivian Wilson had defended another boy on Eve's caseload who had been accused of a crime, and gotten him off, too. Eve had been impressed with her dedication, a courtroom style that was about logic instead of theatrics, and the fact that she didn't talk down to kids. What's more, she'd just plain liked Vivian, who was model-thin and close to six feet tall. The one time they'd walked out to their cars together, Eve had had to scuttle to keep up with her long, confident stride, but could forgive her her stature.

Since then, they'd had coffee a couple of times when their paths crossed at the courthouse, but maybe because both were so busy, hadn't pursued a friendship.

Vivian managed to fit her in that morning. She listened when Eve told her about Joel and agreed immediately to represent him, insisting she would do so *pro bono*. She then asked a million questions, jotting down notes on a yellow legal pad. Occasionally, without explanation, she circled a particular note and drew an arching line linking it to a previous note. From upside down, the lines began to look like a spider web.

"I have an appointment in about ten minutes," she said finally, "but right after that I'll go over to juvie and talk to Joel. Then I'll get in touch with the DA handling the prosecution and, of course, the investigators."

Eve grabbed her bag and rose to her feet. "I can't thank you enough. Joel might have gotten lucky with a court-appointed attorney, but he might not have, too."

"I hate to admit it, but it's a crapshoot," Vivian agreed. "Frankly, unless the investigation turns up some better evidence than it has so far, I don't foresee any difficulty in getting him released. Of course his fingerprints were on the baseball bat! It was his. Anyone at all could have put on gloves and used it to kill the victim. Evidence that Joel had been in the victim's house, now, that would be a lot harder to explain when he denies ever entering."

"I spoke to the detective last night, and I think he'd have said if they'd found anything like that." It was her first reference to having talked to Ben last night, and would be her last.

Vivian held out her hand. "Let's talk later this afternoon. I may have new information for you."

They shook, and Eve departed, feeling a whole lot better where Joel was concerned. For herself... well, that was another story.

Numb was the best she could hope for.

LOCKER ROOMS ALL smelled alike. Given the typical high ceilings and concrete floors, they sounded alike, too, with the clang of metal lockers, running showers, and voices calling across the cavernous space.

Ben had taken a seat in the football coach's office, one of several that opened off the boys' locker room. Duct tape had been used to cover several slits in the vinyl of the chair. Coach Keefe's own desk chair wasn't in much better shape, but he wasn't using it anyway. Instead, he half sat on his battered metal desk, one foot swinging, his beefy arms crossed, using the elevation to glare down at Ben.

"You ever come out to a game?" he asked.

"Yes, in fact, I have. I've made it to several home games each of the past couple years."

"Then you've seen Joel play."

"He's in a class of his own at this level," Ben acknowledged.

"Yes, he is."

The glower hadn't lessened. Ben suspected it served well to control hormone-ridden teenage boys.

"Do you know what his greatest weakness is?"

If Eve were to be believed, Joel didn't have one. "No, I don't," Ben said politely.

"He's not aggressive enough."

Ben had to blink at that.

"You heard me," Coach Keefe growled. "Kid has all the physical ability in the world. He was blessed with the size to play pro ball if he wants.

But the truth is, he worries about hurting someone. He knows every other player on the field is smaller and weaker. We've come a long way, but he still pulls back. I'm hoping at the college level he can let loose." He shook his head. "I'm telling you flat out, there is no way Joel Kekoa took a baseball bat to a man's head. It's not in him." His tight-jawed glower said, *And that's all I have to say.*

Ben rose to his feet. "I'm guessing you know Joel as well as any teacher here at the high school. I appreciate your assessment of his character."

"You remember it."

Ben offered his hand. The coach grudgingly shook it.

Boys were hurriedly dressing, some still emerging from the shower room, others stuffing their PE uniforms in lockers and slamming them. Aware of stares, Ben made his way out, crossing an open courtyard and reentering the main building. He'd been told Bruce Golzynski, wrestling coach and government teacher, had a planning period next. To be sure to catch him, Ben wanted to be outside his classroom before the bell rang.

He just made it, and was glad to be able to flatten his back to the wall when the flood tide of students poured into the hall. Unlike with freeway traffic, kids going one way didn't stay to the right, kids going the other way to the left. Instead, it was the same, mad jostle he recalled from high school.

Then, he hadn't noticed the scrawny kids struggling to avoid being trampled underfoot. Now, he shook his head. High school was no picnic.

He earned some glances, but Gavin Shaffer, strolling out of Golzynski's classroom, didn't see him. Somehow, space opened up for him. Ben watched as a phalanx of other good-looking boys fell in behind him and girls all sneaked looks at him. His blond hair shone. He was the kind of kid all the others wanted to be, which meant plenty of them hated him. The arrogance in his stride said, *It's all about me.*

Yeah, Ben could see why Eve disliked the boy. But cocky and insensitive didn't translate to cold-blooded killer. A lot of decent people had been cocky and insensitive as teenagers.

When Ben saw his chance, he entered the classroom, to find the teacher sitting at his desk, a pile of papers in front of him. When he heard the door click closed, he glanced up.

Ben introduced himself and explained that he was gathering background on a couple of boys as part of an ongoing criminal investigation.

Turned out Golzynski had heard about Joel's arrest. "Don't know that I can see it." But he shrugged. "He's withdrawn. Sullen-looking sometimes."

Which also didn't translate to cold-blooded killer. But his analysis also suggested not everyone thought Joel Kekoa was too sweet for words.

Golzynski had been hired as a social studies teacher, he explained when Ben asked, but a few years back had taken on the wrestling team, as well. He'd been a high school wrestler himself. He wouldn't have been big enough to play basketball or football, even in a small high school, but even now had a lean build that suggested a wiry strength. Although prematurely balding, he probably wasn't older than early thirties, at a guess.

When Ben mentioned Gavin's name, Golzynski's expression became cautious.

"He was new this year, you know."

"I am aware," Ben agreed, stretching out his legs. He'd chosen to sit in a student desk in the first row.

"With his record, I considered myself lucky to get him for the wrestling team."

Past tense, which was interesting.

"How'd he do this year?" Ben asked. Wrestling was a winter sport.

"He's good. Quick, strong. Wants to win real bad. Team made it to the regional finals, and Gavin was part of the reason why." His tone had a constraint as interesting as that use of the past tense.

Did *wants to win real bad* translate to *has a killer instinct?* "What weight class is he?" Ben asked mildly.

"One hundred fifty-two pounds."

That was about what Ben would have guessed.

Gavin was maybe five foot ten, a couple of inches shorter than Ben was, and would probably gain more bulk given a few more years. He might even grow a little taller. Nonetheless, he was a lightweight compared to Joel, who without carrying any noticeable fat had to weigh in over two hundred pounds.

"I see you have him in class, as well," Ben remarked.

"I do."

"Can you give me your impressions of him?"

Golzynski hesitated. "Can you tell me what this is in relation to?"

"I'd rather not at this point. He is not accused of a crime." He paused, hoping the teacher heard the subtext. *Yet.* "What I'm hoping is to get a sense of his character. I can promise what you tell me won't go in any police reports. It's useful background information, that's all."

Expression troubled, Golzynski said, "Nobody wants to admit it, but teachers all have favorite students, and we have students we don't like. I do my damnedest to hide my feelings either way. I don't let them influence my grading."

"Understood."

"Gavin is smart, and he turns in his work. Every so often, I catch his sneer. He's two-faced."

"Looked like he's popular with his peers," Ben said, nodding toward the hall.

"He has his fans. Didn't take him any time last

fall to become one of the big men on campus. The girls buzz around him."

"I saw that," Ben agreed.

"But I'm not so sure he's liked. Got to say, he has a nasty tongue and excels at making a laughingstock out of anyone who annoys him. Beyond that, I don't know. Sometimes, though, I have the sense..." He hesitated, flushing. "I shouldn't say this, but I will. Everyone walks softly around him. I don't know what he's done." He shrugged. "I'm not sure I want to know."

"I appreciate your frankness. You've confirmed what I heard from at least one other source."

Golzynski now appeared deeply uneasy. Probably regretting having said as much as he had, he couldn't—or didn't want to—suggest anyone else Ben might talk to. Ben repeated his thanks and left, glad to escape the building before the next bell rang.

Tomorrow, he decided, he'd visit Cascade High School and, depending on what he learned, possibly the middle school Gavin had attended. He'd like to talk to some of Gavin's former neighbors, too.

The contrast between what the coaches had said about the two boys was striking. Walking out to his car, Ben shook his head in disbelief. Had he let his investigation be manipulated by a *kid*?

Everyone walks softly around him.

No, he wouldn't jump to any conclusion. After

all, Golzynski hadn't much liked Joel, either. And Ben himself had found him to be sulky during their lengthy interview.

That said…if Gavin Shaffer had murdered that old man, he was going down.

CHAPTER ELEVEN

"I'M GLAD YOU stopped by," Kirk Lawson said in his mild way, as he and Eve walked down the alley leading behind his autobody shop. They detoured around Dumpsters and a delivery truck backed up to the carpet store, ignored trash the wind had blown up against the chain-link fence. Beyond the fence were detached garages and peeks into backyards.

"I wanted to talk to you without Mom around," she admitted. "It's such a nice day, I got a craving for tacos."

He chuckled at that. Only Eve knew how often he cut through the alley to buy lunch from the taco truck that parked most days in a vacant lot at the corner. Mom worried about his cholesterol and would have disapproved. What she didn't know wouldn't hurt her, Eve figured. Too late today anyway—he and Eve had already purchased their lunch, which he carried in a white paper bag.

The break room for his business, such as it was, consisted of a couple of molded plastic lawn chairs placed on the asphalt just outside the door, some piled cinder blocks serving as makeshift tables.

Mostly, the young employees came out here to smoke, rain or shine.

Today was balmy, even for the third of April. A forsythia on the other side of the alley poked branches covered with bright yellow flowers through the wire links of the fence. Eve had seen viburnums in bloom already, too, along with crocuses and snowdrops. The forsythia failed to make the alley an attractive picnic spot, but when Eve was troubled, she felt more comfortable here than she did in the home where she'd grown up. Here she could talk to her Dad.

Plus, these were the best tacos in the world.

He went inside and returned with cold sodas from the machine available to employees and customers. While he was gone, Eve had moved the coffee can serving as an ashtray a distance away, although the stale smell of smoke lingered.

The two of them sat, each unwrapping a taco. It was Dad who said, "Something on your mind, Eve?"

"Don't I ever visit you just for the pleasure of your company?" she said lightly.

He smiled at her, his eyes kind. "Sure you do. But I can tell the difference."

She sighed. "I had a huge blowup with Ben last night. It…had to do with some of my insecurities."

"Hope."

"She's part of it." She told him what Ben had

said, and was gratified by the spark of anger in her dad's eyes.

"Maybe he was right to ask," she said finally, so quietly it was as if she was talking only to herself.

"Of course he wasn't!" Kirk snapped, with rare forcefulness. "Have you ever given any thought at all to the race or skin color of the kids whose welfare you oversee?"

"No." She thought she was being honest. "I mean, it's sometimes a factor in their placement."

He nodded, understanding. Their rural county was primarily white, but with an increasing population of Mexican and Central American immigrants. Black and Asian families were rare.

"It wasn't race he was talking about anyway. It was…not belonging. And Ben is right that Joel's situation had some parallels with mine." In the long hours of the night, she'd had to admit he'd seen something that hadn't occurred to her.

"Eve, to start with, I don't think it would have mattered what Hope looked like. Your mother doesn't want to see it, but I don't know how you could have helped but feel overshadowed by Hope." He shook his head. "Her being blonde and blue-eyed, what difference does that make?"

"It's—" She had to stop, bite her lip, start again. "She looks like you and Mom. I don't."

And there it was, the raw truth.

Her dad had the blue eyes he'd passed onto

his daughter, but he wasn't a handsome man. His craggy face looked well worn, she'd always thought.

"You always had the promise of beauty, even when you came to us." Not looking at Eve, he smiled as if he was seeing that wild-haired, terrified little girl. "Your mom and I, we didn't care one iota what color your eyes were. We wanted a little girl who needed us."

She had to say this. "I always thought you asked for a child who *didn't* look like Hope. So I wouldn't remind you too much."

She saw grief on his face now. "No, Eve. It was probably better you didn't look like her, but we wouldn't have turned you away if you had. We loved you right away."

"I always thought—" Her throat closed up again. She had always thought so many things. She sneaked a peek to see the sadness she'd awakened in this man she loved so much.

"What did you think, Eve?" he asked gently.

"That I was supposed to be, I don't know, a substitute. But I hadn't been enough for either of my parents, so I knew nothing I could ever do would be good enough to make up for not being Hope for you, either."

He had an uneaten taco in his hands. Now he set it down. "I have never, for one minute, been disappointed in you, Eve. Can't imagine I ever will be. I can't deny we mourned for Hope. I guess we were too obvious about it." He didn't say, *especially your mother*, even though they both knew it was true. "But we didn't measure you against her. How could we? We didn't know her at nine or ten or fifteen or twenty. She stayed a little girl in our minds."

"Until she came home."

"Having our first daughter back, that means the world to us. But it doesn't change how we feel about you at all. Truth is—" he hesitated, lines deepening on his forehead "—and I wouldn't say this in front of Bailey, but you're woven into our lives in a way she can't ever be. All those thousands of memories, the fights—" he smiled at that "—the proud moments, the silly ones, we'll always have those, and we don't with Bailey. Doesn't mean we don't love her and aren't grateful every minute that we'll have a chance to be her parents again, but you're ours in every way. I thought you knew that."

She suddenly became aware that tears streamed down her face. "I do," she wailed. "It's just sometimes—"

He laughed. "We all get mixed up. Come here."

He stood, pulled her up, wrapped his arms around her and let her sob against him. Nothing in the world was more comforting than his smell, the rumble of that chuckle, his business logo embroidered on the chambray shirt that soaked up her tears. Most of her tears over the years had been shed on this shirt or an identical one.

"Daddy," she whispered.

She pulled herself together at last. They finished their tacos and talked a little more, some about Joel, some about Bailey, and a little bit about her mother. Eve knew he'd never criticize his wife, but he said a few things that confirmed her belief he'd seen enough to understand the tension between her and Mom.

At the end, he said, "If he apologizes, you might want to think about forgiving Ben."

She stared at him in shock. "Why would I?"

"Because I'm thinking he's used to asking hard questions of people, trying to figure out what drives them. Maybe he did what he thought he had to."

She shook her head. "He couldn't have said anything like that unless on some level he holds me in contempt. In a way, I can't blame him. I've allowed myself to feel so much resentment. But you understand and still love me. You wouldn't have needed to ask that question. He understands and still had to ask."

"Don't jump to conclusions."

Eve forced a smile and rose on tiptoe to kiss his cheek. "My ever-wise father."

He looked troubled, but let her go. He'd said so much that was healing, but he would never understand what it had done to her to know that people always looked at her family and wondered how she fit in. She had hungered so for that sense of belonging. And there Ben was, saying the words that told her he 100 percent got it.

The outsider, darker-skinned. Biological child, blond, handsome, favored. Anyone looking at them would know.

Hope's reappearance had resurrected feelings Eve had thought she'd long since overcome. She'd had her moments, emotions rising like ghosts from the past. But she'd told her dad the truth today: she had felt loved by her parents. Especially by him. A few petty moments did not mean she'd let her insecurity growing up warp her.

Obviously, Ben thought differently. *That* was what hurt most.

BEN PUSHED HIS chair back and rose to his feet. After shoving his weapon in his holster, he grabbed his jacket from the back of his chair.

Seth, who had just hung up the phone, glanced over his shoulder. "You going to lunch?"

"I'll probably grab something on the way, but I'm visiting Cascade High School in Everett. Hoping to talk to some teachers and coaches, maybe some kids, who knew Gavin Shaffer."

"Shaffer?" Seth looked blank.

Ben reminded him who Gavin was.

"Why are you looking into his background?" Seth looked surprised.

"Eve has been uneasy about him from the beginning. She thinks he resented Joel. Might have started this shit with the goal of getting rid of him."

Seth clasped his hands behind his head and scrutinized Ben, who had paused by his desk. "The victim was convinced Joel was tormenting him. The murder weapon had Joel's fingerprints on it. It was hidden in his locker."

"It was his bat. It would have had his fingerprints on it no matter what. There were none on top of the blood. And putting it in his locker could have been a setup."

"So." Seth sounded incredulous. "Have you looked seriously into Joel's background? Or are you depending on what Eve's told you about the kid?"

Ben's irritation was checked only because he could see the justification in Seth's questions. "Today, I interviewed teachers at the high school about both Joel and Gavin." *But wasn't my real goal to find support for Eve's belief?*

No answer.

"There must be a dozen teenage boys within a couple-block radius of Rowe's home," Seth continued. "So why Gavin in particular?"

"I've checked out other neighbors, too. But what I heard today raised some red flags where Gavin is concerned."

"All right," Seth said slowly. "But I think I need

to say this. I know how much pressure Eve is capable of applying to protect one of 'her' kids. Given your relationship, watch your step. Be sure you're thinking like a cop, not her boyfriend."

Ben stared in disbelief that was a thin covering for his fear that Seth was right about his motivation, even though he wasn't Eve's boyfriend. Not anymore. *My fault.*

He struggled for his usual detachment. Eve didn't like Gavin. One teacher at the high school didn't like him, either.

Everyone walks softly around him.

"Gavin had the same advantage of proximity that Joel had," he said. "I've learned enough about him. I'd be irresponsible if I didn't follow up."

Seth let his hands fall to his sides and nodded. "Okay. Go forth and do your job."

"Gee, thanks." Gritting his teeth, Ben walked out. He bounded down the stairs, shoved through the swinging half door and stalked across the parking lot to his sheriff's deputy car.

Behind the wheel, he made himself take some deep breaths. He felt more like burning rubber, which wasn't smart.

Instead, he gripped the steering wheel with both hands, flexing, loosening, flexing, loosening.

Goddamn. What if Seth was right? Had he done a one-eighty not because Gavin was a real possibility, but because he felt guilty for what he'd said to Eve?

JANICE KAY JOHNSON 243

Yes, maybe. But he did respect her judgment, too, even if he hadn't acted like it. She knew the two boys a hell of a lot better than he did. If he and Eve had no history, if she'd been just a social worker he was consulting, he would have paid attention to what her instincts told her. That was common sense.

Too bad he hadn't given her as much credit as he would have if she were a woman he'd never met until he sat down to interview her. Instead, he'd not only questioned Eve's judgment, he'd questioned her deepest values. Her character.

Because…why? He'd thought she might be a little too passionate in Joel's defense, and of course that meant she was biased? Instead of taking a step back and thinking, *huh, maybe she really believes in this kid because he's everything she says he is.*

She might be happiest never to hear from him again, but she deserved an apology and she'd get one.

He made himself let go of the wheel, rotated his shoulders a few times to lessen the tension, and finally started the engine.

I-5 NORTH FROM Everett was stop-and-go for miles, steady but still slow even north of Marysville. This was Friday afternoon. He should have started home half an hour sooner, Ben thought, disgruntled. Now he shared the freeway with commuters leaving work and everyone trying to get out of town for the weekend.

His mood was lousy to start with.

He'd cornered half a dozen of Gavin Shaffer's former teachers and coaches. A couple of them seemed to genuinely remember Gavin as a smart, handsome, athletic and likable kid. A shining star. Their opinions had initially sowed some doubt in Ben's mind.

Another couple barely remembered him at all.

Two of the teachers who'd known him best, though... If Gavin had been under arrest, if Ben had some physical evidence linking him to a crime, they might have been more willing to speak out. As it was, he could see them thinking about lawsuits and their desire to keep their jobs.

He had new respect for Coach Golzynski, who'd gone out on a limb, relatively speaking.

Today, he'd watched shifting expressions and known that those two former teachers had felt distinctly uneasy with this boy. They, the adults, the authority figures, had obviously walked softly around him. It was the same instinct that made humans afraid of snakes. When they looked into Gavin's eyes, they didn't see what they should be seeing.

That was the most honest anyone had been with him today: a Mrs. Wyman, who had had Gavin in sophomore English as well as Debate, had said,

"He has a way of looking at you." She'd shuddered, then tried to make her expression blank.

Mrs. Wyman had also stopped him after he checked out at the office and said in a very low voice, "You might want to talk to Rick De Luca. He taught Spanish and was the wrestling coach, but he quit last summer to start a business. He knew Gavin." She'd slipped him a folded piece of notepaper, on which he'd found De Luca's name and a phone number.

He tried the number before pulling out of the high school parking lot, but was thrown right to voice mail and chose not to leave a message. He'd try again later.

He might have gotten further talking to students, but hadn't even tried; the administration would never have condoned that, given that he was basically on a fishing expedition. As it was, he wouldn't be surprised to get a call from someone at the Everett PD.

The sum total of his afternoon's work was a little more unease, but given the differences of opinion, nothing he could call fact. Since this wasn't his weekend to have Rachel, he thought he'd go back to Everett tomorrow and hope to catch some of the Shaffers' former neighbors at home. They'd have less reason to hold back. He'd have started with them, except few were likely to have been home on a workday afternoon.

He'd just exited the freeway and was driving

eastbound toward Stimson when his phone rang.
He glanced at the number. Seth.

As tired as he was, he hoped like hell he wasn't
being summoned to a gory crime scene. He answered anyway.

"Ah...don't remember if I told you Bailey was
coming to town this weekend," Seth said. "She
called from the airport to let me know she's on
her way north."

"Don't count on seeing her in the near future."

"Slow going today?"

"It's Friday. Uh, how long is she staying?"

"Only until Tuesday morning. It was my turn to
fly down there, but I haven't been able to get away
for an entire weekend so she upped and bought
a ticket."

If Ben remembered right, Bailey's last visit had
been almost two months ago. *The weekend I met
Eve.* That was a long time to not see the woman
you loved.

"We thought maybe you and Eve could make
it over either Saturday or Sunday night for dinner," Seth continued.

"Check with Eve, but you'll have to count me
out." It took everything he had to sound off-handed.
Gee, no, can't make it this weekend, sorry. Too
bad Seth or Bailey hadn't talked to Eve first. That
would have saved Ben from this awkward conversation.

"Is there a problem?" Seth asked. "Is this about what I said?"

"No," Ben said. "Talk to Eve."

The slight pause told him the message had been received.

"All right, I'll do that. I'm, uh, going to do my best not to come into work until Tuesday."

"I can take anything new. I don't have any plans."

Seth thanked him and they signed off.

Ben sank back into brooding. Was there any chance Eve would be ready to hear an apology?

Why would she? He'd seen the stricken expression on her face. No, he had to get somewhere on his quest to prove he actually had listened to her before he tried to get through to her.

That had him frowning, remembering what Seth said. *Be sure you're thinking like a cop, not her boyfriend.*

He finally was. Pranks aside, reason told him Gavin could far more easily than Joel have slipped out of his house Sunday night, committed a murder and sneaked back in. He could have stripped, maybe hosed himself off, right there. Remembering a hose coiled beside the back faucet of Rowe's house, Ben made a mental note to ask the CSI crew if they'd fingerprinted it and the faucet handle as well as checked for blood. Gavin wouldn't have wanted to use the hose at his own house, because water running in the pipes might have awakened Lynne or Rod. Same held true if the killer was someone else. Whoever he was, he'd have been most likely to leave a fingerprint when he was cleaning up.

After a day of unease, Ben...settled. He was using his head now. Doing the job he should have done in the first place, instead of leaping to the easy conclusion.

EVE SET DOWN the tortilla chip she'd been about to dip into spicy salsa when she saw her sister walk in the door of the restaurant. Smiling the moment her eyes met Eve's, Bailey waved off the hostess and came straight to the booth. Eve slid out to give her a hug.

"I can't believe Seth let you out of his sight so fast."

Bailey laughed. "He wasn't thrilled. I think he had in mind not getting out of bed today. I did promise to bring him food."

"The way to a man's heart."

"Oh, I don't think that's it," Bailey said wickedly.

They both laughed. Eve hoped her sister couldn't tell her own laugh was fake.

They ordered before Bailey looked across the table at her, her expression serious.

"I'm going to guess Ben isn't just busy this weekend."

"No. Our relationship was short-lived. I'm hoping that won't make it awkward for you and Seth."

Bailey shook her head. "Who cares if it does? Will you tell me what happened?"

Oh, God, did she want to? She was a little bit horrified to discover that she did. Why else would she have agreed to this lunch? She could have made an excuse, avoided seeing Bailey until enough time had passed and this burning hurt in her chest had turned to cold ashes.

She picked up a tortilla chip again, using it as an excuse to avoid meeting Bailey's eyes. "It started when he arrested one of my kids. I don't know if Seth told you about that."

"Joel something? A football player?"

"Right." She summarized the sequence of events that led to her removing Joel from his former foster home. "I really believed that would be the end of it. Except then Mr. Rowe was murdered."

"And Ben is primary on the investigation."

"Unfortunately." Eve grimaced. "Or maybe I should say fortunately. Our…conflict over Joel brought out some stuff that I'd have figured out eventually. Sooner is better than later." She almost managed brisk.

"Some stuff."

This was really hard to say. Eve had trouble swallowing the bite she'd put in her mouth.

"He...knew how I felt about you. I mean, before you actually showed up."

Bailey nodded, the look in her eyes unnervingly similar to what Eve had seen in her father's eyes at lunch yesterday.

"It always bothered me I didn't look like Mom or Dad. That anybody could tell at a glance I was adopted."

"You don't buy the line about how being adopted means you were chosen, versus your parents getting stuck with whatever came out?"

Eve surprised herself with a giggle. "Whatever came out?"

"Yeah. I mean, who is to say Dad didn't desperately want a son. A lot of men do. But what did he get? A little princess-wannabe girl."

It wouldn't have been so funny if either had thought for a minute Dad had been disappointed to have a daughter. Two daughters, as it turned out. As it was, Eve felt a whole lot better by the time she finished laughing.

Then Bailey's amusement vanished. "What did he say?"

Eve knew exactly which *he* her sister was asking about. So she told her.

It seemed to take her a minute to absorb that. "What a creep."

"I don't know if he's that. It's more that..." She shrugged. "He seemed sympathetic. You know? But really, he couldn't have liked me very much, not if he thought something like that. I misread him, big-time. So…eventually, I'll be okay with running into him at your house, but not so much at the moment. As it is, I'll likely still have to deal with him where Joel is concerned." She frowned, thinking about it. "Or maybe not, now that Joel has an attorney. I probably need to back off, except for staying in touch with Joel to let him know I believe in him."

Their entrées came, and while they ate Bailey asked more questions about Gavin and about what evidence Ben had.

"I've got to say, there seems to me to be plenty of room for reasonable doubt," Bailey said finally. "You're sure Ben hasn't come up with more?"

Eve huffed. "Like he'd tell me. I don't know. Laura Santos—she and her husband run the group home where I placed Joel after I moved him— says Ben came to talk to them again. I guess he's been back to the original foster home, too. I called Rod yesterday. I could tell he didn't want to talk to me. He was really twitchy."

"It's awful about that old man. I mean, being grumpy shouldn't be a capital crime."

"No." Eve's sinuses burned. Spicy food, she told herself. "Enough about me. Um…do Mom and Dad know you're in town?"

Bailey wrinkled her nose. "Yes, although I didn't call until this morning. Mom always gets so excited, and mostly this visit is about Seth. But she'd be hurt if she found out I'd been here and not called, so..." She gestured, losing a glob of sour cream from her fork. "Oops." She used the napkin to swab it up. "We're having dinner there tomorrow night. You'll undoubtedly be getting an invitation."

"I'm still mad at her for pushing me to drag Ben to dinner there." She made a face. "Even though it's mostly my fault for *letting* her push me."

"She has it down to a fine art," Bailey said sympathetically. "She must have honed her pressure tactics all those years when she was leaning on the cops to keep looking for me when they were more than ready to quit. And, hey! Why let your skills get rusty?"

This time Eve's laugh was rueful but genuine. Bailey was right; home-baked cookies, sad eyes, pictures of her adorable little girl—those were only weapons. Eve admired her mother's persistence and sheer determination. How could she not?

"I get along better with Dad," she admitted.

"Me, too." For a moment, Bailey appeared reflective. "He doesn't try to make things happen or to change people. Mom... I don't know, I suspect she's more of a dreamer. She sees us through rose-colored glasses."

Eve nodded. "I think you're right. Maybe it's because that one awful thing happened, and she's tried ever since to be positive."

"Or she might have been born an optimist."

They looked at each other. Eve's mouth curved. "And what does she have for daughters? The two of us."

They laughed again.

She had the sudden, disconcerting thought that she hadn't felt even the slightest hesitation at saying that. She, too, was her parents' daughter, every bit as *real* as Bailey, who had once been Hope. And Bailey said Mom and Dad so easily these days.

Impulsively, Eve reached across the table and squeezed Bailey's hand. "I can hardly wait until you're back to stay after you graduate."

For just an instant, Bailey's expression was unguarded. Then she bit her lip and squeezed back. "Me, too," she said simply.

THE ELDERLY LADY in dainty gardening gloves and a wide-brimmed hat tied beneath her chin said, "May I see your badge again?"

"Of course." Ben unclipped it from his belt and handed it over.

She scrutinized it while saying fretfully, "I wish I had my reading glasses."

He hadn't gotten to the Shaffers' old neighborhood as early in the day as he'd intended, because he'd made the decision to track down Rick De Luca first. De Luca, who now sold supplies to eager amateur home brewers, had been blunt enough to turn Ben's uneasiness into out-right alarm.

But he still needed more ammunition before he openly questioned the kid. The houses here were modest, aging clapboard homes on small lots. Probably some renters, some new homeown-ers, and some old-timers like Mrs. Finster. On a Saturday morning, several of the near neighbors were out working in their yards. A guy a couple yards down was using a gas-powered rototiller to prepare what was presumably a plot to grow vegetables.

Not wanting to give any reason for her to feel threatened, he stayed on the sidewalk side of the white picket fence. He'd gone to her first, because she lived right next door to the house where Gavin and his mother had lived until Lynne married Rod Carter.

"I'll be glad to wait while you go get your glasses," he said patiently. "But I promise you my badge is the real thing."

Her gaze was unexpectedly shrewd. "I'm sure it is. Now, what is it you want to know, Detective?"

"How long have you lived here, Mrs. Finster?"

"Near fifty years. I'm widowed now, but my husband and I bought this house not long after we got married."

"Did you know Mrs. Shaffer and her son when they lived next door to you?" he asked.

Evelyn Finster looked at him as if he was crazy.

"Of course I did. They moved in after her divorce. That boy was nine or ten then."

"Were they good neighbors?"

"Well, *she* was all right, except for being sure her nasty little boy walked on water. I was relieved when they moved, to tell you the truth."

His hunting instincts came to attention. His easy tone was pure front now. "And why was that, Mrs. Finster?"

She sniffed. "We had a whole lot of unpleasant incidents in this neighborhood while that boy lived here. Not a one since he left."

"For example?"

"Mr. Tran down the street caught Gavin keying his car. I believe that's what it's called."

"It is."

"He spoke to Mrs. Shaffer, and the next thing he knew someone smashed all the glass in the small greenhouse he had in his backyard. Since I saw Gavin running away myself, I called the police and spoke to his mother." Her face tightened and her voice acquired a tremor. "I had an elderly cat. I found her decapitated on my front doormat the next morning. I knew who had done it."

The back of his neck prickled. Jesus. The kid had been practicing his cruelty all along.

"I'm very sorry," he said, and meant it.

"I'm not the only one in this neighborhood who breathed a sigh of relief when that U-Haul truck pulled out," she told him. "My cat wasn't the first pet tortured or killed around here. Nobody could ever prove he did it, but I knew."

How young had the little creep been the first time he killed an animal for fun? Ben wondered.

"That wasn't all he did," Mrs. Finster continued. "He found a way of paying anyone back for getting in his way. He and several friends threw eggs at the Bakers' house over there on the corner." She pointed. "They made such a mess, poor Mr. Baker ended up having to repaint. Only a few weeks before, his daughter had broken up with Gavin, you see."

Oh, yeah, Ben saw.

"Was that the end of it?"

"Unfortunately. I urged him to call the police, too, but he said how could he prove Gavin was behind it, and what good would that do anyway? It was true, every time they came out, officers would nod but they never actually charged him." She fixed a firm gaze on Ben. "What's that boy been up to now?"

He smiled at her. "I'm afraid I can't tell you that, but I will say I'm not surprised by anything you've said."

"Are you going to allow him to keep getting away with murder?" she demanded.

It took him a second to realize she was only using a figure of speech and had no idea how accurate she'd been.

"No, ma'am." He held her gaze, letting her see he meant it. "I will not."

"That's fine then," she said with a nod. "If you don't have any more questions, I believe I'll get back to my gardening. Everything takes me longer than it used to, but the weeds haven't slowed down any."

He laughed. "No, Mrs. Finster, and they're not likely to."

Her chuckle was more of a giggle, unexpectedly young-sounding, which had him still smiling as he circled his car to get in. As he buckled his seat belt, though, his smile died. He thought back to the last thing Rick De Luca had said.

"That Shaffer kid is an arrogant little prick."

Now Ben found himself thinking Gavin Shaffer was something else altogether: he was a sociopath. He fit the description to a T, from the superficial charm and high intelligence to the lack of remorse and pathological egocentricity.

But like Gavin's former neighbors, Ben couldn't prove it. Not yet. But he would. The kid might be smart, but the arrogant part, yeah, it fit. Gavin was incapable of believing anyone could bring him down. Why would he, when it sounded as if he'd always gotten his way?

He must have been seriously annoyed when his adoring, supportive mother remarried, and he not only had to adapt to her new husband but was forced to share his home with an older boy who was a football star being recruited by a bunch of major universities. No, Gavin wouldn't have liked that. All he'd have had to do was overhear Clement Rowe blasting Joel for daring to set foot in his yard, and Gavin would have seen how he could reclaim the premier place in his household. He might have figured a few nasty tricks would be enough, but still Joel stayed. Given Gavin's personality disorder, escalation was almost inevitable. He might have enjoyed killing Mr. Rowe, he might not have, but it wouldn't have meant any more to him than squishing a bug—or beheading a friendly old cat.

Despite Ben's cold certainty, he knew he had to proceed carefully, and for a lot of reasons. Starting with the possibility that Joel Kekoa also suffered from a personality disorder. It wouldn't be surprising if his upbringing hadn't left him with some scars. His father had been sentenced for armed robbery, after all. Investigators had suspected him of killing a convenience store clerk in an earlier robbery, but weren't able to prove it. Some people would say, *Like father, like son.* Traits could be learned.

But Ben had arrested Joel himself and seen his stunned bewilderment. His first words had been "Somebody killed Mr. Rowe?" as if he couldn't believe it. That might have been grief mixed with his shock, as if despite everything he didn't like to think of anything bad happening to the old guy.

In later interviews, he'd been sullen, maybe even simmering with some anger. But who wouldn't be angry, falsely accused of murder?

Turned out that, despite everything, Joel Kekoa was a lucky kid. He had Eve in his corner.

One step at a time, Ben reminded himself. Right now, he needed confirmation of what Mrs. Finster had told him from some of the other neighbors.

CHAPTER TWELVE

"I SHOULD BE taking off, too," Eve said, about two seconds after Bailey said it. "Tomorrow's a working day." She narrowed her eyes at Seth, who'd claimed an early workday with a straight face when she knew darn well he had no intention of going in at all.

Behind his soon-to-be mother-in-law's head, he winked at her.

Eve would have rolled her eyes, had Mom not turned just then. "Oh, I'd so hoped you'd stay for a few minutes, Eve," she said, not hiding her disappointment.

"For a little bit, Mom." As if she could say anything else.

Mom hugged Bailey close, murmured something in her ear, then gave Seth a squeeze, too, which he reciprocated. Dad settled for kissing Bailey's cheek and shaking hands with Seth.

A moment later, Eve trailed her mother back to the kitchen. Dad disappeared into the living room, and she heard the TV come on. Did he know what Mom wanted to talk about and was hiding out? Or was just giving them some girl time?

"Another cup of tea?" Karen asked.

Eve hopped up onto one of the stools at the breakfast bar. "That sounds good."

Setting the teakettle onto a burner to heat, her mother started fussing. "I'm so sorry Ben couldn't make it tonight. I had Seth ask him, you know."

Eve stiffened. "Seth, instead of me?"

Mom looked startled. "I happened to be talking to him. Since they work together, I suggested he invite Ben and you. Since I don't talk to you as often as I used to."

Eve's temper rose to a simmer. "Oh, that was low."

Nobody could do innocently surprised better than Karen Lawson. "What on earth do you mean?"

"I take your calls whenever I'm not in the middle of a meeting. I have dinner here nearly once a week. In fact, when you called to invite me for dinner tonight, I answered. I call *you* on a regular basis."

"But not as often as you used to."

Guilt spiced the temper, because it was true. Eve had considered Mom to be her best friend—until Hope's resurrection, which had stirred all these complicated feelings. Too many of them involved Mom, so how could she talk to her about them?

But maybe *not* talking to her had been more damaging to their relationship than being honest would have been. Dad had listened and not seemed hurt. Mom, too, might have the right words to heal Eve's sore places, and having her daughter talk to her openly might heal some of Mom's.

"This last year has been a little bit hard for me. Mostly, I'm embarrassed at what I've been feeling, so I didn't want to tell you."

Karen stared at her, not moving even when the kettle shrieked. "I don't understand."

"The water is boiling."

"I *know* it's boiling," Karen snapped in a rare display of temper. She snatched the kettle from the stove, poured water into both cups and turned off the stove. She set one in front of Eve, but stayed barricaded on the other side of the breakfast bar herself.

Wow, Eve thought. *I'm going to have to come right out and say it. She really* doesn't *have a clue.*

"Hope," she said. "Bailey."

Mom didn't so much as blink.

"It started when I first mentioned Hope to Seth." She gave a small, wry smile. "You remember how excited he got."

"I will bless him forever." Mom's fervency came through loud and clear. Her voice rang with joy. "And to think he's marrying her."

Totally oblivious.

"That's all fabulous from your point of view." Eve couldn't help it if she sounded sharp. "But try to remember that *I* was dating the man. Suddenly, he was obsessed with her instead." She took a breath. "And so were you."

"What are you implying?"

"I'm not implying. I'm saying. From that moment on, all you could think about was Hope. I started wondering if I hadn't been as good a substitute for her as I'd thought I was."

The shock on Karen's face made Eve's heart cramp. She closed her eyes. "I shouldn't have said that, Mom. I'm sorry."

"But you meant it, didn't you?"

The hand on her lap, the one her mother couldn't see, tightened into a fist. Her fingernails bit into her palm. "I'm telling you my feelings were hurt. I know it was irrational. I can't help it. I suppose I have a...core of insecurity. From before."

Mom's expression softened but remained puzzled. "You're twenty-nine. You've been our daughter for twenty-one years. I suppose I thought—"

"I'd gotten over all that?" Suddenly there was an edge in her voice again, because she couldn't believe she was having to say this. "Well, here's news. With a beginning like mine, you never get over it, not entirely. And I know you love me. You and Dad." A lump rose in her throat. "I believe that. But I've still struggled with the way you light up for Bailey, as if she's the center of your existence. With the fact that Seth dumped me for her the second he set eyes on her." She gave a short laugh. "No, even before that. I think I lost him when he saw that damn age-progressed drawing."

Neither of them had so much as taken a sip of tea.

"It just...all got tangled up in me. I felt like an outsider. Reality is, if Hope hadn't been abducted, you'd never have taken me in. Never have adopted me. And now...you have her back."

The bones in her mother's face had never been sharper, more defined. Lines that Eve had never seen aged her. "You really think that."

"No!" Eve cried. "That's what I'm trying to tell you. I don't, but there's this little voice inside me that sometimes whispers, *You never were good enough. You don't look like them. Anybody can tell you're not really their daughter.*"

"Oh, dear God." Mom pressed fingers to her lips.

"Dad—I think he understands. But you never even noticed." Her sinuses burned. "So, I guess I did stay away. Not because of you. Because of *me*. Because I'm ashamed. I knew none of what I was feeling was true, but I felt it anyway and I had to deal with that."

"I thought you liked Hope." Her mother sounded utterly bewildered. And, of course, still fixated on Hope. Always Hope. "That you welcomed her home, too."

"I...did. I was glad for you." The shame burned, because at first, she hadn't. "We've really become friends." She shook her head. "More than that. Sisters. We have, Mom. But…it took time."

"And I've been completely blind," Mom whispered.

This minute, her eyes looked glazed. Eve suspected her mother didn't see her in truth.

"I should have been more open with you." No, she thought hopelessly. She should have been a better person than to clutch such petty resentments to herself, as if she was the one who had been wronged. How ironic that she'd always known how lucky she was to be taken in by these kind people. Loved by them. *Oh, God, what's wrong with me?*

Her mother gave a funny little nod. "If you'll excuse me, I don't think I want this tea, after all." She very carefully lifted the tea bag from the cup, dropped it in the trash can under the sink, poured out the liquid and set the cup on the top rack in the dishwasher. Then she walked past Eve, and a moment later Eve heard a door close quietly down the hall. Mom had taken refuge in her bedroom, or perhaps her quilt studio.

Eve didn't move for a long time. The television provided white noise. She had no idea what was on.

Finally, she slid off the stool and, like her mother, dumped out her tea and carefully placed the cup in the dishwasher, leaving the counters so clean they shone.

Then, just as quietly, she let herself out of the house. These had been the worst few days of her life since she was a confused, hungry, filthy child too young to understand crack addiction or why Mommy didn't wake up. Who waited and waited and waited, until she was finally desperate enough to leave that squalid apartment and knock on the neighbor's door, even though they were scary people.

The scene with Ben had been devastating. She'd loved him. Probably still did, but couldn't think about that. Now, she'd hurt her mother terribly in the name of honesty. The woman who had given her stability, normalcy, love. *But she didn't give me understanding,* whispered a voice in her head. That was the one thing her mother had always withheld.

More pettiness. *Me, me, me.*

Social worker, degree in psychology, and she was officially pathetic.

LYNNE CARTER WAS not happy to see Ben again. Gavin in contrast started out relaxed, amiable.

Ben had parked on the street outside the high school, watching as teenagers flooded out of buildings after the last bell of the day, a few lining up to catch buses, others setting off down the sidewalk in packs or completely alone, the majority piling into cars.

The ones walking alone worried him, but he

kept his attention on a souped-up Chevy with flames painted along the sides. Gavin sauntered out surrounded by his own little coterie but split apart from them to get into his car. It started with a throaty roar.

He drove about the way you'd expect—in jerks and lunges, stops raising smoke from beneath the tires. *Idiot*. Ben's thought might have been tolerant, if not for everything else he knew about Gavin Shaffer.

Boy drove straight home, wonder of wonders, and pulled into the driveway. He'd reached the porch when Ben pulled up, blocking driveway and souped-up car.

As Ben got out and strolled up to the house, Gavin appeared puzzled but friendly. There was absolutely no emotion visible in his sky-blue eyes.

Next door, yellow crime scene tape still blocked entry to the front door and presumably the back. No reason it couldn't come down, but there still seemed to be some question about who Clement Rowe's heir might be. Turned out he'd had a daughter, but she was dead, and any grandkids were proving elusive.

Remembering the way everyone on the block in Everett had been out gardening Saturday, Ben felt a pang. Given another few weeks of rain and sunshine, Mr. Rowe's lovingly cared for lawn would be shaggy, maybe start creeping into pristine flower beds.

Ben's face hardened when he looked at the teenage boy who waited on the porch. "Gavin," he said with a civil nod. "Your mom home?"

The mask in place, the teenager shrugged. "Probably. How come you need to talk to her again?"

"I'm actually here to talk to you," Ben said, "but I need her to be present, or at least to clear it."

The eyes literally darkened. "Me? You're kidding, right?"

"Why would I be kidding?" He tipped his head toward the door. "You going to ring the bell or unlock?"

He unlocked and, before the door was wide-open, bellowed, "Mom!"

She appeared from the kitchen. Sounded as if she had a radio or the TV on in there. Her gaze took in her son before turning anxiously to Ben.

"Detective Kemper. My goodness. I didn't expect to see you again."

"Well, ma'am, murder investigations take time. The obvious answer isn't always the right one. I imagine you know that." Out of the corner of his eye, he saw Gavin stiffen.

Mrs. Carter squeezed her hands together. "Of course. Do you need to look in the garage again? Or see Joel's room?"

"No, I was actually hoping to talk to Gavin today. Since he's a minor, I need your permission."

She went utterly still. "Why would you need to speak to him?"

"Just have some questions." Ben kept his tone easy.

Her gaze darted to Gavin. Then she squared her shoulders. "I'm sure he won't mind. Will you, honey?"

The kid's lip curled. Ben couldn't blame him. No self-respecting teenage boy appreciated his mother using an endearment in front of anyone else.

But then he met Ben's eyes, his own guileless. "No, why would I mind?"

"Good. Do you mind if we sit down?"

Ben politely declined Lynne's offer of coffee. She hovered uncertainly in the doorway to the living room as he settled on one end of the sofa and her son in a recliner.

"Gavin, I'm going to walk you back through the assorted incidents with Mr. Rowe."

"But…why?" he asked blankly.

"I wasn't the responding officer and, even though I'm able to read police reports, I like to get my information firsthand."

"You should ask Joel, then. Why would I know anything?"

Ben smiled. "You live right here. Any kind of uproar, you pay attention, right?"

Gavin still looked cocky. "I guess." He shrugged. "Sure."

The trampled rose canes? He hadn't known anything about those until Mr. Rowe came roaring over. No, he hadn't noticed anything wrong when he parked in the driveway only a few feet from the mangled shrubs. "They were just, like, brown sticks anyway."

"Neat brown sticks until then," Ben observed mildly.

Damned if he wouldn't swear secret amusement lurked in Gavin Shaffer's eyes. No, he might be seeing what he'd expected to see, given his skin-crawling dislike of this kid.

The rock through the window? No, sir, he hadn't heard that. He often fell asleep with his earbuds in and his iPod still playing.

Lynne abandoned the doorway to ease into the room and sit on a glider off to Ben's left. At least she was being cooperative so far, not intervening. Too many parents felt compelled to speak for their kids.

Ben asked if he and Joel had hung out at all. Maybe shot baskets together, tossed a football. "There's a baseball diamond, what, half a mile away at Jefferson Middle School. You two ever pitched a few balls for each other?"

Gavin's eyes narrowed. Ben could almost see the wheels turning. Was there any way he could have left a fingerprint on that baseball bat?

"Yeah, I guess we might have a few times," he decided.

Nobody ever said Gavin was dumb. His mother, though, wasn't as good an actor. She gave a start of surprise.

The fire. Ben understood why Gavin hadn't heard anything, since he'd been listening to music, but since he was awake and his bedroom was on the back of the house, it was surprising he hadn't smelled smoke.

"It was winter. My window was closed." But he was starting to look wary and, maybe, just a little mad.

"Wood smoke, though," Ben mused, "it's insidious. Although you have a fireplace. You folks ever light a fire in it?"

Well, yes.

Did he know where the matches were kept?

As if irresistibly drawn, his gaze slid to the mantel. Ben took note of the bottle of gel fire starter and a box of extra-long fireplace matches. The fire marshal had suspected fire starter had been used. The decking wouldn't have been easy to get burning, not after months of on-again/off-again rain. Gasoline had been poured down the side of the house, but whoever lit the blaze might have been afraid to throw that match right onto wood soaked in gas, because of vapors. A dumb kid might not have thought of that; budding arsonists were known to set themselves on fire. But Gavin was smart—as, for that matter, was Joel. And the fire starter was handily available. Ben wondered, if he checked, whether he'd find the bottle mostly empty. Or maybe not; the kid—whichever kid—might have replaced the one he'd used up. Might be worth checking at retail outlets.

Ben let his eyebrows rise and his eyes linger on that fire starter. He made sure to look speculative when he turned his attention back to Gavin.

Speaking of fire—he was betting Gavin had a short fuse.

"Did you know your neighbor fed cats?" he asked.

He shrugged carelessly, his indifference obvious. "There were always bowls out on the deck."

"Any of the cats friendly?" Ben said it as if he was just making conversation.

"Gavin's allergic to cats," his mother offered. "We can't have one."

"Dogs?"

"We've mostly lived in rentals," Lynne said nervously.

"I see." Ben let the silence draw out. "Joel mentioned that particular cat was really friendly. Always winding around his legs when he walked from the bus stop."

He waited for an outburst from Lynne. Something along the lines of, *Then how could he do something so awful?* But she didn't say a word. He turned his head to see her staring fixedly at her hands.

She knows, he thought, what had been his own

near-certainty solidifying. God, what would it be like to have your own child be utterly without conscience, capable of such monstrous acts? Was shielding him from consequences what any parent would do? But Ben didn't believe it, even though he could imagine how wrenching such decisions could be.

He asked questions about the Sunday night when the murder had taken place. Gavin claimed to have hung with friends, then worked on a paper for school. He guessed he'd gone to bed by ten. "I mean, school starts really early."

How conscientious. He hadn't wanted to have to hide a yawn from his first period teacher.

"You do chores here at home?" Ben asked.

"Like what?"

"Say, do your own laundry."

A flush rose on his cheeks. Nope, not stupid. "Mom does all of ours together."

Ben turned enough to smile at her. "Is he known to throw a load in now and again?"

To her credit, she looked perplexed. She didn't realize her darling boy would have been saturated with Clement Rowe's blood after battering him to death.

"I suppose I might ask him to if he came in muddy from a soccer game or something," she said uncertainly.

"Oh, well." Careful to sound vague, Ben stretched and rose to his feet. "Just something to think about." He let some steel show when he nodded at Gavin. "We'll be talking again. Mrs. Carter, thank you."

She fluttered around him and showed him out. Gavin didn't so much as move a muscle. He seemed...stunned. A little scared? Ben could only hope.

Departing, he was fully satisfied. He'd put the vicious little shit on notice that he was a person of interest—and he'd stoked that temper. The ability to keep it tamped down was unlikely to be one of his sterling qualities, and he was, after all, a teenager. Sixteen-year-olds weren't good at impulse control.

And if you're wrong? he asked himself. Then no harm done, he decided. Killer or no, Gavin *was* a vicious little shit who needed to find out that not everybody was as blind to his behavior as his mommy was.

Eve assumed Joel's attorney would have let her know if she'd learned anything significant, but she called her law office anyway, only to learn that Vivian was likely to be in court all day.

Even though she had nothing new to tell him, Eve squeezed in a visit to Joel, who looked utterly defeated, his massive shoulders rounded, his eyes making her think of a cowering puppy.

He liked Ms. Wilson, he said. He'd only seen her the once, Friday afternoon. "She said the evidence the police have isn't good enough to convict me. I think she was just trying to make me feel better."

"No, Joel. The bat in your locker is such an obvious setup."

He lifted his head, his expression despairing. "But who would do that?"

Eve shook her head. She couldn't even begin to hint at what she believed to be the explanation. It sounded so outlandish. No wonder Ben had been unwilling to seriously consider Gavin as a suspect. Why would he? The killer could just as well be any other neighbor who had disliked Mr. Rowe—and it sounded as if they all did—or someone from his past. The vandalism, even the cat, might be unrelated to the murder.

Yeah, right.

She left dissatisfied and not sure she'd raised Joel's spirits at all.

She did several home visits and made calls to find out whether a mother who had been allowed to retain custody of her two children was actually attending AA meetings and counseling. Eve had had grave doubts about giving her another chance, but she was pleasantly surprised to find that the woman had attended three AA meetings that week alone and the counselor felt her attitude was good and they were really making headway.

Eve reached her father, too, who said in surprise, "Your mom didn't say anything about an argument. At bedtime she told me she'd gotten some progress done on a quilt she promised by Friday. She might not have been as upset by whatever you said as you think she was."

Call Mom.

And say what? I didn't mean a thing I said? I did, but I'm sorry I said it? You fell and hit your head on the corner of the cabinet and anything you thought you heard was a delusion?

She attended what proved to be a brief dependency hearing, the kind she liked best, when the judge ruled the court supervision at an end because parent and child—in this case, a father and son—had completed all requirements and were doing well. Sometimes she still harbored doubts at this point. Too often she was right, and six months or a year later, the kids were again abandoned, or a school counselor called to express concern because they were dirty and hungry—or trying to hide bruises. This time, Eve was confident. She shook the dad's hand and hugged the boy, who blushed but looked pleased anyway.

At almost six o'clock, she walked into her apartment—her own space—feeling a relief akin to letting a heavy pack slide from her shoulders. It didn't take her five minutes to shed heels, hose and suit, and change to black yoga pants and a faded, saggy sweatshirt that had once belonged to her father. Yanking the pins from her hair took a couple more minutes. She brushed it and chose to loosely braid it.

Then she pretended she had an appetite and went to the kitchen to consider possibilities.

She had the freezer door open and was letting cold air pour out wastefully—she could hear her mother's *tut tut*—while she studied the contents when her intercom buzzed.

"Wonderful," she mumbled, and closed the freezer. "Please don't be Mom, or—" Her imagination boggled. Friends might drop by on a weekend, but not usually on a weeknight. They all worked full-time plus, too.

She pushed the button. "Yes?"

"Eve, it's Ben. I'd like to talk to you."

She bumped her head against the wall. Did she *have* to do this?

Yes. For Joel's sake.

She buzzed him in rather than answering, looked down at herself in alarm and tore into the bedroom to switch out the sweatshirt for a drapey red sweater. A girl had some pride.

She whisked back to the living room just as he knocked.

As he stepped in, she stared in shock at him. "You don't look so good" were the first, not very clever words out of her mouth.

"Thanks," he said wryly.

"I mean it." He'd aged a decade or more. "What's wrong?"

Those blue eyes, bloodshot, met hers. "What do you think is wrong, Eve?"

Her knees sagged and she sank onto an ottoman as terrible possibilities raced through her mind. He was a police officer. Mom, Dad. Bailey? Seth? That would be bad because of Bailey. But...why would Ben be the one to let her know?

"Tell me."

He shook his head and gave a short, gruff laugh. "You really don't get it."

She gaped at him. He was talking about *them*?

"I hurt you. I'm having a hard time dealing with that."

Her back straightened. "Why? It's not as if you really know me."

"I do." Ben sounded unutterably weary. He nodded toward the sofa. "Do you mind if I sit down?"

Before you fall down, she thought, saying hastily, "No. Of course not."

He sat. She stayed where she was.

After a moment, he shook his head a little. "I came to update you." He managed to sound almost dispassionate. The cop instead of her lover.

"If you haven't released Joel—and someone would have called me if you had—what's to update? Seemed to me your investigation was done."

"No, Eve, it wasn't. I had to arrest Joel after finding the bat. But, contrary to your opinion, I did listen to you. I may have said something stupid—I did say something stupid—but that doesn't mean I don't respect you and your instincts. I know you'd never judge a kid because of the color of his hair or anything superficial. I was… I don't know what. Feeling defensive? Trying to think of a reason you were wrong about what your gut was telling you?" He grimaced. "I don't know," he repeated.

Emotions rose in a flood tide beyond her ability to control. Spun every which way, she couldn't think.

"I don't understand."

"I shouldn't be telling you what I've learned, but I'm going to anyway." He scrubbed a hand over his face. The shadows in his eyes were darker than ever. "I've been looking into the two boys' histories."

"Two?" she echoed, stunned.

"I'm here to say your instinct about Gavin Shaffer was right on. I talked to teachers and coaches both here and in Everett. Some didn't see any deeper than the smart, good-looking kid. But there were a few who didn't want to come right out and say anything that could be actionable, but hinted. He made them uneasy, too, at the very least."

He kept talking, told her what he'd learned from former neighbors of Lynne and her son. About the smashed greenhouse, the keyed car, about a suspicious fire. And then there were the pets gone missing or gruesomely killed.

"I've been back to talk to him. Made him nervous."

"You think he murdered Mr. Rowe."

"I can't prove anything yet," he warned her. "All I've found are red flags. A forest of them."

She was going to cry. He'd listened to her. He believed her.

"Excuse me for a minute." She shot to her feet and raced for the bathroom. Safely locked in, she covered her face with her hands and cried. Silently, and not for long, but she needed the release. Then she splashed cold water on her face and used makeup to try to hide the ravages before she went back out.

She could see that she'd failed. Ben was on his feet, his gaze penetrating, devastated. He closed his eyes for a moment. "Eve."

"No." She went back to the ottoman. "I'm sorry, I just needed a minute. I've been…scared for Joel." *And missing you,* but she wasn't going to say that yet. Maybe not ever. She didn't know yet.

He stood looking down at her. His hands closed into fists before he seemed to deliberately loosen them. After a moment, he sat back down without his usual easy grace.

"What are you going to do?" she asked.

"Keep the pressure on him." He hesitated.

"That's one reason I want Joel to stay where he is for now. Gavin can't get to him there."

Horrified, she said, "You actually think…?"

"I don't know, but if we're right about him, he's already escalated to killing. He's used to sliding out of trouble, partly because his mother protects him."

Eve had met parents like that before. Most refused to believe their little darlings were capable of ugly behavior.

"Is there any way he can find out where you live?" She had to ask.

"I'm not listed, but anything's possible. Harder to get into an apartment, though, and I'm lucky because the parking is gated. Not to say he couldn't slip in behind a car, but if anyone vandalizes my vehicle, I'll know who did it." Gaze somber, he said, "You be careful, too, Eve. He might be smart enough to trace my lack of gullibility back to you." Ben grunted. "He'd even be right."

"How will you ever prove he did it and Joel didn't?"

"I started at the high school today. If I have to talk to every damn kid at that school, I will. Somebody had to have seen him put the bat in Joel's locker. Or heard him brag about it, but in Gavin's case—" He seemed to mull that over. "No. I think he hugs his pleasure to himself because he thinks he has everyone conned."

"He smirks," she heard herself say flatly.

"He does."

They sat and looked at each other for a minute. Those extra lines carved into his face made her want to put soothing hands on him. Stroke his face, knead away the tension she could feel from ten feet away.

"What I said to you was crap," he said explosively, half rising to his feet before forcing himself to sit down again. "You're beautiful, and it breaks my heart to know you don't believe anyone really loves you. Then what did I do but poke you where it hurts most. I'd give anything to be able to take it back."

Her mouth trembled as she tried to smile. "I think you just did."

This time when her eyes filled with tears, she all but dove across her small living room into his arms, sending him sprawling back along the sofa. But those arms had closed around her, so tight she might not be able to breathe, and he pressed his cheek to her head and said brokenly, "Eve. *God.* I'm sorry. Eve. Please."

When she managed to lift her face to his, his mouth closed over hers, hot and hard and frantic.

CHAPTER THIRTEEN

THEY TORE AT each other's clothes. Never did get completely naked, just enough. Ben tried to be tender. Eve deserved that, but his need felt desperate, and hers seemed to be, too. His hands shook and he knew he gripped her too hard, but, God, he had to keep hold. She cried out when he sucked her breasts, and used her teeth on his neck and earlobe.

He was about to come without ever getting inside her, but she must have been close to the same because she was whimpering. Since she was on top, she was the one to take him inside her. The feeling of her body, wet, silky, tight, closing around him was indescribable. It took him a couple of thrusts to think, *I'm not wearing a condom.* Pleasure so acute it was agony made speech impossible.

And then the ripple of her convulsions squeezed him and he couldn't have stopped if there'd been a gun to his temple. Her head tipped back, she screamed his name as he lost it. He wasn't watching the fireworks, he was one of the rockets, shooting into the sky and bursting into all those nameless colors, sparkling against the velvet black until he floated out of existence. He wasn't sure he hadn't passed out for a microsecond.

Eve slumped down onto him, seeming boneless. He'd pulled out her braid at one point, and now masses of black curls covered her face and spilled over his chest. His heart felt as if it was going to jackhammer right out of his chest. His vision remained blurry. He stared up at the ceiling and tried to suck in enough air.

"Wow," he finally mumbled.

Her head bobbed—he thought, and hoped she hadn't meant to shake it.

Ben regained enough strength to lift his hand and smooth it over that glorious mane of hair and down lower, to the silky skin of her back and buttocks. He became fascinated by each tiny knob strung together to form her spine. Delicate, like all the rest of her.

He winced, thinking about what they'd just done. It hadn't been all him, but…damn. He'd been trying to tell her without actually using the word that he loved her, and instead he'd come unglued and been on her like a rabid wolf.

Except…he tipped his head a little to one side, feeling a sting. Then became aware of another, and another. Teeth marks, he was pretty sure. On his back…fingernails.

He worked his mouth before trying to form more words. "Hey," he got out.

"Oh, my." Eve lifted her head and used one hand to push her hair back. She looked as dazed as he felt. "That was…it was…"

He didn't share his vision of being a rocket exploding in the night sky. "Amazing," he supplied.

"I guess so." Pink was already heating her cheeks even before she focused on his neck and her eyes widened. "Oh, my God. *I* did that?"

He touched the wound that had her transfixed. "What, that?" Suddenly, he was grinning, a big, loopy, unbelievably happy grin. "That was the sexiest damn thing I've ever felt."

Eve giggled and laid her head back down on his chest.

After a minute, he said, "I didn't use a condom." Normally, that would have been a statement to strike terror in his heart, but instead it was only an observation. God help him, he liked the idea of her pregnant.

She stirred. "I'm on the pill."

He gently squeezed her ass. "I didn't mean to do this."

Her muscles tightened. "Make love to me, you mean?"

"Well, I didn't think I'd have the chance." He closed his eyes for a moment. "I didn't *deserve* to have the chance."

"No, that's not true." She lifted her head again, this time propping a forearm on his chest to brace herself so she could look down at him. "I think I overreacted. I have a way of doing that," she said, sounding both sad and rueful.

"Not this time." He cupped her face in a hand, rubbing the pad of his thumb over her lips. "I insulted you. Went right for the jugular."

"I thought—" She shook her head, her hair tickling his chest and neck. "Never mind."

"Tell me."

She lifted one shoulder. "I sort of figured you were letting me down not-so-gently. I mean, there's you and Rachel, and there's me."

Anger fired in his belly and he jackknifed to a sitting position, lifting her as he rose. "Please tell me you're kidding."

She shook her head.

"What's that supposed to mean? Me and Rachel, and then you?"

"Just...what you said. That I have a lot in common with Joel. Outsider. Anyone looking would know I didn't belong."

Ben spat out a word he rarely used, one that had her eyes widening.

"Didn't belong? Did I say that?"

"Um... I can't remember your exact words."

"You translated what I said about an echo of your family to believe I was telling you there was no way you'd ever look like you belonged with *me*."

"Do you blame me?" she fired back.

"Yes!" He couldn't remember being so pissed.

"You're the most beautiful woman I've ever seen in my life. I have trouble believing you're interested in me. What, you have this idea couples have to be bookends? What would make you think anything like that?"

The turbulence inside her darkened her eyes to bitter chocolate and killed his case of mad. She actually believed shit like that.

"I…wouldn't have said I did," she said in a soft voice. "I thought—I actually believed—I was a reasonably stable human being." Her laugh had nothing in common with the giggle that lightened his heart. "But lately, all this stuff has been stirred up. I guess it had settled at the bottom, so I didn't know it was there anymore." Her forehead crinkled, and suddenly she was looking deep into his eyes. "Did you mean that? About me being the most beautiful woman you've ever seen?"

"Yeah." He had to clear the gruffness from his voice. "You're so…dainty, and so fiery." He touched her face. "You move like a gypsy dancing, graceful and spirited. You have these huge brown eyes that give away how much you feel. You're strong and determined and passionate in defense of your kids. You'd never give up on one of them, would you?"

Her smile shook. "The legal system sometimes doesn't give me any choice."

He nodded. "I have that problem, too." No, he wouldn't let himself get diverted. "Eve, how can you not know that men all turn and gape when you go by?"

"Because they don't?" A dimple quivered in her cheek. "Maybe there's something wrong with your eyesight." Her voice became husky. "I'm glad."

"You know how sold on you Rachel is, don't you?"

The naked hope on her face squeezed his heart, and hard. "I really like her. We've had fun."

"Yeah." He touched his forehead to hers. "We have. We will. In fact, if it isn't pouring, I thought Saturday we'd go look at daffodils. Tulips, too, if they're out."

She looked as stunned as if he'd just gone down on bended knee. "You're planning to take on the Tulip Festival traffic? Are you serious?"

He grinned, his mood taking a hot air balloon ride. "I thought Rachel would like it. And why buy you a bouquet when I can take you for a stroll through acres of the prettiest ones that can be found?"

She blinked and sniffed. "Damn it, you're going to make me cry again."

"Again?"

"You listened to me. You did something about it. That made me cry."

"Okay. I don't have to buy you flowers or chocolates, huh?" he joked, trying to lighten her mood. "All I have to do is listen?"

"Worth truckloads of flowers," she assured

him. Her forehead crinkled. "This is your week-end with Rachel?"

"Our weekend with Rachel," he said. "As much as you're willing to tolerate."

Her eyes filled with tears again.

He swore and pulled her close, laying his cheek against the top of her head until she sniffed and drew back.

"Really, I was just going to ask if you think Rachel will enjoy driving around to look at flowers."

Ben couldn't dismiss the glow, because she was thinking first and foremost about his daughter. But he grinned and said, "You haven't noticed she's a girly girl? Flowers? Girl? I don't plan to drive miles through the fields. I thought we'd walk through the RoozenGaarde display garden, then take a little bit of a hike. And I'm not above using the flashers to clear the road, you know."

Eve's giggle was everything he remembered—and loved.

TRYING TO KEEP a cap on his frustration, Ben strode toward the doors that would let him out of the high school near the separate gymnasium building. School had let out for the day; the halls were empty, although he knew the baseball team was out on the field for practice and he'd passed one open classroom door where some club or maybe the school paper or yearbook crew had a meeting. There might be other stuff like that going on in different wings.

Day two of trying to find a witness who'd seen the bat placed in Joel Kekoa's locker had been another failure. Ben was beginning to fear that nobody *had* seen. Originally, he wouldn't have believed the little creep could pull it off, but take now. The hall was empty. He hadn't heard the clang of a locker closing for a while.

Alternative said he was an adult—worse, a figure of authority—and any potential witness was a teenager. Natural enemies, from their point of view. He'd been leaning on the truth that Joel was one of them, too, but seeing nothing but blank expressions.

He shoved open the door and blinked momentarily in the bright sunlight. Maybe that was why he heard the voice before he actually saw anyone.

"Mister? I mean, Detective?"

Not liking to be taken by surprise, he stopped, to see a girl rising from where she'd been sitting on the top step, a bulging daypack beside her. She was slight, pale, with light brown hair. Wispy, he thought, about the hair and the girl.

"You know who I am?"

"Yes, sir."

"Were you waiting for me?" He aimed for calm and friendly.

"Yes, sir. Well, kind of. I'm waiting for my mom, too." She glanced toward the street. "She picks me up here, but she's usually late because of when she gets off work."

He nodded. No car approaching on this side street, which was good. His anticipation had risen.

"Detective Kemper," he said, holding out his hand. "Ben Kemper."

She shook shyly. "My name is Kylie Burke."

"Nice to meet you, Kylie." He paused. "You've heard the questions I've been asking?"

She bit her lip and nodded. "I should have talked to you yesterday, but…well, Mom was earlier than sometimes, and I guess I had to think about it. Because—" she drew a deep, visible breath "—I'm kind of scared of this boy. The one I saw putting something in Joel's locker."

A savage triumph filling him, it took everything Ben had to keep his manner mild. "This boy?"

"Oh! His name is Gavin. Gavin Shaffer."

"I see." He smiled at her. "Why don't we sit down?"

"Okay." She perched back where she'd been, her feet on the step below so her knees were all but pressed to her chest. She kept her arms in tight, too.

He put a few feet between them and stretched his legs out. "Okay, Kylie. First, you know I'm interested in a particular locker."

Her head bobbed. "Joel's. Everyone knows he was arrested. And I don't believe he would kill someone." She sounded as if she were talking about little green men landing on the football field. "He's *nice*. I mean, to everyone. He doesn't make fun of people, and…and if you, like, bump into him, he's good with it. You know?"

"I know."

"So, my brother's locker is only three away from Joel's."

"He doesn't hitch a ride with your mom?"

She shook her head. "He drives now, and he has a job right after school. Plus a girlfriend." Her nose wrinkled. "So he drives *her* home."

Ben hid a grin at her disgust.

"Mom doesn't really like me getting home before her, so mostly instead of taking the bus I wait here for her. Sometimes when it's raining, I have to wait inside.

"It was kind of, like, drizzling that day. The one before Joel got arrested. But, I don't know, I came outside anyway, but I was sort of huddling in the corner there, 'cuz it's under the eaves."

Ben saw where she indicated. She'd have almost been pressed up against the glass, but also partially shielded from being seen from inside by the start of the wall. And, yes, it had drizzled that day, off and on.

"I was bored. You know. And watching for anything happening out here, and in there, too. There are, um, some cool guys on the JV team." Pink touched her cheeks, but she forged on. "So I paid attention when I saw this guy coming down the hall. I knew who it was right away." She sounded matter-of-fact. "A lot of the girls think he's the best-looking guy in the school. But one day I saw him when he was leaving the school. He has his own car."

Ben nodded encouragement.

"He was pulling out into the street, and this old, fat, little dog that lived in that house—" she pointed "—was waddling out into the street. He hit it. I think he did it on purpose. Then when he saw Mr. Witter standing there—Mr. Witter is a science teacher," she explained. "Anyway, Gavin jumped out and acted really sorry, but I know what I saw." Her chin jutted defiantly.

"I believe you," Ben said.

The chin came down. "Plus I've seen him be mean to kids. Mostly people don't notice me."

She sounded surprisingly okay with that, but he wondered. All he said was, "All right. You saw him in the hall."

Kylie nodded. "He kept looking around. I thought it was strange he was still here, because he isn't doing any sports right now and the parking lot was practically empty. Mom was really late that day. Anyway, he opened his locker, so I thought he came back because he forgot something, but he took out this black plastic bag, and I could tell it had something long and not very wide in it." She demonstrated with her hands. "He walked really fast to Joel's locker, and he opened it and put the bag in it."

"Into Joel's locker," Ben repeated. "How did you know it was Joel's from here?"

"Because after Gavin left back the way he'd come, I went in. I wasn't absolutely positive, but it was one of, I don't know, three or four lockers along there. And I know it wasn't in James's. That's my brother," she added.

"Did you hear what we found in Joel's locker?"

She shook her head. "Only that it was something bad. People said it had blood on it."

"It did."

"I think he had something on his hands, too. I only caught a glimpse, but later, I figured out he didn't want his fingerprints on the bag."

Five-year-olds knew not to leave fingerprints these days.

"Something? Like gloves?"

But she shook her head. "Uh-uh. I think it might have been, like, sandwich bags. He stuffed something in his pockets as he walked away."

Sandwich bags, goddamn it. That would work. Wouldn't matter if he dropped one, because this was a school. Who'd think twice?"

"I should have said something after I heard about Joel," Kylie said, shamefaced. "But I wasn't sure, and you must have had other reasons to arrest him or you wouldn't have been looking in his locker, so…" She trailed off. "I was scared," she said again. "I know he could get to me."

She had good reason to be scared. Ben didn't want to say that, but he wanted her to stay safe.

"You're smart to be cautious," he said finally. "This is a murder we're investigating. What I want you to do is tell no one about what you saw."

"Even my mom?"

"Will she keep it to herself?"

Kylie hesitated. "She's a hair stylist. In a salon. They talk a lot."

"Can you wait to tell her? Give me a couple of days?"

After a moment, she nodded.

"In the meantime, I'd like you not to be alone."

He saw incomprehension, then she looked around. "Like after school, you mean."

"Exactly."

"I can walk to the library with friends. I'll tell Mom I have to research something and she'll pick me up there."

The public library was only eight blocks or so away, and filled to the max every day after school with kids from the high school and middle school. Ben made a practice of avoiding it then.

"Excellent." Out of the corner of his eye, he saw a small blue car turn the corner. "That your mother?"

"Uh-huh." She jumped up, swung her pack over her shoulder and started down the steps.

"Oh, Kylie?" he called after her.

She paused halfway down and looked at him.

"If necessary, will you testify as to what you saw?"

She gave a sturdy nod.

"Your phone number?"

She called it to him as she bounded down the rest of the steps and hurried to the curb, where her mother had stopped.

Ben ambled after her, but turned toward the parking lot.

Damn, he did love getting the break he needed in a successful investigation. He was already plotting his next step before he'd unlocked the car.

MOSTLY BY CHANCE, Ben hadn't seen much of Seth the past couple days. Having the man he considered a friend question his motives for looking harder at Gavin had stung a little. But keeping each other on track was what partners did.

Hell, even if Seth had been downright offensive, he might have had cause. Ben winced at the recollection of a few things he'd said when he thought Seth was spending time he couldn't afford on the pursuit of the scum who'd abducted Hope. Or had he said "wasting" time? Truthfully, Ben hadn't believed Seth would actually be able to track down the guy. After twenty-three years? How could that be possible? But the thing was, Les Hamby had *kept* snatching girls, all pretty, blue-eyed blondes like Hope, and Seth had hunted him relentlessly, finding patterns. The FBI jumped in, and damned if the guy wasn't sitting now in jail in Arizona. Early on, he'd fought extradition to Washington, but according to Seth had recently given up, mostly because the girl he'd had with him when he was arrested had finally been identified and returned to her parents—who lived in Arizona. So he now faced charges in three different states for the kidnap of the three of his victims who had been identified, starting with Hope.

What Seth had done was extraordinary.

No matter what, when Ben, steaming, stalked into the squad room, he didn't give a damn that Seth was at his desk or that his eyebrows rose.

Ben flung himself into his chair and scowled into space. *Grab the files you need and get out of here,* he told himself. *Thank God it was the end of the day.* Why was he sitting down at all? Much as he wished he was seeing Eve again tonight, it was probably just as well he wasn't, given his shitty mood.

"Can't get a date for prom?" Seth asked.

Ben had no problem transferring the scowl to his sometime-partner. "What, now you think I go for underage girls?"

Seth held up both hands. "Hey, it was a joke. Because you've been hanging around at the high school."

"You mean, interviewing potential witnesses," he said tautly. "Who are sometimes students there."

His friend contemplated him. "I take it you struck out."

"No, I found my witness." He got more satisfaction than he should have at saying that. "Girl saw Gavin Shaffer, looking around and obviously thinking he was alone in the hall, take a long, narrow item in a black plastic bag out of his locker and put it in Joel's or one on either side of it."

A smile broke out on Seth's face. "Then you've got the little son of a bitch." The smile faded. "Eve's instincts were right on."

"Why does that surprise you?"

"It shouldn't," Seth admitted. He shook his head, apparently trying to clear his thoughts. "So what's wrong?"

"I just had a meeting with Cavender." Don Cavender was with the DA's office. "He says the girl's testimony isn't enough to get a warrant. She could have a grudge. She can't absolutely swear the object she saw—assuming she really saw it at all and didn't describe it the way she did because she heard through the grapevine what we found in Joel's locker—was actually put in his locker, versus one on either side." He said a very obscene word then. "Despite the fact the unlikelihood of something that resembled a baseball bat wrapped in black plastic was placed in a locker near Joel's but not *in* Joel's by a boy who lives next door to the murder victim." He was snarling by the end.

"Cavender never likes the testimony of kids," Seth said sympathetically. "Bad draw, getting him."

"Especially considering the currently accused is also a kid."

"Especially."

"You could go over his head."

Ben grunted. "I will if I can't find some supporting evidence or another witness." But they both knew how touchy that would be.

"Good. Let me know if there's anything I can do." Seth pushed back his chair and stood, gathering his phone and a couple of files from his desk. "I'm sorry about Eve. I don't know if I said that."

Okay, Ben's mood took an upswing. He grabbed what he needed, too, and the two men started toward the door.

"We've worked it out."

Seth stopped dead. "You've what?"

"You heard me. We're back on. You may duly report to your girlfriend."

"Fiancée," Seth said with satisfaction.

Ben grinned at him without malice. "Caught in a noose."

"You're jealous," Seth said amiably.

"We'll see." He just laughed when Seth hooted.

"OH, MY GOD," Eve said, when Ben told her what the freshman girl had seen. Delight burst in her, even if he hadn't been able to get the warrant he wanted to search Gavin's bedroom and locker at school. He would; of course he would. Then her mind took a sideways jump. "This was yesterday? I wonder why Vivian didn't call me right away. I mean, I'm not her client, but..."

"I haven't told her yet."

"What?" She gaped at him, setting down her glass of wine on his table. She'd been watching him cook. "Why? Isn't full disclosure a rule?"

He turned from the stove. "Before trial, sure. In the middle of an investigation, we have more flexibility. Plus, you and I know Joel won't be going to trial."

"But..."

"Eve, I want him to stay where he is. You know that. It's even more important now, because I don't want Gavin wondering if someone saw him and who that could be. I asked the girl not to wait where she usually does for her mom until I clear her, but you never know with kids. Or Mom may insist. If Gavin gets nervous and lurks after school for a few days, sees her just outside those glass doors every day..."

Chilled, she said, "He might decide to take care of her."

"She saw him hit a dog with his car, she thinks on purpose. I know the old dog she was talking about. I wondered not long ago why I hadn't seen him, figured his owner had had to put him down."

His voice was grim. "Instead, the son of a bitch saw his chance and took it. Quick thrill, no conscience."

"I hate him," Eve said fervently, fists clenched. "I'm so glad he's not part of my caseload."

"What would you do if he was?" Ben sounded really curious.

"What I absolutely had to do for him, and I'd cooperate with the police investigation. And breathe a huge sigh of relief when you made the arrest."

"Good to hear." He smiled at her. "Grab the silverware, will you?"

They sat down to a stir-fry that turned out to be good. He laughed at her when her first bite must have been noticeably cautious.

"Think I'm going to poison you?"

"You don't sound like you do a lot of cooking."

"Not as much as I should, but I don't like eating out all the time, either." He shrugged. "You learn."

"Your mother didn't make you learn?"

His face went blank. *Bang.* She'd intruded unknowingly, and he was shutting her out.

Eve concentrated on eating for a minute.

"I was mostly raised by my father."

Surprised, she looked at him. He was frowning, his gaze unfocused. His voice was slow, reluctant. Didn't want to say, or didn't want to remember, she wasn't sure.

But he surprised her by going on. "She took off

when I was seven. She and Dad fought a lot," he said, divesting the simple statement of emotion. He might as well have shrugged. It happened. No big deal.

"You mean, they got a divorce?"

"Huh?" His eyes, darkened to navy, met hers. "Oh, eventually. But no, she just…packed and went. I came home from school and no one was there. There was a neighbor lady who watched me sometimes after school. We both figured Mom had had something come up and forgotten to clear it with Mrs. Gunderson, or else I'd forgotten what Mom told me to do. Mrs. G called Dad, who I guess figured the same. Only, when he came home he found Mom's half of the closet and share of the drawers empty. Plus," his mouth tilted wryly, "their joint checking and savings accounts were just as empty. Mom did a flier."

"Oh, Ben," Eve whispered. "I'm so sorry."

His eyes focused again, briefly, on her. "It was a long time ago."

"Yes, but—"

"Dad was… I don't know if he was hurt as much as enraged. I was bewildered. She was kind of careless, as mommies went, but really beautiful and special to me."

Remembered pain bled into his voice whether he knew it or not. Eve hurt for him, and was ashamed at how much she'd whined about her own wretched childhood without ever wondering how wholesome *his* had been.

And then his description of his mother as *beautiful* hit. Just...*oh. Oh. I get it. Finally. No,* she thought, shaking her head, *more like, I should have guessed.*

"Your looks came from her, didn't they?"

His smile was almost genuine. "Good one. Must be that degree in psychology."

"No wonder you aren't full of yourself, the way most guys who look like you are."

He picked up and pondered his glass of wine. "I could always tell it bothered my father some, seeing her in me."

"Did you keep a relationship with her?"

"You mean, did she bother doing the every-other-weekend thing? No. I've...never seen her again." He tipped the glass up and took a long swallow.

Her hurt deepened, spread, but she suddenly became conscious of wariness, too. Rachel might have inherited the bright blue eyes and sunny blond hair from Ben, but...

"What's Nicole look like?" Eve blurted.

CHAPTER FOURTEEN

WELL, SHIT. WASN'T it just yesterday Ben had reminded Seth how smart Eve was? Too smart, he thought now.

But he also knew this subject would have arisen eventually. He didn't have any photos of Nicole out here at the apartment, but sooner or later Eve would have asked to see one.

"Yeah," he admitted, "I've been thinking about this lately. Are you going to find me too creepy if I say, although it never occurred to me until recently, that Nic looks a lot like my mother?"

Eve had withdrawn some, and he couldn't blame her. The idea had been oozing out of his subconscious and bothering him, too, even as it illuminated a whole lot of his psyche.

"No-o." Although she sounded doubtful. Then she frowned at him. "How could you *not* know?"

"I thought I liked blondes." He shrugged. "A lot of guys do."

"Did you ever date women who weren't?" She sounded a little combative this time.

He lifted his eyebrows. "You mean, until you?

Of course I did." He grimaced. "It's just… I told you Nicole grew up in foster homes, right?"

Watching him with her beautiful chocolate-brown eyes, Eve nodded.

"She was placed locally about halfway through seventh grade. One day, there she was in a couple of my classes. First time I saw her, I felt a punch in the chest. She was, shall we say, more mature at that point than I was?"

"Physically?"

"Oh, yeah." He had a flash of memory, extraordinarily vivid. The swell of the pretty new girl's breasts, the way her hips swayed. She'd give her head a small shake, making her shiny blond hair shimmer. He saw it, like a slo-mo in a movie when the stunned boy gapes. He could still feel that punch, if muted by time. "Of course, I was skinny and clueless about how to get the girl. Until her, I wasn't a hundred percent sure I *wanted* the girl." Yeah, make a joke out of it. He'd been getting too serious. "Except in fantasies, which involved buxom women who didn't look anything like middle school girls."

Eve rolled her eyes. "I can imagine."

"Yeah, you did middle school, too."

"And have something like fifteen middle-school-age kids on my caseload."

He found himself grinning, another surprise. Instead of feeling scarred because he was remembering himself at that age, he was amused.

And instinct had him wanting to shut the door now, but he knew Eve well enough now to be sure that would be a mistake. He had to get this out, a realization that stomped dead any amusement at all.

He cleared his throat. "Despite a certain amount of yearning, I didn't ask my friend to ask her friend if she'd go steady with me."

That earned him a quick smile, and the tightness in his chest eased.

"In fact," he continued, "nothing started for us until our sophomore year in high school, and, like I told you, we split up while I was away at college. Even though I wasn't that far away. I went to Seattle U," he added. A smile twitching irresistibly at the corners of his mouth, he said, "A good part of the student body at SU is female. So I can't claim to have gone into a decline, or been celibate."

Eve made a face at him.

"Still, Nic was always there, in my head. And, honest to God, I never once thought, hey, does she remind me on some subliminal level of my mother? Although you'd think I should have."

"Most of us aren't that self-aware. Especially—" she wrinkled her nose "—when we're eighteen or twenty. And anyway, do you think it was that straightforward?"

"No. No, I don't." He hadn't known until now how much thought he *had* been giving this. Or maybe *thought* wasn't the right word. It had been more like a computer working, just a quiet, background hum. If he was to let go of what he'd felt for Nic, he had to figure this out. And before he let his relationship with Eve move forward, he had to be sure he *had* let go. Mostly, he thought he had. But there were pangs of regret and maybe still something more when he saw Nic's name on the screen of his phone and knew she was calling, or when she let him see her unhappiness. To Eve, he said, "I didn't—don't—point like a setter every time I see a pretty blonde." Bailey, for example, hadn't done anything for him.

No, he'd convinced himself he was desperately in love with one particular woman. Other pretty blondes wouldn't have measured up. Which gave him the idea that Eve had broken through initially because she *didn't* remind him in any way of Nic.

When she'd broken up with him partway through fall semester his first year at SU, he'd been shattered, sure, but also, deep down, believed he'd find her again. As he had.

Too bad he hadn't been smart enough to see she'd been an echo for him, one that kept bouncing off walls, never quite going silent. His mother was long gone, out of his reach, and always had been. But Nicole, she was there, attainable.

"Man." Now he rubbed a hand over his face, feeling exposed and even pathetic. "I'm an idiot."

"No." Eve pushed away from the table and came around to his side, bending to wrap her arms around him. "No more than me or anyone else who got messed up as a kid."

He pushed his chair back, too, enough so that she could sit on his lap and he could not only hold her, he could rub his cheek against her thick, glossy, black hair and remember how it felt tumbling over both of them in bed.

Part of him wanted to drop this subject. But he had to get it all out. Say aloud what Eve needed to know.

"Nic was screwed up, too. She had a lot in common with my mother. Always dissatisfied, restless, hungry for something she didn't have."

Eve's head bobbed, bumping his chin. "Kids who don't receive the validation and love they need from parents or anyone else are left with a hollow place inside. I must have had one myself, but I was lucky because the Lawsons filled it. It doesn't sound like Nicole had anyone."

Of course she understood.

"I thought I could be that person for her." He was just as glad Eve still had her head tucked in the crook between his neck and shoulder so she couldn't see him when he said, "What I didn't get was that I was looking for her to fill a hollow place in me, too."

But she straightened, then, so she could look at him. "Hindsight is a wonderful thing."

"Yeah, it is. The moral of this story is, I was stupid. I set myself up for a replay of the worst thing that happened to me when I was a kid. And then I was hammered when it did happen—twice, once when she broke up with me after high school, second time when she suddenly announced she wanted a divorce." He shook his head. "What I called love was a lot more complicated than that. Which makes me realize I can't blame it all on Nic. If I'd been a happy, completely stable guy, I might have had more to give her."

Eve was shaking her head *and* a finger at him long before he finished. "No, no, no. First thing, don't use the word *blame*. Nicole can't give what she doesn't have. The fact that she doesn't have it is not her fault. The fact that you didn't recognize it was missing in her is not yours, either. Who even thinks to look for something like that?"

"At least until we have a degree in psych." He went for light again.

"Often, not even then. There are majorly screwed-up psychotherapists." She wrinkled her nose. "And social workers. God. Look at me."

"I am." His voice went husky. "Eve, you give and give and give. You aren't missing a single thing."

Just like that, her eyes were wet. "That's… wow."

"Did I say something wrong?"

"No, right." Her smile shook. She bent forward to wipe now damp cheeks on his shirt. She went very still for long enough to worry him. Before he could say anything, she lifted her head again. The expression in them deeply serious, her eyes held his. "One last thing. I doubt love is simple for anyone. We're all looking for someone to fill our own needs. Plus, what woman doesn't look for a man who shares some of her father's qualities—or is totally unlike him. Ditto for men and their mothers. Our childhoods form us. Don't... denigrate what you felt for Nicole."

Compelled by her eyes, a rich color that brimmed with a whole lot he couldn't quite interpret, Ben couldn't seem to so much as blink. He felt a muscle twitch in his cheek. At last he said, "Okay."

She slid off his lap. "You can't tell me it hasn't occurred to you to wonder why *I'm* attracted to you." Her voice had an edge. It was almost hostile.

Ben was taken aback for an instant before he got it. Same song. He shook his head in disgust. "Don't start with that crap. You're harking back to my idiocy, right? I'm supposed to be worried that you only want me because I fit your image of what ideal people look like."

"Isn't it true?" she yelled.

One minute she'd been rational, compassionate, the next she'd flipped out. What had happened here? He fought to keep calm, to understand and not just react. Was this a deliberate attempt to push him away? Or had she panicked because it suddenly struck her that this was a logical follow to what he'd said about him and Nicole?

"Bullshit!" he heard himself snap.

"How do you know?"

"Because, yeah, we had a ping of attraction that was physical. Of course it was."

Eve blinked a couple of times. Confused. Good, he thought.

"I've met plenty of beautiful women. I bet you've met plenty of guys with my coloring. This is the Northwest. We have our share of Scandinavian descendants."

She couldn't argue, because it was true. Forget Kiwanis, Freemasons, Elks—around here, Sons of Norway were big. "Why me?" he asked.

"I...don't know."

He had her on the run now, he thought with satisfaction.

"The first hit for me was when you smiled at Rachel," he told her. "You were genuine, gentle, not condescending. Then you hugged Bailey, when I knew—" He stopped, bracing himself for outrage.

"Seth has a big mouth," was all she said.

He let himself grin. "He does." Then he let the silence ride.

Her forehead crinkled. "I liked the way you were with Rachel, too. And you touched me."

Had he?

"You listened to me. You expressed some of the same worries I have, about letting people down who depend on you."

"You care," he murmured. "That's what got to me." He lifted a shoulder, determined to be honest. "Plus, back to the beginning. You're incredibly sexy."

Miracle of miracles, she laughed. "Lucky for me, so are you."

"Eve, I know why you're sensitive. I can only tell you I want everyone to know you belong to me." Hearing what he'd said, he hid his wince. *With* me. That's what he should have said.

Once again, she confounded him. She whispered, "Thank you. For saying that. And…"

His eyes narrowed. She'd better not thank him for his interest or kindness or any other crap like that.

"Putting up with my insecurities."

"Funny thing." He held out his arm, inviting her to come to him again. "Mostly, when I look at you, I see strengths."

"Well, damn." She swiped at her face. "Here I go again." But she also sat on his lap, wrapped an arm around his neck, and pressed her lips to his scratchy cheek.

The combination of tears and touch had his heart swelling.

EVE LET HERSELF into the house. "Mom?"

"Eve?" Her mother popped out of the kitchen. "Honey, I didn't expect you!"

"No, I just, um, brought my lunch—" she lifted

the brown paper sack "—and thought I'd see if you were home."

"That's wonderful." Karen beamed. "But I'm sure we can do better than whatever you have in there."

"Actually, it's not half bad. Ben made a really good stir-fry last night, and sent me home with leftovers. If I can use your microwave..." She hoped she wasn't giving away the nerves she was battling. Maybe this was a really terrible idea.

"Of course you can." Her mother, trim as always, in jeans and a tucked-in striped blouse plus polished loafers, led the way to the kitchen. "I'll share my salad with you, if I can have a taste of your stir-fry."

"Deal."

Eve set her bag on the counter and began removing the contents, including a can of soda, a small bag of red grapes, and the plastic-lidded container holding the chicken and cashew main course.

They could just visit, she thought. Talk. It would make her mother happy. She didn't have to say anything that would make Mom *un*happy.

But...everything she and Ben had said last night had kept turning in her head while she was trying to sleep. She thought he'd meant every word, settling a part of her that had remained uneasy. Which gave her the idea that she and her mother could have the same kind of resolution. If Eve could make her mother understand...

She waited until they were sitting at the table, food in front of them, before she said, "I know I've upset you lately."

"Oh, the less said about it the better."

Why was this one of the moments when Eve was unnerved by awareness of how much Mom looked like Bailey? Except it was the other way around, of course.

"I just...wanted to say I'm sorry." Oh, there was a major cop-out.

Her mother smiled gently. "Love means never having to say you're sorry."

Eve set down her fork. "Isn't that a bumper sticker?" She couldn't help herself. Snide just slipped out.

Mom chuckled. "That doesn't mean it isn't true."

"We *should* say we're sorry when we behave badly."

"Eve, we understand more than you think."

Suddenly, she found herself mad. "Then why—" Oh, no. She'd sworn she wouldn't do this.

"Why what?" Mom looked pleasantly puzzled. Yep, there she went again. Not a clue what was brewing in her daughter. Had she never noticed undercurrents? Did she actually think she understood anything?

Eve said it very quietly. "Why did you never notice how jealous I was of Hope?"

They stared at each other.

Mom very subtly...withdrew. "We love you."

"I don't doubt you love me. I've never doubted that."

"Then what's this all about?" Karen Lawson was an attractive, mild-mannered woman whose most powerful emotions had always been grief and guilt. Emotions having to do with Hope, never with Eve.

"I don't think you ever let yourself see how it felt to me to know I couldn't set foot into that bedroom across the hall. The pretty, perfect bedroom. To know *I* couldn't have a pink bedroom, oh no, because Hope's already was. To be talking to you, and realize your gaze had strayed past me to the mantel, and sadness would fill your eyes. To always suspect you'd trade me in in a heartbeat to have her back."

The gradually dawning shock on her mother's face found an echo in Eve. Why was she so driven to say these things, despite her best intentions? What had she hoped to accomplish?

"That's cruel," Karen said in a voice that shook.

"I don't mean it that way. I do understand how hard it all was for you. I count my blessings every day. It just...bothers me that you can't see why I struggled sometimes to believe I mattered, too."

"I grieved for Hope. I doesn't mean I came to love you any less."

"I know that. I do know it. In my head." Eve touched her fingers to her forehead. "In here—" she touched her breast "—it was harder. Can't you understand that, Mom?" She heard herself begging, and saw the resistance even before her mother answered.

"You haven't asked your father, have you." It wasn't a question.

"I think he saw me more clearly."

"Maybe because *he* had no reason to blame himself for what happened to Hope. We both knew it was my fault."

Eve's mouth fell open. "He never blamed you."

"Of course he did. He should have!" Her mother stood, gathered up her untouched lunch, and marched into the kitchen. "I can't do this, Eve. You'll have to excuse me." Again—always—she vanished down the hall, and Eve heard a door close quietly but firmly. Not slam, oh, no, Mom never vented that way. Or at all.

Eve looked down at her own, equally untouched lunch and, after a moment, carried everything into the kitchen. She scraped it into the garbage, rinsed out dishes and put the plastic container back in the brown paper bag.

She'd blown it, big-time. Damaged her relationship with her mother yet again, maybe irreparably.

But then she felt a small spurt of her own anger.

If you loved someone, weren't you supposed to listen? Had Karen really not understood how broken that little girl she and her husband took in had been? Why was she determined to remain totally blind to why Eve had been jealous and felt undermined when Hope reappeared in their lives?

Letting herself quietly out of the house, she nourished the spark of anger rather than sinking into the depression lurking beneath.

Face it. Her mother had been blind. Or hadn't wanted to know.

Maybe she'd been so damaged by the loss of her daughter, she'd only had so much left to give. Maybe, because of her own pain, she'd been looking inward instead of at the other people in her life. If so…poor Dad.

Lord, Eve hoped this empty feeling inside *her* wasn't the kind of hollow she and Ben had talked about.

BEN HAD BEEN back to the high school. Back to Clement Rowe's neighborhood. He'd searched Rowe's house, top to bottom, looking for something, anything, that would help. Wouldn't you think Rowe might have started watching for the next trick? Even set a trap? Maybe used a digital camera to try to catch someone in the act?

But he didn't own a computer, a cell phone or a camera, not even a Polaroid.

Ben didn't find a diary, either. Binoculars, yes,

sitting on an end table in the living room where the old man could grab them anytime. Which set Ben to wondering how good Rowe's vision had been. He had clearly used reading glasses—Ben found a pair in just about every room. He had maintained his driver's license, although there wasn't much to the vision test. Like every other cop, Ben was unhappily aware someone could pass it who had no peripheral vision, or had a blind spot, trouble with depth perception.

But Rowe had believed his tormentor was Joel Kekoa, not Gavin Shaffer. Why? Only because Joel had taken the one, defiant step onto his lawn? Had Rowe ever seen even movement in the dark?

Ben had to leave, knowing no more than he had when he arrived.

A troop of teenage boys was passing as he walked out, a couple on skateboards, one wobbling on a bike because he was pacing them, another one walking. They were issuing challenges to each other, laughing, reaching out to take mock swings at each other, but went quiet when they saw him.

"Got a minute?" he asked them.

They stopped. One of the boys with a skateboard kept a foot on it, while the other picked his up. "Uh... I guess," he said.

"Do you live around here?"

Only one lived on the block, almost to the corner. Ben turned to see the house he was indicating. The others' homes were spread along the next eight blocks or so.

He asked if they knew Joel and Gavin.

They exchanged cautious glances with each other.

"I'm on the football team," the biggest kid said. "I mean, I'm a freshman, but I kind of know Joel. He's *awesome* out there."

Two others were sophomores. Only the boy on the bike admitted to being a junior and having a couple classes with Gavin, although he insisted he didn't really *know* know him.

"What about Mr. Rowe?" Ben nodded at the house.

He got shrugs. Sure, they'd seen him out in his yard sometimes, and otherwise he watched them from the front window.

"To be sure we don't go in his yard or drop trash or anything," the football player said with rolled eyes. He looked embarrassed then, probably having remembered what happened to Mr. Rowe.

Ben finally let them go, having failed to learn a single useful fact.

Which pretty well summed up the two days since Kylie Burke had approached him. Good thing he was used to this kind of frustration. It pretty well defined his job. What he'd learned was, keep poking, keep looking around corners, keep talking to people you've already talked to three times. Secrets were really hard to bury forever. They had a way of leaking out.

He sat in the car for a few minutes, trying to decide what his next move should be. He still hadn't started the engine when he saw Gavin's car coming. Heard it coming, too.

Gavin spotted him and slowed almost to a stop, then turned into his driveway only a few feet away from where Ben was parked. What Ben wanted to do was just keep sitting there. Play chicken.

Impulse, but not the smart thing to do. Gavin must already be on edge; he'd know Ben was still asking questions at the high school. Too much pressure could be dangerous.

Ben put the car in gear and pulled away from the curb as Gavin got out. Ben nodded, raised a hand as if at a casual acquaintance, and kept driving. In the rearview mirror, he saw Gavin staring after him, then turning to saunter toward the porch.

No problem, he'd be telling himself, reassured at Ben's lack of interest in him. The police tape was still on Mr. Rowe's house. No surprise the cop was taking another look.

Too bad, Ben thought. He'd have enjoyed making the kid sweat.

Yeah, but would Gavin have sweated? he wondered. Your average teenage boy got stupid when he was nervous. A tough street kid might become more aggressive.

But there was a third option. Nerves implied some kind of conscience, or at least an awareness of fallibility. Gavin Shaffer might remain completely cool, because hadn't he always gotten away with everything?

"Not this time," Ben murmured. Somewhere, there was another witness, and by God he was going to find him.

EVE JERKED AWAKE and lay very still, listening. She would swear she'd heard something…

A grunt—a *snort*?—stirred her hair. And then she became aware that an arm lay heavily across her, and that a body, hot and hard, spooned hers.

She wasn't alone in bed.

She shouldn't have been startled, because— now that her mind was clearing—she remembered making love with Ben. They had mostly quit eating out the evenings they got together, and instead cooked for each other, or, after an especially long day, bought takeout. Last night he'd come to her place. It was just that he'd never spent the night. She was pretty sure he hadn't intended to this time, either.

Either Ben's forearm or hand were blocking her view of the lighted numbers on her clock. She had to lift her head a little to see them.

Five forty-seven.

Eve almost groaned, before it occurred to her she should be glad she had woken up when she did. Presumably, she and Ben both had fallen asleep while cuddling, which meant she hadn't set the alarm. Which she *would* have set for six thirty.

Had his arm just tightened around her?

Yes, because the hand was no longer blocking her view. Instead, it squeezed her breast gently. And, if she wasn't mistaken, an erection pressed against her bottom.

"You're awake," she murmured.

"Mmm." His hips rocked, and his hand skated down to slip between her legs, his fingers deft considering she'd swear he'd been asleep thirty seconds ago.

But, oh, it felt good. She tried to turn over, but he held her in place.

"Let me," he whispered.

There wasn't much she could do except reach back and stroke his flank, all lean muscle, hard bone and sleek skin.

Morning sex had never held much appeal for her before. She tended to wake up grumpy, her mood not improving until after at least one cup of coffee. Plus, there was the bad breath issue.

But there was something deeply arousing about not really being able to participate. The hard ridge of his erection jerked when she wriggled a little against him. And, oh, heavens, what he was doing with his fingers. She suddenly wanted more than his fingers.

"Ben."

That was all she had to say. He gripped her topmost thigh and lifted it forward, and was between her legs, nudging her where she ached. Eve groaned, and he pushed slowly inside her. Retreated as slowly. It was torture.

She tried to move, to lift her hips to meet him.

"Patience," he said in a gritty, early morning voice, and maintained the steady, almost languid rhythm that had her belly tightening even as it made her crazy.

"Please. Please."

He laughed, low and husky, slid one finger between her folds and pressed. The climax that grabbed her and then let her fly free was shocking in its intensity. Ben made a sound, lifted her to her knees and thrust a few times hard and fast until he made a raw sound and she felt him jerk inside her.

Then it was his turn to groan as he fell back onto his shoulder, letting her collapse, face buried in her pillow. Eve turned her head and blinked a few times, trying to bring the green numbers on the clock into focus.

At last she succeeded. 6:08.

"Oh, my God," she mumbled. Twenty minutes. Probably less. And she felt... She had to think about it before reaching a conclusion. Amazing. "You're still here," she said.

"You noticed." He pushed hair aside and nuzzled her nape. "I'm flattered."

Eve giggled. "That was a surprisingly nice way to wake up."

"I thought so." He made a grumbly sound and said, "I wish it was Sunday."

"So you could go back to sleep."

"Yeah." His teeth closed gently on the tendon running up the side of her neck, sending a zing through her. "Then wake up and do it again."

"Too bad, so sad."

Ben laughed. "Unfortunately, I have to hustle enough to get home and change clothes." There was a pause. "Do you think anybody would notice if I wore the same clothes as yesterday?"

She mulled that over, not in any hurry to move. "Given that you wear basically the same kind of pants and shirt every day—probably not."

"I can skip the shorts," he said thoughtfully. His hand roved over her hip and waist, cupping her breast again. "Not enough time to go back to sleep. The doing it again, though…"

Pressed against her as he was, she couldn't miss the way his penis thickened. Already. She would have sworn she couldn't get aroused this soon. She'd been wrong.

"Maybe," she whispered.

"I like a positive woman."

Astonishingly, they still had time for breakfast.

CHAPTER FIFTEEN

THINKING ABOUT EVE visiting Joel this morning, Ben hoped like hell she could resist sharing information she shouldn't. No, not fair; she kept promises. And it was hard to worry about much of anything when he felt so exceptionally relaxed. Man, he wanted to wake up like that every morning. Sleep every night with his arms around her.

He wasn't shocked or even mildly surprised by the realization. Maybe falling asleep in her bed last night had been one of those accidental-on-purpose things. He'd begun to hate the nights when he wasn't getting together with Eve. He wondered how she felt about living with a man.

Guaranteed, Nicole wouldn't like it. Which had him wondering, as he so often did about her. Would she object because she liked jabbing at him? Or because she was jealous? And if she was... So what, he told himself, frowning.

And give her some credit. She might also be genuinely trying to protect Rachel from getting hurt down the line if/when Eve disappeared from her life.

Damn it, focus, he told himself. He was walking

into the mortgage company where Lynne Carter worked. He felt the need to take another shot at her and her husband—and to do so individually, instead of meeting a united front. This time, he wasn't taking any chance Gavin could overhear, either.

Called from her office, Lynne did not look thrilled to see him.

"Can you get away for a few minutes?" he asked, conscious of the receptionist and a couple who were waiting for a mortgage consultant and looking curious. He hoped it wasn't Lynne they were waiting for. "We can get a cup of coffee or just go for a walk."

She sighed, looked at the clock on the wall, and sighed again. "I have twenty minutes before my next appointment."

Ben smiled and held open the door for her.

Outside, she blinked in the sunshine. "It's really a nice day, isn't it? Why don't we just walk. I've had my morning quota of coffee."

"Me, too," he lied. "I'm hoping the weather holds. I'm taking my daughter and my girlfriend to look at the daffodils."

"What a nice idea. Except for the traffic," she added, which was the default for locals, even newly minted ones like her. The Tulip Festival brought in substantial business, but visitors en masse had a way of gumming up the works.

After a moment, she asked, "What did you want to talk to me about?"

"Just hoping we can run through the various incidents with Mr. Rowe again." He held up a hand, forestalling the expected protest. "I know we've done it before, but people remember things. I'm pretty well lacking any real evidence tying Joel to the various tricks."

"Oh, but—" She'd hurried so much, her speech stumbled.

"But?"

"Well, his window screen wasn't quite attached."

"And could have been that way for months."

He encouraged her to talk about her first encounters with Rowe, anything Rod had said about him, both the boys' complaints.

She seemed genuine initially, wrinkling her nose when she described her first meeting, when she was being friendly and hoping to get to know the neighbors. But as she continued, her tone became more and more constrained.

Reading between the lines, Ben thought she *hadn't* actually seen anything. But she wasn't stupid. Every one of the vicious pranks—if you could call them that—were replays of incidents that had occurred in her former neighborhood. Ones for which she must know neighbors there believed her son to be responsible. A loyal mother to the bitter end, she wasn't saying, though.

They circled the block once, and he thanked

her for her time and let her go, pretending not to notice her relief.

Ben checked his watch. Time for a follow-up interview for another investigation, then he planned to corner Rod Carter at his lunch break.

SLUMPED IN THE chair across from her at the small table, Joel gazed beseechingly at Eve.

"Can they just keep me here, without there even being a trial?"

"It's only been a week since your arrest." She counted. "Eight days."

"But I didn't *do* anything." He looked so miserable, her resolve wavered. If she could just hint…

I promised. She suppressed a sigh.

"I know you didn't, Joel. Just hang on. Detective Kemper is still investigating."

His dark eyes smoldered. "He's the one who arrested me."

"I know he is. That's because he's primary on the case. It also means he's responsible for having enough evidence to convince a prosecutor that he can convict you at trial."

"There's nothing to find," he muttered.

"If the baseball bat was planted, other evidence could be," she felt obligated to remind him.

He stared at her, his shock apparent. "But… like what?"

"I don't know. He's asking a lot of questions,

and not just about you. He knows finding the bat where it was isn't definitive."

"What's that supposed to mean?"

She talked around what she knew, not saying anything she hadn't before, and that his attorney wouldn't also have told him. The bat *could* have been planted. The fact that Joel's fingerprints were on it meant nothing, unless one had been planted in the blood, and she knew for a fact that wasn't the case.

"But what are they *doing* to find out who killed Mr. Rowe?"

"Mostly asking questions, I think," Eve said. "I've talked to Detective Kemper frequently—" over breakfast this morning, for example "—and he says he still has avenues to pursue." Although she didn't quite know what. She also didn't know why the girl's statement that she'd seen Gavin put the bat in a locker that was likely Joel's wasn't sufficient to justify another search warrant, but Ben had seemed unsurprised if also frustrated.

As she talked, Joel let his head hang, his body language reflecting his feeling of impotence.

"Have you had visitors?" she asked.

His mouth twisted. "A few. Tony and Laura both came."

"I assumed they would."

"And Coach Keefe came. Plus Mr. Dennis. He's the assistant coach."

Eve nodded.

"I guess everyone at UO must know I was arrested, huh?"

"I have no idea." God, she hoped not.

He shrugged.

When she left, Eve didn't know if she'd done him any good. Except she had to believe it would be worse if she *didn't* come.

She walked out to her car, wondering what Ben was doing right this minute.

And whether he'd want to stay the night if she suggested dinner again.

ROD CARTER WAS even less happy to see Ben than his wife had been. The first words out of his mouth were a flat, "You again."

Ben had had to wait in the lobby of the public utility district building while Rod was summoned. Now he smiled. "Following up, and then following up again is my job, Mr. Carter. I appreciate your patience. I know you want to help, given your relationship with Joel."

Ben was encouraged to see a shadow cross the other man's face, one that naturally seemed to be open and good-humored rather than secretive.

The PUD building had a small café on the ground floor, and they both bought cups of coffee, but took them to a bench on the far side of the lobby from reception rather than sitting in the half-full café where they might have been overheard.

They sipped in silence for a minute, Ben mentally tossing the dice. That expression had looked a lot like guilt to him. Carter might feel it only because he hadn't supported Joel, hadn't even gone to visit him in juvie. But Ben had seen his discomfort before and wondered.

First he asked for permission to record the conversation. Then, his strategy decided, Ben said, "I'm going to be frank with you, Mr. Carter. I'm starting to have real doubt that Joel committed the crime." He paused deliberately. "Any of the crimes."

Joel's foster dad flicked an alarmed look at him. He hadn't missed the subtle emphasis on "any."

A big, buff guy, Carter had a boyish quality about him. Ben doubted he was capable of subtlety and probably wasn't any mental giant, but he seemed likable. The admirable impulse that had led him to take in a foster son said something important about him.

The fact that he'd then abandoned that boy had to be eating at him.

"But then—" He swallowed. "Who?"

"I have ideas about that, too," Ben said, almost gently. "And I suspect you do, too."

Rod turned his head sharply away and stared straight ahead for a long minute. Then he groaned, and his shoulders slumped. "How can I say anything to Lynne? Jesus." He bent his head and pinched his nose. "She'd never believe it! I tried to convince myself—"

"You can't let Joel be convicted for a crime he didn't commit. He trusts you."

The big shoulders shook on what was almost a sob.

"What do you know, Mr. Carter?"

"The fire," he mumbled, head still hanging. "I heard the door from the garage close and stepped out of the bedroom. He didn't see me. He was putting matches and that can of fire starter back on the mantel."

"He."

"Gavin."

"I see."

"It was a few minutes before any of us smelled smoke or knew there was a fire. How could I say anything?" He lifted his head to gaze imploringly at Ben. "Lynne and I have only been married a few months! He's her kid. She thinks he's damn near godlike. At first, I thought she was right. He's smart, a hell of a wrestler, never sullen like teenagers can be." Carter brooded for a minute. "When he and Joel didn't hit off, I thought it was Joel."

"But you don't anymore."

With back bowed and shoulders rounded, Rod Carter looked diminished. Ben suspected that, in his own eyes, he was. He'd lied to himself for the sake of household peace, or maybe so he wasn't looking at his wife's back when he got into bed at night. All understandable, if not admirable.

But now he shook his head. "He's...sneaky." His voice was low, defeated. "I don't like him, or the way he treats his mother sometimes."

"I interviewed former neighbors of your wife and her son. I heard some ugly stories. I suspect that, deep down inside, she knows what he's capable of."

Carter's forehead creased. "She's always so... perky around him. You know? Jumps right in on his side if he complains about anyone. Insists he's always right. The best."

"On some level, she might be afraid of him," Ben suggested.

Carter looked appalled. "God."

"I understand why you feel torn. This can't be easy for you. Even so, I'm going to ask that you not retreat from what you've told me. For Joel's sake, if for no other reason. I'm also going to ask you not to say anything at all to Lynne or Gavin until I've acted on this information." He hardened his voice. "It is absolutely essential that neither have any warning. Do you understand?"

He squeezed his eyes closed and his Adam's apple bobbed. "Yeah," he said gruffly. "I understand." He huffed out a breath. "I don't know what this is going to do to Lynne."

"It can't help but be tough on her. She'll need you."

"Need me?" Carter's incredulity was plain. "More likely, she'll blame me."

"If her son battered an old man to death, he has to be stopped."

Rod bent forward again, elbows braced on his thighs. Pain was apparent in every line of his beefy body. "I know. God." His voice rose in something like anger. "Just do what you have to, all right?"

"I will." Ben flicked off the recorder and rose to his feet, feeling pity as he looked down at a man reduced by the choice he'd made. "Thank you for your honesty, Mr. Carter," he said quietly, and walked away.

As Ben returned to his vehicle, he checked his watch. He wanted to believe Rod Carter would keep his word—and his mouth shut. Ben wasn't a 100 percent convinced, however. He doubted Rod would call his wife this afternoon. He'd probably be glad to get back to work, to be able to put off facing the consequences of his admissions to a police detective. Once he was home, though, faced with his new wife...all bets were off.

Which meant Ben needed a warrant in hand and to be ready to serve it by the time Rod and his wife got off work.

As he drove, he called Don Cavender, the assistant DA, who agreed to be available. Twenty minutes later, he was listening to the recording.

"That should do it," he agreed. "Poor sucker. The wife's not going to take it well."

Cavender had a son and daughter, Ben knew. The girl was a freshman or sophomore in high school, he thought. Yeah, if anyone would understand what Lynne Carter faced, he would.

"Probably not." Ben grimaced. "What parent would?"

"My prediction is, she won't accept it," Cavender said flatly.

That was Ben's take, too. She'd fight tooth and nail for her perfect son. Her new marriage would soon be history. Rod had been right; she'd convince herself he'd lied because she couldn't think the worst of her precious son.

The prosecutor promised to let him know the minute he had a warrant signed.

Back at the sheriff's department headquarters, Ben was relieved to find Seth at his desk. He could have taken someone else with him to serve the warrant, but Seth had already been in on this, and Ben trusted him.

He explained, and Seth nodded.

"Thank God. And I don't say that lightly." He grunted. "Usually I don't approve, but in this case, I hope the district attorney's office decides to try him as an adult. I don't like the idea of him ever getting out of prison."

Picturing an older, tougher, embittered Gavin Shaffer walking out, a free man, was enough to send a chill up Ben's spine. Season a sociopath with a good, long stretch in the pen, then let him loose on society. That was a recipe for horror.

He wanted to call Eve, but couldn't let himself. They weren't home free yet; Kylie's testimony and Rod's—if he stuck to his guns—should be enough to get Joel off the hook. But to convict Gavin? Not a chance. They needed tangible evidence. And Ben was all too well aware that Gavin had the brains to have ensured there wouldn't be any to find.

What Ben was counting on was the boy's arrogance. He'd set up Joel, and at every step his mother and stepfather bought in—or at least had appeared to. That would make the kid even cockier, sure no one would ever consider him. He might have enjoyed the process enough to already be plotting the downfall of someone else who'd annoyed him.

Ben couldn't settle. He didn't usually get antsy, but this case had become personal for him. Because of Eve, sure, but also because he didn't like being played. First he wandered over to pour a cup of coffee he didn't drink. Then he prowled until Barb Asher, the sole female detective, scowled at him. "Go pace somewhere else! You're making me crazy."

He dropped into his desk chair and managed to stay there for five minutes before he shot back to his feet. When Seth glanced at him, Ben said, "I'll be—"

His phone rang.

"Got it," Cavender said with satisfaction.

Seeing Ben's fierce grin, Seth rose to his feet.

"We're on our way," Ben said.

THE TIMING WORKED FINE. Gavin must have done something with friends after school, because Ben saw him parking and going in the house as they turned onto his street. The garage door stood open and Lynne's car was there, but apparently Rod hadn't made it home yet.

Ben parked behind Gavin's car, blocking it in, and he and Seth moved fast. Seth stood out of sight while Ben rang the doorbell.

Lynne came to the door. The moment she saw him, fear transformed her face.

"I need to speak to Gavin, Mrs. Carter," Ben said. "Right now."

"Gavin?" she called.

Her son appeared from the kitchen. He was cool enough not to react visibly, but he took a step back. "You want to talk to me? Let me put my stuff in the bedroom first."

"No." Ben crossed the threshold. "I need you to come here right now."

"I don't understand," his mother said.

"This is bullshit!" Gavin announced. "If I want to go to my room, I'm going to my room."

"I'm sure we can straighten everything out…" Lynne began.

"Mrs. Carter, I have a warrant to search Gavin's bedroom, car, personal possessions like his pack, and his school locker. I need him to stay in sight while we conduct that search."

Gavin broke away and took off toward his bedroom. Seth was right behind him. The kid screamed invectives as Seth bent his arm behind him and pushed him back into the living room. Out of the corner of his eye, Ben saw Lynne, backed up to a wall, press her fingers to her lips.

"Mrs. Carter. I need to ask you to look over the warrant."

"But…you arrested Joel. The two boys didn't even *like* each other! Gavin never would have co-operated with Joel in doing mean things like that. Why would you need to look at Gavin's room?"

Mean things? Like slamming a baseball bat into a man's head? They all heard another vehicle pull into the driveway.

Lynne cried, "Rod!" and turned to him the minute he appeared, but then her mouth formed an O and she backed up when she saw his face. He'd aged today. Weariness, guilt and resolution combined.

"I'm sorry," he said to his wife, and turned to Ben, who felt some admiration. The guy hadn't crumpled, after all.

He perused the warrant briefly and handed it back with a nod that set Gavin off again.

"We'll have to cuff Gavin and put him in the

back of our car if he can't sit quietly and allow us to work," Ben said, raising his voice to be heard over the screamed obscenities.

Rod turned to him and snapped, "Sit!'

"I don't have to," the boy snarled.

Rod looked at Ben. "Do it."

His wife began to scream at him. Seth pulled out plastic cuffs and had Gavin face against the wall. Then he walked him out, leaving Ben to make sure the mother didn't rush to her boy's bedroom to take care of whatever it was he didn't want them to find.

Returning, Seth said, "I'll take the car."

Rod handed over his own keychain. "I have a spare for his car."

Lynne stared at him in shock. "What are you *doing*? You said he'd be your son, and you're letting them treat him this way?"

Anguish flickered in his eyes. "And I'd expect a son of mine to be a half decent human being and to cooperate with the law."

Accompanied by Rod, Ben took Gavin's book bag to his bedroom. Rod stayed in the bedroom doorway watching. Snapping on gloves, Ben first went through the bag, but found nothing out of the ordinary except a baggie of marijuana, which he held up for Rod to see. Marijuana was still illegal for minors in Washington state. Under normal circumstances, Ben might have pretended he hadn't seen it. It wasn't a priority for law enforcement anymore unless someone using was also driving and clearly impaired.

The room was neat, which made his job easier. He pulled back covers, looked under the pillow and mattress, and then under the bed itself. Dresser drawers held only clothes, which didn't surprise him; chances were Lynne put away his clean clothes, neatly folded. Desk drawers held a more interesting jumble, including a roll of twine that was a match for the twine used to hang the cat from Clement Rowe's eaves. As he lifted it out of the drawer, he heard a pained sound from Rod. Ben placed it in an evidence envelope, as he did the rolling papers to go with the marijuana. Schoolwork, textbooks. Condoms. Lots of scrawled notes—he'd leave those for now and come back to them.

Once he opened the closet doors, he proceeded methodically, starting with the shoes. Those he examined carefully. High-top Converse, cleats for baseball or soccer, dress shoes, sandals. Gavin had been wearing typical athletic shoes; all else failing, Ben intended to look at those, too. Crouching, he saw a duffel bag. It was limp enough to be mostly empty, but he could see something clunky in there. He set it on the bed and unzipped, to see an old, battered pair of athletic shoes similar to what Gavin had been wearing.

Ben's pulse took a jump. The shoes were stained: by grass, and by streaks of something that had dried to a rust color. When he turned them over, he saw more of the crumbling rusty substance caught deep in the treads. Ben knew dried blood when he saw it. Gavin had wiped them off, then shoved them out of sight.

Gotcha, Ben thought, but didn't say out of deference to the man watching silently from the door. When Ben glanced over, though, he saw that Rod had fixed a horrified stare at the shoes.

Ben bagged them and went back to searching.

He didn't find any bloody clothes, which didn't surprise him. Those could be gotten rid of in a Dumpster behind a business or a garbage can set out at the curb a mile away from home. He might be questioned about the shoes, however, if he tried to wear one of his good pairs to mow, say. He'd probably figured he could hose them off on a sunny day and just hadn't done it yet.

Arrogance.

Seth appeared, shaking his head. Then he spotted the brown paper bag open on the bed and looked in to see the shoes. His eyebrows rose. At Ben's request, he took a closer look at the desk, even pulling it out to check behind it, and slid Gavin's laptop into a bag.

Rod started forward a step. "Why are you taking that? He probably has school assignments on it."

"We'll need to make a copy of the contents, Mr. Carter," Seth said politely. "It's not uncommon for teenagers to write what they're thinking, if only for their own satisfaction. And, of course, we'll need access to the social media sites he frequents."

"Oh, God," Rod groaned.

Finally, they thanked him. Ben explained that they would be releasing Gavin, and that it was his parents' responsibility to ensure he didn't take off.

Ben let Seth go ahead to deal with the little creep, and paused himself on the front doorstep. Lynne seemed to have frozen in place. Ben would have felt more pity for her if he hadn't seen Rowe's battered body.

At his cop-neutral best, he explained that they would also search Gavin's school locker first thing in the morning, and would be in touch to let Rod and Lynne know whether anything of interest had been found.

Jaws clenched, Rod nodded.

"Thank you for your cooperation. I'm sorry you've had to go through this experience."

As if they'd both just been in a car accident, they stared at him without much comprehension. Rod put an arm around his wife. She didn't seem to have noticed.

Ben stepped aside to let Gavin pass him and enter the house. The boy's burning stare promised retribution.

Evidence bags stowed in the trunk, he and Seth got in the unmarked unit and sat for a moment.

"I owe Eve a profound apology," Seth said into the silence. "That kid makes my skin crawl."

"Oh, yeah." Ben had reached to start the engine when he felt a punch of relief. "He kept the shoes."

They grinned at each other like a couple of fools.

"WHAT? YOU GOT A search warrant? How?" Eve demanded.

Midday, Ben had called to say he might not get free this evening, but ten minutes ago, he'd buzzed to ask her to let him in. When she opened the door to him, he had a jubilant grin on his face. His first words were, "I think we have him, Eve."

"Gavin?"

"Who else?"

He grabbed her and swung her in a circle. Laughing when he set her down, Eve sobered. "Are you sure?"

Ben explained what they'd found—and what they hadn't found. Although tomorrow was Saturday, the principal was meeting him at 6:00 a.m. to allow him to search the locker.

"Can't believe he'd have stashed bloody clothes there, though. And if he had, I'm betting he disposed of them when he heard I was right there at the school this week, still asking questions."

"Joel?"

Ben shook his head. "We have to wait to be

sure that's human blood on the shoes, and, if so, that it's Rowe's blood."

Eve hugged herself. "How soon?"

"Prelim? By Monday for sure. We'll know what type it is. If that's a match with Rowe's, they'll look at DNA. I think the blood type alone is enough for me to arrest Gavin. Given the witness statements I also have, I want him in custody."

She gave herself a little shake. She hated to imagine what Gavin was thinking, or what he was capable of doing when cornered.

"Have you eaten?"

"No, but you don't have to feed me."

"Don't be silly."

She got as far as the kitchen before she came to a sudden stop. "Wait. You never said how you persuaded a judge to sign a warrant. I thought they were refusing."

Ben half sat on a stool. "Rod Carter."

What he told her made her sad. She'd already been disappointed in Rod, but this... Eve shook her head.

"How could he keep something like that to himself?"

Ben's blue eyes never left her face. "I think he'd convinced himself that the fact Gavin pulled one of the 'pranks'—and I use that word advisedly—didn't mean he'd actually killed a man."

"But he was okay with thinking Joel had?" she said, still steamed.

"He came through in the end."

Eve huffed a sigh. "Fine."

Ben chuckled. "You saw Joel today?"

"Yes. He looks defeated. Do you think his scholarship offer will be withdrawn after this?"

"Not if he's released when the real culprit is arrested. Even if his first choice school releases him, someone else will want him." He hesitated. "This experience is something else he'll have to live with, though."

"Now he knows how it feels to be incarcerated like his father. And it's so unfair!"

He didn't say, *Shit happens*. They both knew that well enough.

"Maybe we're celebrating too soon," she said suddenly. "I mean, you don't know for sure. What if the blood is from, I don't know, the cat? Or it's the wrong blood type?"

"That's one reason I don't want any of this to get to Joel," he admitted.

She nodded, but said softly, "I just want to be waiting when they release him. To hug him and say, it was all a mistake. You know?"

Ben could look so hard sometimes, unfeeling, and yet he'd turn around and let her see tenderness instead. The contrast was so striking, Eve wondered if she'd ever entirely understand him.

The gaze that rested on her now held sympathy. Softness. "I do know," he murmured.

The timer dinged and she removed the garlic bread from the oven, putting it on a plate and giving it to him.

He thanked her, then said, "Eve...do you have a washer and dryer in your unit?"

"Actually, I do." Warmth spread through her veins. "Now, why would you want to know that?"

"It crossed my mind to invite myself to spend the night. Only then I remembered I've been wearing the same clothes for two straight days already."

Leaning back against the kitchen counter, she crossed her arms. "I do believe we could wash them, Detective. Of course, that would leave you without anything at all to wear."

Ben gave her a wicked grin. "Would the sight of me naked disturb you?"

She had to laugh. "It might. In a good way, of course."

Two nights in a row, she thought. When Ben let down his guard, he didn't hold back.

Wow. Was she ready to consider living with him?

If Eve had discovered anything about herself amidst all the turmoil since Hope returned, it was that she needed to feel secure. Which made her breathless and edgy at the idea of taking what would be a gigantic risk if he wasn't being entirely truthful about how he felt about his ex.

But there he sat: big, vital, sexy, smart, kind in unexpected ways, and she knew she was kidding herself. The answer was yes—except that she was still scared, too.

CHAPTER SIXTEEN

FRIDAY MIDDAY, BEN had had to call Nicole and ask to either change weekends or see if he could pick Rachel up Saturday morning, shortening his weekend with her. "I'm involved in something at work," he'd said briefly.

On the rare occasions in the past when he'd had to ask for a change, she hadn't been able to resist being snippy. He waited for her usual. *But of course it's different when* you're *the one wanting to change our arrangement*. Instead, all she said was that she had plans Saturday night and would prefer he went ahead with this weekend.

When he arrived Saturday morning to pick up Rachel, she was bouncing with excitement. No surprise, she clutched her current favorite doll.

"I'll walk you out," Nicole said, pulling Rachel's small pink suitcase. His mouth opened and then closed. She might be pissed to see that Eve was with him, but this had to happen sooner or later.

Once they stepped outside, he released his daughter's hand so she could dash to his SUV, where Eve was already hopping out to greet her.

The two women took a long look at each other. Eve smiled and called, "Hi," then turned to open the back door and help Rach climb in.

Ben braced himself and glanced at Nic. She hadn't moved, maybe hadn't even blinked. The sadness on her face took his breath away.

"Nicole?"

She seemed to shake herself and then looked at him. Her smile had an odd twist. "You could have said."

"I'm sorry." He groped for words. "I didn't think meeting Eve would bother you."

"I didn't realize she'd be with you." Her eyes searched his with unexpected intensity. "It's funny, too, because I'd been thinking—" She shook her head. "Don't listen to me. You'd better get going. All Rachel can talk about is flowers." She even smiled before she turned to go back into the apartment building.

Just for a moment, he watched her go. The pang he felt might be pity. Even so, he had an impulse to go after her, find out what was wrong.

I'd been thinking... What?

What difference did it make? he asked himself impatiently. Eve and Rach were waiting.

During the few long strides that took him to the SUV, he hoped Eve hadn't thought anything of his brief conversation with Nicole, then frowned. Because they shared a daughter, he and Nicole were forever linked. That was something with which Eve had to deal.

Traffic was a bitch after they crossed I-5 and headed west into the heart of the tulip country, but Rachel was happy to chatter and, eventually, play some kind of word game with Eve. He laughed too much to be impatient with tourists who braked in the middle of the road so they could lean out to take pictures of sweeps of scarlet and yellow and purple.

RoozenGaarde was one of the big bulb farms and, Ben had been told, had a particularly spectacular display garden. He followed an attendant's directions and parked in a huge field across from the garden. Getting out, he stepped into a mud-filled rut and grimaced. Despite gravel, intermittent rain and sunshine and a battering from multiple vehicles had left the field a mess. Could have been worse, he reflected; he hadn't planned an alternate activity if it had rained today.

It only being the second weekend in April, quite a few of the tulips weren't in bloom yet. Enough were, though, along with a huge variety of daffodils, hyacinths in purples, pinks and whites, and some other, dainty flowers grown from bulbs he didn't recognize. Eve had taken a catalog when they arrived, and each patch of flowers in the beds intersected by winding grass paths was labeled.

"Now I really wish I had a garden," she grumbled. "I suppose I could put a few bulbs in a pot on my minuscule balcony, but it doesn't get much direct sun, so… Oh! Look at that double tulip! Isn't that glorious?"

Ben wandered, smiled and enjoyed Eve's and Rachel's enjoyment. Both had worn colors as bright as anything nature created, as if in anticipation. The flowers were pretty. His daughter was pretty. Eve was gorgeous. The hyacinths had an extraordinary, sweet fragrance that filled the air. He didn't have any desire to know each hybrid of any of the flowers by name, but might like having a garden down the line. *If Eve wanted one,* he found himself thinking, imagining a house, a swing set in the backyard. And, yeah, he felt nothing but relaxed acceptance and even anticipation about where they were heading.

He'd succumbed without much of a fight, he realized, in part because he hadn't liked the bachelor lifestyle. He had no hankering to sample a different woman a week.

Gaze resting on Eve, he smiled. He couldn't seem to get enough of her, in bed or out.

Only the memory of the expression on Nicole's face shadowed his mood.

Eventually they strolled through the gift shop, and they chose two ceramic pots, each planted with a hyacinth bursting with buds. One for each of his ladies.

Rachel stared at hers. "I bet my bedroom will smell really good when it's blooming, huh?"

"I know it will." Eve tipped her head gently against his shoulder in thanks. "At this time of year, I usually buy one at the grocery store for my windowsill, but I'll bet this one will be bigger and better."

At the last minute, he frowned. "Let's pick out one for your mom," he told Rachel. He'd call it a peace offering.

"That's a good idea," Eve said. If she was bothered, he couldn't tell. "I'll get one for my mother, too."

If it were him, he'd just grab one, but as it was, he and his daughter had a long discussion about Nicole's favorite colors with him aware of Eve listening. Rach waffled until he finally grabbed one and said, "Purple. Yours is pink, this way you'll have one of each."

"Okay," she said, looking satisfied.

They headed back to the SUV, but after they'd carefully set their pots on the floor, he suggested a walk along the next field, filled with rows of daffodils in brilliant yellow bloom.

Rachel grabbed his hand. "Yay! I'm not tired yet. At all!"

Probably used for tractors or harvesting equipment as well as giving visitors opportunities for photos, a dirt track paralleled the field. Rachel raced ahead. Ben kept an eye on her, but also appreciated a few minutes to talk to Eve.

He took her hand in his. "Having fun?"

Her smile had an extra glow. Sunlight gleamed off her hair and showed gold flecks in her warm brown eyes. "Of course I am," she declared. "Aren't you?"

"Yeah. This is a good day." Ahead, Rachel had caught up with a family walking their dog and had apparently been given permission to pet what looked like a yellow lab. Seeing the flapping tail, Ben let go of any parental concern. "Hey, have you talked to your mom again?" he asked Eve.

Eve had told him about their last conversation. Not a lot, but enough. Ben had been careful not to say what he thought, but was beginning to wonder if he should. He didn't like taking the chance that he might hurt Eve, though. He'd done that once, and hated remembering the expression on her face.

She didn't answer right away, but her expression had dimmed. "No. I mean, it's only been a couple of days."

He gave her hand what he hoped was a reassuring squeeze.

"I just want her to, oh, acknowledge that I have grounds for feeling the way I do. Is that so unreasonable?"

Ben hesitated. Here was his chance. She'd asked, right? "I have to admit," he said, picking his words carefully and trying to keep his tone nonjudgmental, "I don't completely understand what you're going for. Do you need your mother to admit she invested so much of herself in grief, she shortchanged you? Or is it something else?"

Eve quit walking. He turned his head to see she was staring at him, her lips parted as if she'd opened her mouth to say something that never popped out. Was she mad? He couldn't tell.

Then she moaned. "That's what I've been asking for, isn't it?"

"I don't know."

"I told myself I needed her to understand, but that wasn't it at all." Her voice was so soft, she might have been talking to herself, not him. "I wanted Mom to grovel because she was so sorry she'd hurt me." Her laugh lacked all humor. "And that's ridiculous." Her head turned suddenly until she spotted Rachel, giggling now as she hugged the dog.

Ben discovered how much he liked the fact that she, too, was keeping an eye on his daughter.

"Ridiculous?" he prodded after a minute.

"Why would I need that from her? Oh, God. Why would I even *ask* for it? I was…so lucky to have them. My parents. And here I've been— what?—wanting to make sure they loved *me* the most? How childish is that?"

Ben chuckled and bent his head to kiss her lightly. "Completely normal, I suspect."

"But I'm a grown-up!" she wailed.

"In theory," he agreed, tongue in cheek.

Eve punched his belly, making him laugh. Then she gave a huff. "I'm an idiot."

"No, you're not. You just needed to know you were really wanted."

Her eyes searched his for a moment. "Of course I was," she murmured. The smile that took shape and slowly bloomed was more beautiful than any flower in the display garden.

"And are," he said, voice low and gritty.

He saw only her. The flicker as her pupils dilated then shrank, the faint quiver of her lips, the sweet curves of her cheeks and forehead. Astonishment was supplanted by hope. Or was it belief? Only a distant awareness that Rachel would be rejoining them any minute kept him from snatching Eve into his arms and kissing her voraciously.

She swallowed. "Thank you," she whispered.

He had to clear his throat. "For?"

Eve's smile took on an impish quality. "Wanting me."

"Will you spend the night?"

He saw resistance on her face even before her lips shaped the word "No. You know we shouldn't until…"

"Until what?"

"I suppose…" Her forehead crinkled. "There's a commitment Rachel can trust in."

He let out a hard breath. "I know you're right. But, damn."

"Daddy!"

Ben jumped. He hadn't even seen his kid coming.

"You're not supposed to say *that* word," she chided him.

From somewhere, he found a laugh. "You're right. Oh, darn. Is that better?"

"Uh-huh. Did you see the dog, Daddy? He *licked* me." Her smile became sly. "I wish *I* could get a dog. Mommy says we can't, but *you* could keep my dog for me."

Ben heard Eve laughing. "Good try, kiddo," he told his daughter. "But I work too many hours, and I don't have a yard."

She scrunched up her face. "Oh, poop."

He tipped his head. "Is that an okay word?"

"Poop?" She giggled. "Of course it is. There's a book, you know. It's called *Everyone Poops.* Really," she assured him, seeing his expression. "My teacher read it to us last year, in kindergarten."

"Good God," he muttered.

Rachel decided she was tired and needed him to carry her. He had been pleasantly surprised she'd made it this long, and crouched so she could clamber onto his back. To her delight, he jogged toward the parking lot, circling back a couple of times to Eve, whose face was lit with laughter.

Beautiful. His heart constricted painfully. Thank God neither Eve nor Rachel seemed to notice.

He'd promised pizza on the way home, but wasn't surprised to look in his rearview mirror and see that Rachel had nodded off, her neck bent awkwardly.

They'd just reached the city limits when his phone vibrated. He glanced at it, and tension gripped him. The caller was Jen Nysether, the lab tech from CSI he knew had Gavin's shoes. "You have something this fast?" he said.

"I do," Jen told him. "It's blood, and it's a match for Clement Rowe's. As it happens, only about two percent of the population have B-negative blood. We'll run the DNA for confirmation, but I think this is enough of a green light for you to bring in the owner of the shoes."

"I owe you one." He ended the call to see Eve watching him. "The blood type is a match," he said.

"Oh." She closed her eyes for a moment. "Oh, thank God."

"I have a neighbor who will watch Rach." He kept his voice down, hoping she wouldn't hear. In the rearview mirror, he saw that her eyes had opened to half-mast.

Eve shook her head. "Why don't you drop us off at my place? I'll take her out for pizza, or order one in. She can use my bed if she needs a nap."

"You don't mind?"

"Of course not. I have fun with her. Plus…" Sparks lit her eyes. "I assume you'll be arresting *him*."

He allowed himself a smile that might have scared her under other circumstances. "I will."

"You won't go alone?" Eve sounded anxious.

"No, I'll call Seth, and if he's tied up, I'll find somebody else."

"When this is all over," Eve declared, "I'm going to track down Officer Pruitt and give him a piece of my mind."

Ben laughed.

Rachel protested until she learned she'd get her pizza and could stay with Eve until Daddy was done. When Ben dropped the two of them off, Eve gave him a last look.

"You'll let me know? So Joel can be released?"

"I will," he promised.

Eve hurried into juvenile hall, relieved when she spotted Ben and Seth but no Joel. It had taken her a while to drop Rachel at her parents' house, along with one hyacinth in bud.

Both men turned when they heard her footsteps.

"Does he know yet?" she asked, sounding breathless after her mad dash from the parking lot.

Ben grinned. "Nope. We figured you could give him the news."

"Thank you." She lifted her face for his kiss, then blushed when she remembered Seth was there. "I have a problem, though. The Santoses have filled his bed. In a pinch they'll put an air mattress on the floor for tonight. I have a couple of other calls in, but—"

"I can take him," Seth said.

Eve knew her mouth had dropped open. "But…"

"I'm licensed." He looked a little embarrassed. "There was that kid last year. No, I guess he wasn't yours. But, uh, he needed short-term placement. I imagine the license is still good."

"You did say something." She only vaguely remembered, except his willingness to take in a kid in need had made him even more appealing to her when they started dating.

"Why didn't I know about this?" Ben asked.

"It's not something we usually do," Seth muttered, "so I didn't advertise it. He was only with me a week or two."

Relieved, Eve said, "If you can keep Joel until I find a place for him, that would be great."

He moved his shoulders, looking uncomfortable. "No, I talked to Bailey, and she's good with this. We want him to stay with us until he leaves for college."

Of course Bailey would be good with it. Eve was disconcerted to feel the sting of tears in her eyes. Ben wrapped a long arm around her. "Hey. You okay?"

"Yes. Just…" She offered Seth a wobbly smile. "This is amazing. Thank you."

"Ben tells me he's a good kid. I've watched

him play ball a few times. What did you say he's decided on, the U of O?"

"Yes. Unless…"

His expression hardened. "I'll take 'em on if they try to weasel out."

She had to hug him, murmuring a "Thank you" in his ear. He hugged her back. Then she left the two of them waiting and went in to get Joel.

When he shambled into the conference room, he looked scared. "I didn't think you'd be back so fast. Did something happen?"

"Something did." Eve smiled broadly at him. "Detective Kemper arrested Gavin for murder. We just need to do some paperwork, and you're out of here."

He burst into tears. Ignoring the guard, she put her arms around the hulking boy who had such a sweet nature, he'd gotten to her in a way most of her kids didn't.

Eventually, Joel swiped his tears on his shirt-sleeve. "Do I go back to the Santoses'?"

"No, I have a permanent placement for you." She still had trouble believing it. "You've met Detective Chandler, haven't you?"

Joel drew his head back, alarm in his dark eyes. "He was there when I was arrested."

"Yes, but he's been helping Detective Kemper prove you didn't have anything to do with Mr. Rowe's death." She smiled. "My sister, Bailey, is going to marry him. She's in college in LA, but as soon as she graduates next month, she'll be up here. You'll be living with both of them."

"But... I'm turning eighteen in less than a month."

"Seth wants you to stay until you leave for college."

He battled tears again, his face working furiously. "Really?" he finally got out.

"Really." She squeezed his arm. "What do you say? Shall we blow this pop stand?"

A huge grin spread on his face. "I don't know what a pop stand is, but I really want to get out of here."

"Then let's do it."

THE LAWSONS HAD said Rachel could spend the night, but Ben and Eve decided to pick her up anyway.

On the way, Eve mumbled, "I wonder if Mom would have let *her* sleep in Hope's bedroom."

Startled, Ben glanced at her. "Did you want to?"

Her face went through some contortions. "Well...not really. I mean, I would have been afraid to touch anything. It was supposed to stay *exactly* the same, you know." She brooded for a minute, then grinned at him. "I really wanted that bed, though."

She had to explain that it was a canopy bed, and then what a canopy bed was, but finally he got the gist and gave the engine a little more gas. Forget dawdling.

"God, I hope your mom doesn't show Rachel that bed."

Eve laughed. "Because you'd have to get her one."

"She has princess aspirations. You know that."

"And the room is pink, too. Really, really pink."

"You're scaring me." Although he wouldn't mind painting Rachel's bedroom, assuming he was allowed by the rental agreement. He'd have to check.

Karen and Rachel answered the door together. They looked really happy, and something smelled good.

"We baked," his daughter announced.

Ben inhaled. "What did you bake?"

"Cookies! Two kinds," she added with satisfaction. "Chocolate chip, 'cuz those are my favorites, and some that are really dark."

"Ginger-molasses," Karen explained.

Eve moaned. "Those are *my* favorites."

Her mother smiled at her. "I know they are. That's why I made them."

"Oh, Mom." Suddenly Eve dropped her bag and flung her arms around Karen.

Ben put a hand on his astonished daughter's shoulder and nudged her gently toward the living room, where Kirk had risen to his feet and was watching his wife and daughter. He wrenched his gaze away to smile at Ben and then Rachel.

"You've got my wife dreaming of grandkids, you know."

"Is that like sugarplum fairies?" Ben asked.

Kirk chuckled. "I'm afraid so."

Ben's senses were still attuned to Eve. He strained to hear her low words.

"I'm sorry, Mom. So sorry."

He couldn't make out what her mother said in response.

"I've been really silly." Eve's voice hitched. "I always felt loved. I did. Can you forgive all my whining?"

More murmurs. Kirk was looking past him, Ben saw, and finally he had to turn to look, too. Eve and her mother clung together. He could see only Karen's face, wet with tears.

Emotion balled in his throat.

"Daddy?" Rachel tugged at his hand. Her face was tilted up, and he could tell she didn't understand why neither man was paying attention to her. *Because she's completely secure,* he realized, remembering what Eve had said that once. *Whatever Nic and I did wrong, it wasn't this. Our daughter knows how much she's loved.*

Eve, he thought, was beginning to know the same.

"Karen said we could all have some cookies. Do you want one?"

"Yeah." He smiled and bent low to whisper in her ear. "Maybe ten."

She giggled in delight. Out of the corner of his eye, Ben saw that the two women had separated, and that Eve's face was wet, too. She was also smiling, though, tremulous but somehow radiant at the same time.

A band tightened around his chest.

She gave a sniff. "Cookies, huh? I'd better go mop up so I don't make mine soggy."

Rach thought that was funny.

He glanced at Kirk, to see a look in his eyes as he watched his wife that was meant to be private. How many years had those two been married? The constriction in Ben's chest tightened. He wanted what they had.

They all ended up sitting around the dining room table drinking milk and eating cookies, with more heaped on platters in the middle. The two women had puffy eyes, but every so often they smiled almost shyly at each other. Kirk didn't have much to say, but he never did. Ben made some effort, and his motormouth daughter filled any silences.

And, damn, but those cookies were good.

Somehow, he wasn't surprised to find himself clutching a plastic container full of them when it came time for the three of them to leave.

Having to drop Eve off at her place was the

one bummer. He and Rach walked her up. Rachel hugged Eve goodbye, and he kissed her lightly.

"Will you come over tomorrow?" he asked.

Her eyes searched his. "Do you want me to?"

"Do we want Eve to come over tomorrow?" he asked Rachel.

"Can she?" She bounced a couple of times. "Can she, Daddy?"

"We want you," he said, hearing the extra huskiness in his voice.

"Okay." Pink-cheeked, she tore her gaze from his to smile at Rachel. "Do you like tacos?"

Rachel did.

"I'll bring the ingredients for lunch," Eve promised.

"Deal," Ben said, backing away. He really hated to go. "You're sure…?"

Her rolled eyes said she knew what he was asking. "I'm sure." Her door closed firmly, leaving him and Rachel on the other side of it.

He looked down at her. "Guess we're on our own."

Retaining her grip on his hand, she said, "It's practically tomorrow, Daddy."

He grinned at her, gave a last glance at the door, and said, "You're right."

CHAPTER SEVENTEEN

WHEN THE KNOCK came on Ben's door, Rachel panicked. "I don't have Elsa! Where's Elsa?"

Elsa, Ben was all too well aware, was her doll based on the queen from the movie *Frozen*. The one she'd watched eighty-nine million times. She had the Anna doll, too, but Elsa was her favorite. Elsa's hair was the same color as hers, she'd explained, plus Elsa wore a crown.

Princess aspirations.

"Go," he said. "Find her."

Laughing, Eve said, "I'll help." The two of them headed for the bedroom. They would do better finding Elsa than he would. He hadn't seen the doll since that morning, if then. He'd ended up going into work for a few hours today, partly to meet with the attorney Lynne Carter had hired for her son. The son who, reportedly, had attacked a guard last night. Ben had noticed that the attorney repeatedly referred to his client's mother, but never to the stepfather.

Eve and his daughter had seemed pleased when he made it home an hour ago, but he didn't have the feeling they'd languished in misery without him, either.

Ben let Nicole in. She was her usual put-together self. She never went anywhere without makeup that enhanced her vividly blue eyes and darkened the arch of her eyebrows. She still had the figure for pale blue skinny jeans, with which she wore heels. He'd never gotten that, but she'd insisted her legs looked short without heels. Her hair was loose and shining. He had the thought that she hadn't changed that much from the girl he'd fallen in love with. Whereas, he thought wryly, he didn't look much like the skinny, tongue-tied boy he'd been the first time he set eyes on her.

"Hey," he said. "We were all ready, but Rach doesn't know where Elsa is. God forbid she go home without her."

Nic made a face. "I wouldn't hear about anything else."

"I doubt she's really lost." He felt strangely awkward. "More like momentarily forgotten."

She nodded. For a moment, neither said anything. Should he invite her to sit down?

But then, she fastened her blue eyes on him. "Ben, since we have a minute… I've been thinking. A lot." She gave a small shrug. "We have quite a history."

Feeling wary, he didn't know what to say but, "It's true."

"I've been…thinking I blamed you when I felt unhappy, and it wasn't you at all. I'm willing to work on that." Her lips formed a moue. "I know you're dating Eve, but… I miss you." Never looking away from him, she reached up to caress his cheek. Voice soft, aching with regret, she murmured, "Is it too late for us, Ben?"

Momentarily staggered, he didn't move. He grappled with a realization that, not so long ago, that would have had him dropping to his knees in gratitude. Nic wanted him back.

For a moment—no longer—he felt something. Wistful, maybe. It was a shadow of what would once have been a firestorm. This was the woman he'd thought he would love forever.

Now, a familiar if cynical thought sneaked in. Had she liked knowing he still loved her from afar? Was she reacting to the threat she must sense Eve was? Calling him back to heel?

But even that didn't last long. Because the truth was…she'd killed his passionate devotion. Whether she really missed him or not no longer mattered.

He stepped back, so that her hand had to drop to her side. "I'm sorry, Nic." He tried to sound at least a little regretful. "It is too late. You'll always be the mother of my daughter, but—" *Nothing more.* He didn't finish the sentence. Didn't have to.

Oh, hell, he thought suddenly. *Eve.*

He turned to see her standing at the opening to the hall, her expression completely unreadable. Her gaze moved from his face to Nicole's, where it lingered before meeting his again.

"Disaster averted," she said with what he guessed was deliberate lightness. "We found Elsa. Rachel decided she needed to use the bathroom again, though."

God, he hoped she hadn't misinterpreted what she'd likely just heard—or the fact that his ex-wife had been cupping his jaw in her hand.

He held out his own hand to Eve. "Come here. You two haven't officially met."

She took his hand, hers chilly but warming within his grasp. Ben performed the introductions. The two women were polite, although he saw a dangerous flash in Nicole's eyes. He didn't kid himself he was breaking her heart, but he'd stung her pride. There was no getting around that.

Rachel dashed out, saving the day. She remembered the hyacinths and hurried to fetch them from the kitchen windowsill. Nicole at least pretended to appreciate hers. He could tell she didn't like the fervent hug Rachel gave Eve, though. He said his own goodbyes, and then they were gone.

Eve stepped back. "It's time I take off, too," she said, very pleasantly.

She saw astonishment on his face, mixed with something else. Guilt? *Please, not guilt.*

He frowned. "I was hoping we could have dinner."

"Ben, I haven't gotten a blessed thing done this weekend. I really need to do a load or two of laundry and some ironing this evening."

"You iron?"

She found herself laughing at his surprise. What a thing to latch onto out of everything she'd said. "Yes, astonishingly enough, I do."

"Oh." He had a strange expression on his face. "I guess I just need to come out and ask. How much did you overhear of what Nic and I said?"

"Not very much." *I saw her touch you.* Did that count?

"She has it in her head that we should reconcile," he said bluntly.

Dread gripped Eve, even though she thought she knew what he'd told Nicole. *I have to believe,* she thought desperately.

"I...wondered if that's what she was working her way up to," she admitted.

"I've never told you I love you."

"No." It was barely a whisper.

"Only that I want you." Somehow he'd come to be holding her hands in a warm clasp.

"Yes."

"Did you understand what I meant, Eve?"

In an attempt to hide the agony of uncertainty inside, she closed her eyes. "I thought I did."

His lips, warm and soft, touched her forehead. "Then what did I tell Nic?"

Old fears and new collided with the sense of self-worth she had been accepting—a confidence Ben had something to do with. And…was that a smile in his voice?

She took a deep breath and looked at him again, seeing his worry, his…love? What if it was pity? But…she didn't believe that. Couldn't.

"I think—" her voice cracked, but she managed to steady it "—you told her you were sorry, that you're actually madly in love with this spitfire of a woman who keeps you looking beyond the obvious."

Ben laughed, the skin crinkling beside his very blue eyes, the creases in his cheeks deepening. "You're right. I don't think I said *spitfire* and didn't mention anything about you making sure I do my job right, but I did say I was sorry. I told her it was too late."

The relief felt like a flash flood. She took the one step forward that allowed her to lean on him. He groaned and his arms closed around her immediately.

"I was afraid that's why you said you had to go," Ben said hoarsely. "Because you were hurt."

She shook her head. "No. I really do need to do laundry." She hesitated. This was a time for honesty. "I suppose I did think you might want to be alone. If you have any doubts. I mean, you loved her for a long time. And Rachel would really like it if you were back together."

"Maybe." He rubbed his cheek against her hair. "You know Rachel is crazy about you. And *I* realized something yesterday." He waited until Eve tipped her head back so she could see him. "You were right about her. She's amazingly confident. Because Nic and I both love her and give her everything we can. That's one of the things I said to Nic. She'll always be the mother of my daughter."

"And she's a good one, or Rachel wouldn't be so secure." She swallowed. "Which makes me wonder. Remember when I said she might have nothing to give? I had to have been wrong."

But he was shaking his head. "Maybe what you're capable of feeling for your child isn't the same as for a lover or spouse. Nic sees herself in Rachel. I think her most powerful drive is to make sure her daughter has a happier life."

"That…makes sense."

"I worry that won't last." He crooked a smile that smoothed the lines of worry on his face. "If not, Rachel has me." Pause. "Us."

Such a simple word, to be so powerful. *Please, let him mean that,* she prayed.

"The day I met you at Seth's, I parked there in front—remember?—and I helped Rachel out of the backseat. Then I turned around and saw you. You were looking at us—maybe even waiting for us—and my stomach balled up. You've never quite believed I could fall in love with you, have you?"

Her sinuses burned. "It was hard, but... I've been getting there."

"Because I did. I love you, Eve. And I'm hoping a whole lot that I'm not in this alone."

The thread of uncertainty in his voice shook her. Why had she always believed he was the confident one? He'd told her about his mother deserting him. About Nicole leaving him for the thinnest of reasons. Maybe nobody reached their ages unscathed.

And I couldn't have fallen for a man who had, she realized.

"I love you," she said, with all the certainty she could inject into her voice. "I do."

"Damn." This time he squeezed his eyes shut and bent until his forehead just bumped hers. "I was so damn afraid."

She wrapped her arms around him and squeezed, feeling the hard beat of his heart.

"What you said Saturday. About why you couldn't spend the night."

Eve remembered; of course she did. "I don't want to confuse Rachel."

"You were right." His chest moved as he drew a long breath. For courage? "Can we make that commitment, Eve?"

She wanted to ask what kind of commitment he was talking about. Instead, she murmured, "We've only been seeing each other for two months. Are you sure, Ben?"

"I'm sure." He straightened and tugged her toward the sofa, but instead of drawing her down beside him, he pulled her onto his lap. "You have to admit, it's been an eventful two months. We've…gotten a lot deeper in each others' lives than people usually do that fast."

"Hurt each other," she had to say, although he was right.

"I hurt you," he corrected, with that voice as rough as a calloused hand. "I never wanted to."

"You knew enough about me to go for the jugular." Eve didn't like remembering the stiletto sharpness of his accusation.

"But not enough to know how ridiculous I was being." He kissed her gently. "Are we past that?"

Trying to smile, she bobbed her head. "You listened." Did he know how important that was? "You gave Joel back his life."

"You mean, I did my job. With a little help from you."

This smile was a little better. She tucked her head in the crook of his shoulder and neck, and waited.

"We could give Rachel some brothers or sisters," he suggested.

She sat back up again, so abruptly he grimaced and shifted her on his lap.

"What's that supposed to mean?" Eve demanded.

"What do you think it means?"

"I don't know!"

"It means I want you to marry me."

"That's your idea of a proposal?" She tried to scramble off him, but his big hands held her in place.

"No. Of course not. Hold still." When she reluctantly obeyed, he lifted his hands from her hips to cradle her face. "I'm sorry, sweetheart. I was trying not to ask you yet. I figured it was too fast for you. That you need more time to be sure of me. Then my big mouth—" He grunted. "Maybe Rach gets it from me."

Eve pressed her lips together to suppress a smile.

"I just— I was going to ask you to move in with me. Or...me with you." The vulnerability on his almost too handsome face was all she could have wished for. "But I wanted you to know *I'm* sure." His shoulders sagged. "And none of that makes any sense, does it?"

She could no longer resist either the tears or the smile. "It makes complete sense," she said, in a small, choked voice. "And... *I'm* sure, too. Just... I don't want to get married until after Bailey and Seth. Okay?"

"Yeah," he said huskily. "Can I at least buy you a ring?"

"Yes, you may," Eve said primly—just before she pressed her lips to his for the single sweetest kiss of her life.

THEY DECIDED HER apartment was better than his. They agreed, too, that they'd buy a house once they were married. He mentioned a swing set; she confessed to having caught the gardening bug from her mother.

Without any pressure from him, Eve decided it was time to get serious about creating the nonprofit. Getting their act together enough to earn tax-exempt status would be a big job to start with. Then she and her two partners had to build a base of supporters and start writing for grants. Never mind all the little stuff, like coming up with a name, a logo, finding a space that would meet their projected needs. Even with hard work, they were a year or more away from any kind of launch. She'd keep her job until then, and maybe part-time for a while afterward, until they knew they could make it. But Eve was ready for that beginning. When better to change her life?

She and Ben also made the decision to keep mum about their engagement until the following weekend, when Bailey would be in town and they were all invited to the Lawsons' for Sunday dinner.

This was to be Bailey's final weekend visit,

Seth told Ben. "Praise the Lord," he added. He, Eve and her parents were all attending her graduation in May, and after that Bailey would be here for good.

"It's been a long haul," he said gruffly.

"Nine months."

"Since we met."

His expression distant, Seth had to be remembering the day the desk sergeant called to say that a Bailey Smith was here to talk about Hope Lawson. If Hope had never come home, Ben wondered, would he ever have met Eve?

Yeah, he thought. He'd still have arrested Joel. Unless the butterfly effect of them not already knowing each other had changed everything else, too. All he knew for sure was, he'd been hit as hard the first time he saw her as Seth had been when Bailey aka Hope had showed up here, scared, defiant but hungry for family.

As if his thoughts had followed the same path, Seth suddenly focused on Ben. "You and Eve getting anywhere?"

"Yeah," Ben said mildly. "I think so." He grinned. "Bailey demanding an update? You can tell her she has to see for herself."

"You'll be there Sunday?"

"I will. I asked Nic if I could have Rachel again this weekend so she can come, too. Karen and she hit it off big-time." He'd half expected Nicole to revert to her usual attitude, but instead she'd been subdued, that sadness in her voice. And, yeah, he'd still felt a pang, but that was all.

"You know," Seth suggested, "if you married Eve, Rachel would have a grandmother."

Ben's phone rang, saving him from having to comment. He'd already had the same thought. Rachel would love to have a new set of grandparents. His father was fond of her, but not very comfortable with little girls. With Nic having no parents at all... Yeah, a grandma who baked and quilted and grew roses would make a difference for his little girl.

But not as much difference as Eve would. A woman who would fight to the death for "her" kids, Ben thought with satisfaction.

The petite, beautiful, warmhearted woman he loved.

He answered his phone. "Detective Kemper."

EVE LEANED FORWARD until the seat belt cut into her midsection. "Seth and Bailey are already here."

Amused, she saw Ben glance in the rear-view mirror. "If you-know-who hadn't lost Elsa *again*..."

His daughter sniffed. "I know you mean me."

"Who else?" They rolled to a stop at the curb right in front of the Lawsons' modest, well-cared-for rambler. "Here we are," he said.

Rachel unfastened her seat belt in a hurry.

"Karen is nice. She said I can call her that 'stead of Mrs. Lawson. Except maybe now I can call her Grandma. Do you think I can?"

Eve exchanged a smile with Ben before they got out. Now the only challenge would be making their own announcement before his eager daughter made it for them.

Ben rested a hand on her shoulder. "Remember, Eve needs to tell her parents and sister our news herself."

Her forehead crinkled. "Well, she should do it *fast*."

"Hear that?" he murmured in Eve's ear.

She laughed. She'd laughed a lot this week. She felt as if she was walking on air. Ben had brought some of his clothes over and spent every night with her until Friday, when he picked his daughter up for the weekend. Eve had had to work Saturday, so after having dinner with them Friday night and talking with her about their plans, she hadn't seen them again until they arrived for her up a few minutes ago. He'd given notice to his apartment manager, and after this weekend, Rachel would have a bedroom at Eve's.

They started up the driveway together, until Ben abruptly came to a stop. Eve turned to him in surprise, to see him smiling down at her.

One hand still on Rachel's shoulder, he held the other out to Eve. "This is how we met."

"It is." She rose on tiptoe to kiss him lightly, then bent to hug Rachel. "Do you remember?"

She nodded earnestly. "I thought you were so-o pretty."

"I thought so, too," Ben agreed, the crinkles beside his eyes showing his amusement, but there was a glint in his gaze for Eve, too.

The front door opened. Bailey called, "Here we are, dying of impatience, and the three of you are just standing out there!"

Eve hurried the rest of the way to throw her arms around her sister. "And you're still not here for good."

Bailey wrinkled her nose. "I wish. Then I'd be done with finals, too." She greeted Rachel and Ben and led them into the house.

Ben inhaled. "Man, that smells good. What are we having?"

"Pot roast."

"In your honor," Eve said to her sister.

Ben quirked an eyebrow.

"It was my favorite from when I was a kid," Bailey explained. "I think it was when Mom served it that my memories started to come back. Taste is apparently powerful."

Their mother appeared, and soon they were exchanging greetings all around. Joel was here, of course, his discomfiture obvious. Eve was amused to see him sticking close to Dad. Eve tried to keep her left hand tucked out of sight, but knew it wouldn't be long before somebody noticed her ring.

She broke free to hug first her father, then Joel. Suddenly, there was a shriek. Bailey.

"You're wearing a ring!"

Laughing, Eve turned. "I am," she agreed. Ben came to her side and gripped her right hand while she held out her left. Rachel stood on his other side, looking as proud as if she was entirely responsible for the happy ending.

Mom burst into tears and hugged them both. Dad hugged Eve and shook Ben's hand. Seth punched Ben lightly in the shoulder and complained, "You could have told me." Bailey jumped up and down and kissed and hugged them both, too.

In other words, total chaos.

It took them a while to make their way to the dining room. Bailey, Eve and a beaming Rachel helped bring out the food.

After the expected discussion of possible wedding dates and venues, Eve finally had a moment to ask Joel how he was doing.

Alarmed at being the focus of all eyes, he mumbled, "It's really good. I'm mostly caught up with school."

Seth clapped him on the back. "I've put him to slave labor. He's mowed the lawn twice. We're thinking about painting the house this summer."

"I wish I could get a summer job," Joel explained, "but I have to leave to start football practice too early."

Bailey gave her fiancé, then Ben, a fulminating stare. "I can't believe either of you thought for a minute Joel would hurt anyone."

Joel blushed again.

"I could use some temporary help at the shop once you've graduated," Kirk said unexpectedly. "Probably only part-time, but if you'd be interested…"

Joel appeared stunned. "Really? I mean, that would be great. If you're not, you know, hiring me to be nice when you don't really need anyone."

"Oh, I'll have work for you," Kirk warned.

Seth grinned across the table at Joel. "You know the Lawsons have adopted you now, don't you?"

Joel's dark eyes widened. "It's, like, just for this summer."

Seth shook his head. "Joel, as far as I'm concerned, you're ours."

"Of course you are," Bailey said firmly. "Holidays, summers, whenever you need a place to go. That's what I always wanted."

Poor Joel was about ready to cry.

"Of course, we'll expect tickets to every U of O home game," Seth added with a grin.

Karen beamed at him, then Rachel. "What a wonderful head start! Two grandchildren already."

Joel looked stunned, then ducked his head and

took what he probably imagined was a surreptitious swipe at his cheek. Eve felt tears gathering, too.

"And you know," Seth added, "once you have Karen Lawson on your side, man, you have a fierce defender for life. This is the woman who never once gave up on finding her daughter."

Bailey reached a hand kitty-corner over the table for her mother's. "It's true."

Eyes red-rimmed, Joel lifted his head to look at Eve. "Ms. Lawson is like that, too." He had to clear his throat before he could finish. "I guess she got it from her mom."

Damn it, just like that, Eve was crying. The most extraordinary feeling of warmth flooded her chest as she accepted what this boy had put into words as if it had always been obvious. So much that she was came from her parents—the kind man smiling at her, the mother who jumped up to circle the table and hug first Joel and then Eve.

Ben handed Eve his napkin and kissed her wet cheek. For her alone, he murmured, "Never thought of your mom as a spitfire too, did you?"

Eve laughed through her tears. "I should have." Of course Mom was. She'd fought for Hope, and she'd fought just as hard for Eve.

Bailey and she looked at each other, Bailey's expression momentarily as naked, as vulnerable, as Eve felt. Bailey nodded; Eve did the same.

"I don't know about everyone else," Seth said, "but I'm starving."

Glowing with happiness, Karen passed the first dish.

Beneath the tablecloth, Ben's hand found Eve's. He leaned toward her to say softly, "You have quite a family."

Eve brushed his cheek with her lips. "You mean, *we* have quite a family."

She would never forget the expression on his face when he looked around the table, then back at her. In his eyes was the astonished beginnings of belief, she thought.

"We," he agreed, voice husky, before finally letting go of her hand to accept a serving dish.

* * * * *